Other Books in The Vintage Library of Contemporary World Literature

THE FOUR WISE MEN

THE FOUR WISE MEN

MICHEL TOURNIER

TRANSLATED FROM THE FRENCH

BY RALPH MANHEIM

AVENTURA

The Vintage Library of Contemporary World Literature

VINTAGE BOOKS   A DIVISION OF RANDOM HOUSE   NEW YORK

First Aventura Edition, October 1984

Translation copyright © 1982 by Doubleday & Company,
Inc. and William Collins Sons & Company, Inc.
All rights reserved under International and
Pan-American Copyright Conventions. Published in the
United States by Random House, Inc., New York, and
simultaneously in Canada by Random House of Canada
Limited, Toronto. Originally published in France as
Gaspar, Melchior et Balthazar by Editions Gallimard in
1980. Copyright © 1980 by Editions Gallimard. This
translation originally published by Doubleday &
Company, Inc., in 1982.

Library of Congress Cataloging in Publication Data
Tournier, Michel.
The four wise men.
(Aventura: the Vintage library of contemporary
world literature.)
Translation of: Gaspard, Melchior & Balthazar.
Originally published: Doubleday, 1982.
1. Magi—Fiction. I. Title.
[PQ2680.083G313 1984]   843'.914   84-40222
ISBN 0-394-72618-9
Manufactured in the United States of America

Contents

GASPAR,
KING OF MEROË

I am black, but I am a king. One day, perhaps, I shall have this paraphrase of the Shulamite's song—I am black but beautiful—engraved on the tympanum of my palace. For what greater beauty can there be than a king's crown? To my mind that was so solidly established a certainty that I did not so much as think of it. Until the day when blondness burst into my life. . . .

It all began in the last moon of winter with a rather muddled warning from Barka Maï, my chief astrologer. He is an honest, conscientious man, whose science I trust as much as he distrusts it.

I was dreaming on the palace terrace, basking in the first balmy breezes of the year beneath a night sky sparkling with stars. The sandstorm that had raged for eight long days had abated, and with the feeling that I was breathing in the desert I filled my lungs.

A faint sound told me there was a man behind me. I recognized Barka Maï by the discreetness of his approach.

"Peace be with you, Barka," I said. "What have you come to tell me?"

"My lord," he replied with his usual circumspection, "I know next to nothing. But that nothing must not be concealed from you. A traveler come from the sources of the Nile has announced a comet."

"A comet? Explain, if you please, what a comet is and what the apparition of a comet signifies."

"I shall answer your first question more easily than your second. The word comes to us from the Greeks: ἀστὴρ χομήτης, which means long-haired star. It is a wandering star, whose appearances and disappearances in the sky are unpredictable and which consists essentially of a head dragging a train of flowing hair behind it."

"I see: a severed head flying through the air. Continue."

"Alas, my lord, comets are seldom of good omen, though the calamities they announce are fraught more often than not with comforting promises. When, for example, a comet appears before the death of a king, might it not be celebrating the accession of his young heir? And is it not true that lean kine tend to prepare the way for years of fat kine?"

I told him to stop beating about the bush and come straight to the point.

"Just tell me what is unusual about this comet that your traveler promises us?"

"First of all, it comes from the south and is heading north, but with stops, capricious shifts of direction, detours. Quite possibly it will not traverse our sky. That would be a great relief for your people."

"Wandering stars are often said to have extraordinary shapes, to resemble stars, swords, crowns, clenched fists with blood gushing from them, almost anything."

"No, this one is quite commonplace: as I've told you, just a head with flowing hair. Concerning the hair, however, a very strange observation has been reported to me."

"To wit?"

"Well, it seems the hair is golden. Yes, a comet with golden hair."

"That doesn't sound very menacing to me!"

"Perhaps not, perhaps not, but believe me, my lord," he said under his breath, "it would be a great relief for your people if it steered clear of Meroë."

I had forgotten this conversation when two weeks later I was passing with my retinue through the market of Baaluk, famed for the diversity and distant origin of the merchandise displayed there. I have always been curious about the strange things and bizarre creatures that nature has seen fit to invent. At my orders, a kind of zoological reserve has been set up in my parks, and in it remarkable specimens of the African fauna are kept. There I have gorillas, zebras, oryxes, sacred ibises, pythons of Seba, and laughing cercopitheci. No lions or eagles, they are too common, too vulgar in their symbolism, but I am expecting a unicorn, a phoenix, and a dragon, which have been promised me by travelers on their way through. To be on the safe side, I have paid for them in advance.

That day Baaluk had nothing very appealing to offer in the animal line. All the same I bought a consignment of camels, because for two years I hadn't been more than a two days' march away from Meroë and I felt an obscure need for a distant expedition; in fact, something told me such an expedition was imminent. I therefore bought mountain camels from the Tibesti—black, curly-haired, and indefatigable—pack camels from Batha—enormous, heavy, with smooth, light-brown hair, too awkward for use in the mountains but impervious to mosquitoes and horse flies—and, it goes without saying, swift, graceful, moon-colored coursers, those dromedaries as light as gazelles, saddled in scarlet and mounted by fierce Garamantes from the Hoggar or the Tassili mountains.

But what held our attention most was the slave market.

I have always taken an interest in the diversity of the
races. The human genius, it seems to me, thrives on variety
of stature, profile, and color, just as the world's poetry
gains from the interaction of many languages. Without argument I acquired a dozen tiny pygmies, whom I am planning to employ as oarsmen on the royal felucca, which I
use every autumn to mount the Nile, between the eighth
and fifth cataracts, to hunt the egret. I had started back,
paying no attention to the silent, morose crowds waiting in
chains for prospective buyers. But I couldn't help seeing
two golden spots that stood out sharply from all those
black heads: a young woman and a youth. Skin as light as
milk, eyes as green as water. And over their shoulders fell
an abundance of the finest sunlit hair.

As I've told you, I am extremely curious about nature's
oddities, but I am really drawn only to what comes to us
from the south. Not long ago a caravan from the north
brought me some of those Hyperborean fruits, capable of
ripening without sun or heat: apples, pears, and apricots
they call them. Though fascinated by the sight of such
monstrosities, I was repelled, when I tasted them, by their
anemic, watery insipidity. Of course one can't help admiring the way they have adapted to deplorable climatic conditions, but for eating they can't hold a candle to the most
inferior date.

It was with similar feelings that I sent my intendant to
inquire about the origin and price of the young slave girl.
He came back at once. She and her brother, he informed
me, were part of the human complement of a Phoenician
galley captured by Massilian pirates. As for her price, it
was high, because the merchant declined to sell her without the boy.

I shrugged my shoulders and gave orders to buy them

both, but I directly forgot my purchase. To tell the truth, I found my pygmies much more amusing. Besides, it was time for the great annual market at Nawarik, where they sell the most pungent spices, the strongest wines, the most effective medicines, and the headiest perfumes, gums, balms, and musks of the Orient. For the seventeen women of my harem I brought back several bushels of cosmetic powders and for my own personal use a coffer filled with little sticks of incense. For when I perform my judicial and administrative functions, or officiate at religious ceremonies, it seems fitting that I should be surrounded by censers, sending up swirls of aromatic smoke. It confers an air of majesty and makes an impression. Incense goes with the crown as wind goes with the sun.

It was on my return journey from Nawarik that, drunk with music and viands, I chanced to see my two Phoenicians again, and again it was their blondness that called them to my attention. We were nearing the well of Hassi Kef, where we planned to spend the night. After a torrid day of absolute solitude, we saw plentiful signs that water was near: the footprints of men and animals in the sand, quenched fires, axed tree stumps, and a little later vultures in the air, for where there is life there is carrion. As we entered the great hollow, at the bottom of which Hassi Kef is situated, a cloud of dust pointed the way to the well. I could have sent men ahead to clear the ground for the royal caravan. I have been criticized for waiving my prerogatives too often. But my motive is not humility, which would indeed be misplaced. I have pride to spare, and my familiars have been known to perceive it behind a consummate show of affability. But, you see, I love objects, animals, and people, and I find it hard to bear the isolation imposed by my crown. The fact is that my curiosity is often at odds with the aloofness and restraint which royalty imposes. To stroll about, to mingle with the crowd, to stop and gaze, to gather faces, gestures, glances—all that is a delightful dream forbidden a sovereign.

Be that as it may, Hassi Kef, swathed in a ruddy, dusty glory, was a grandiose spectacle. Under the impetus of the slope, long lines of beasts broke into a trot and hurled themselves into the bellowing throng around the watering troughs. Camels and asses, oxen and sheep, goats and dogs jostled one another and trampled the sludge of manure and chopped straw. Armed with sticks and thorny branches, lean, fine-featured Ethiopian shepherds, who might have been carved in ebony, were looking after their beasts. Now and then they would pick up handfuls of muck and throw them at the rams and he-goats, who were starting to fight. The strong, living smell, heightened by the heat and the water, is as heady as pure spirits.

But a god ruled over the hubbub. Standing on a crossbeam above the well, the water drawer moves both arms like the sails of a windmill, seizing the rope at its lowest point and raising it over his head until the full goatskin comes within his reach. A quick torrent of clear water pours into the troughs, where it instantly becomes muddy. The limp goatskin falls into the well, the rope twists like a furious snake between the hands of the water drawer, and the arms resume their windmill movements.

This backbreaking work is often done by a poor, tortured, grunting and groaning body, always looking for an opportunity to slow down or stop, but the overseer is never far off, brandishing a long whip to revive the poor devil's flagging vigor. But what we saw this time was the exact opposite, an admirable machine of muscle and sinew, a statue of light-colored copper, spotted with black mud, dripping with water and sweat, functioning effortlessly, with a kind of enthusiasm, of poetry one might say, more dancer than toiler. And when with a sweeping movement he raised the rope over his head, his face was turned skyward, and there was joy in the way he shook his golden mane.

"Who is that man?" I asked my lieutenant.

The answer, which was soon brought to me, recalled the market at Baaluk and the two Phoenicians I had acquired there.

"Didn't he have a sister?"

The girl, I was told, had been put to work in the millet fields. I gave orders that they should be reunited and taken to the palace at Meroë. What then? I would decide in due course.

In due course . . . this hackneyed formula, connoting immediate execution of an order whose consequences remain a mystery, as though lost in the night of the future, had more serious implications in the present case. It meant that I was giving in to an impulse that I could not deny, though it was not justified by any purpose—not to my knowledge, at least, for conceivably the two foreigners were part of a plan of destiny that escaped me.

In the days that followed I thought constantly of my light-skinned slaves. Unable to sleep in the night preceding my return to the palace, I left my tent and made my way some distance into the steppe without an escort. First walking at random, though as far as possible keeping my direction, I soon glimpsed a distant light, which I interpreted as a fire and chose, with no particular idea in mind, as the goal of my noctambulation. Between that fire and me there was a sort of game, for what with the hollows and knolls, the bushes and rocks, it kept disappearing and reappearing, without, so it seemed, coming any closer. Until the moment when—after a disappearance that seemed final—I found myself in the presence of an old man, squatting at a low table lit by a candle. In the midst of that infinite solitude, he was embroidering a pair of babouches with golden thread. Since it was plain that nothing could interfere with his work, I simply sat down facing him. Everything about him was white, a white apparition floating in an ocean of blackness: the muslin veil that enveloped the old man's head, his livid face, his long beard, his cloak, his long diaphanous hands, and even a mysterious lily in a slender crystal vase on the table. I filled my eyes, my heart, my soul with the sight of so much serenity, so as to gather comfort by returning to it in thought if passion should some day knock at my door.

For a long while he seemed unaware of my presence. Then at last he put down his work, folded his hands over one knee and looked me in the face.

"In two hours," he said, "the eastern horizon will be tinged with red. But the pure heart does not hope for the coming of the Savior more confidently than the sentinel on the ramparts awaits the rising of the sun."

Again he was silent. It was the expectant hour when all the earth, still plunged in darkness, communes with itself in anticipation of the first light of dawn.

"The sun . . ." the old man murmured. "So slowly does He impose silence, that one can speak of Him only in the dead of night. For half a century I have submitted to His great and terrible law; His course from horizon to horizon is the only movement I can bear. Sun, jealous god, no longer can I worship any other than you, but you abominate thought! You knew no rest till you had heavied every muscle in my body, killed every impulse of my heart, and blinded the light of my spirit. Under your tyrannical rule, I am changing from day to day into a translucent stone statue of myself. But I confess that this petrifaction is a great joy."

Again he fell silent. But as though he had suddenly remembered my existence, he said: "Go now, go before He gets here!"

I was about to rise when a perfumed breeze stirred in the branches of the terebinths. Then, unbelievably close to me, the solitary sobbing of a shepherd's flute burst forth. The music entered into me with unspeakable sadness.

"What is that?" I asked.

"It is Satan weeping as he beholds the beauty of the world," the old man replied on a note of tenderness that contrasted with the harshness of the words he had spoken before. "That is the way with all degraded creatures: the purity of things makes the evil in them weep with regret. Beware the creatures of light!"

He leaned across the table toward me and gave me his lily. I went away, holding the flower like a candle between thumb and forefinger. When I returned to the camp, a golden bar along the horizon set the dunes on fire. Satan's plaint still echoed inside me. I wouldn't have admitted it then, but already I knew that blondness had broken into my life and threatened to lay it waste.

The fortress of Meroë—a Hellenized form of the Egyptian name, Barwa—was built on the ruins and with the materials of an ancient basalt citadel of the pharaohs. It is my home. There I was born, there I live when I am not traveling, there I shall most likely die, and the sarcophagus that will hold my remains is ready. It's not exactly a cheerful dwelling, it's more like a military installation with a bit of necropolis thrown in. Still, it offers protection from the

heat and from sandstorms. Besides, I have a feeling that it
resembles me, and in a way I love myself through it. In the
center there is an enormous well, which dates from the
apogee of the pharaohs. Cut out of the rock, it goes down
two hundred and sixty feet to the level of the Nile. Halfway down there's a platform, which camels can reach by a
spiral ramp. The camels are used to operate a noria, which
raises water to a first cistern, which feeds a second cistern,
which feeds the palace pond. Visitors who admire this co-
lossal edifice sometimes express surprise: with all this pure
water available, why hasn't the palace been provided with
flowers and greenery? And it's true that there's hardly
more vegetation around the palace than in the middle of
the desert. That's how it is. Neither I nor my familiars nor
the members of my harem—doubtless because we all come
from the arid territories of the south—can conceive of a
verdant Meroë. But I can see how a foreigner might feel
crushed by the relentless austerity of the place.

That must have been the case with Biltine and Galeka,
who were desperately homesick and, to make matters
worse, rejected by the other slaves because of their color.
When I questioned the mistress of the harem about Biltine,
that Nigerian woman, though accustomed to racial and
ethnic mixtures, gave a shudder of loathing. Allowing herself the liberties of a matron who had known me as a child
and had guided my first amorous exploits, she heaped the
newcomer with sarcasms, beneath which I discerned,
scarcely veiled, the question heavy with reproach: Why,
oh why have you picked up that creature? And she
itemized: the colorless skin, through which little violet
veins can be seen here and there; the long, thin, pointed
nose; the large, protruding ears; the downy forearms and

calves; and other blemishes with which black people think they can justify the disgust they feel for whites.

"And you know," she concluded, "white people claim to be white, but it's a lie. They're not really white, they're pink, as pink as pigs! And they stink!"

I understood her litany, in which she expressed the xenophobia of a people with mat black skin, flat noses, minuscule ears, glabrous bodies, and acquainted with only two smells—both of them reassuring and devoid of mystery—that of the millet eaters and that of the manioc eaters. I understood this xenophobia because I shared it, and I'm sure there was an element of atavistic revulsion in my curiosity about Biltine.

I bade the old woman sit down beside me, and in a familiar, confidential tone calculated to flatter her and touch her heart with memories of my early, initiatic years, I asked her, "Tell me, my dear old Kallaha; there's something I've wondered about ever since I was a child. You must know the answer if anyone does."

"Can't be any harm in asking, boy," she said with mingled benevolence and distrust.

"Well then. About blond women—I've always wondered about their three crops of hair. Are they, too, blond like their heads or are they black like our women's, or are they some other color? Tell me. You who have made the foreign woman strip naked."

Kallaha rose brusquely to her feet. Her anger was back again.

"You're asking too many questions about that creature. You seem to take quite an interest in her. Would you like me to send her to you? Then you can investigate for yourself."

This old woman was going too far. It was time to remind her of the respect she owed me. I stood up and spoke in a very different voice.

"Good. Excellent idea! Make her ready and send her to me two hours after sunset."

Kallaha bowed and backed out of the room.

Yes, blondness had come into my life. It was a kind of sickness that I had caught one spring morning while looking about the slave market at Baaluk. And when Biltine, oiled and perfumed, appeared in my apartments, she merely embodied that turn of my destiny. The first thing I noticed, against those somber walls, was the brightness she seemed to emanate. In that black palace Biltine shone like a golden statuette in an ebony coffer.

Quite at her ease, she squatted down facing me and folded her hands in her lap. I devoured her with my eyes. I thought of Kallaha's hateful remarks. She had spoken of downy forearms, and indeed, in the flickering torchlight I saw her bare arms spangled with reflected fire. But her ears were hidden by her long, flowing hair, and her finely cut nose gave her face an air of insolent intelligence. As for her smell, I dilated my nostrils in an attempt to catch a whiff of it, but more out of desire than to test what Kallaha had said—that old calumny—about whites. We sat there for quite some time, watching each other, the white slave and the black master. With voluptuous terror I felt my curiosity about that strangely constituted race changing to attachment, to passion. Blondness was taking possession of my life. . . .

At last I framed a question, which would have been more pertinent on her lips than on mine, if slaves had the right to ask questions: "What do you want of me?"

An odd question and a dangerous one, for though Biltine already belonged to me she might have thought I was asking her price, and indeed this is how she seemed to take it, for she replied at once:

"My brother Galeka. Where is he? We are two Hyperborean children, lost in the African desert. Don't keep us apart. My gratitude will reward you."

The very next day brother and sister were reunited. I, however, had to contend with the mute hostility of the whole palace, and old Kallaha was not the last to condemn the inexplicable favor I was showing the two whites. Every day I thought of some pretext for having them near me. We would go sailing on the Atbara, visit the city of the dead at Beghera-wieh, watch a camel race at Guz-Redjeb, or simply spend the hours on the high terrace of the palace, where Biltine would sing Phoenician songs, accompanying herself on the cithara.

Little by little my way of looking at brother and sister changed. As I grew accustomed to their shared blondness, it ceased to dazzle me. I saw them more clearly and found them, though of the same race, less and less alike. Specifically, I became more aware of Biltine's radiant beauty, and I felt my heart filling with darkness as though her increasing grace must inevitably strike me with disgrace. Yes, I grew sad, irritable, melancholic. The truth is I no longer had the same picture of myself. I thought myself crude, bestial, incapable of inspiring friendship or admiration, not to speak of love. Let's face it: I began to hate my negritude. And then I recalled the words of the sage with the lily: "That heartbreaking music is Satan, weeping as he beholds the beauty of the world." The poor black man I was conscious of being was weeping over the beauty of a white woman. Love had made me betray my people deep in my heart.

Yet Biltine gave me no cause for complaint. As long as
her brother took part in our excursions and entertainments, she was the most playful of companions in pleasure.
The caresses she lavished upon me made me drunk with
delight and the thought of them will remain in my memory, bitter as the aftermath of those happy days may have
been. Obviously I had no doubt that she would become
my mistress. A slave cannot deny herself to her master's
desire, especially if he is a king. But I put it off, for I had
not done looking at her and watching my view of her
change. The curiosity aroused in me by a physically unusual, troubling, and vaguely repugnant creature had given
way to the profound carnal thirst which can be compared
only with the plaintive, tormenting hunger of a drug ad-
dict in a state of privation. But the savor of the unknown
still had a good deal to do with my love. In that somber
palace of basalt and ebony, the African women of my
harem blended with the walls and the furnishings. Better
still, there was a kinship between their hard, perfectly
shaped bodies and the objects around them. One might
have supposed them to be carved in mahogany, sculptured
in obsidian. With Biltine I felt that I was discovering flesh
for the first time. Her whiteness, her pinkness, gave her an
incomparable aptitude for nudity. *Indecent:* such was Kallaha's irrevocable judgment. I fully agreed with her, but
that was what most attracted me to my slave. Even
stripped of all clothing, a black is always dressed. Even
with every inch of her covered, Biltine was always nude.
Nothing is so becoming to an African body as bright-
colored garments, solid gold baubles, and precious stones,
but on Biltine's body these same adornments seemed heavy
and borrowed, as though denying her vocation for nudity.
Then came the feast of the fecundation of the date

palms. Since the date palm blossoms at the end of winter—
the male trees a few days in advance of the female—fecundation occurs in the fullness of spring. The male trees cast
their pollen into the air, but in the plantations the proportion of female to male trees—twenty-five to one, a faithful
image of that between women and master in the harem—
necessitates human intervention. This is the duty of men,
but only of married men. They break off male branches,
point them by turns toward each of the four cardinal
points, shake them over the female flowers, and finally set
them down in the center of a cluster. While the insemina-
tors are at work, groups of young people sing and dance at
the foot of the trees. The festivities, which last as long as
the fecundation process, are the traditional occasion for arranging betrothals, while the marriages are celebrated six
months later at the harvest festival. The ritual fecundation
dish is a haunch of antelope marinated with truffles and
seasoned with red pepper, cinnamon, caraway seed, cloves,
nutmeg, and amomum seeds.

We mingled with the joyous crowd, drinking, eating,
and dancing in the great palm grove of Meroë. Biltine
insisted on joining a group of dancing girls and did her
best to imitate the almost imperceptible swaying of the entire body, the total immobility of the head and minuscule
movements of the feet, which give the women's dances of
Meroë their hieratic air. Did she feel, as I did, what a
shocking sight she was in the midst of those girls with their
tight-braided hair, their scarified cheeks, and their lean,
scrupulously dieted bodies? In her own way she must have
sensed it; it obviously cost her a great effort to perform
this dance, which concentrates all the exuberance of
Africa in a minimum of movements.

I was all the more pleased to see her do honor to the

haunch of antelope after making free with the traditional
introductory tidbits, salad of flowering tarragon, humming
birds *en brochette*, zucchini stuffed with puppy brains,
plover roasted in vine leaves, sautéed ram's cheek, and the
inevitable ewes' tails, which are pouches of pure fat. Meanwhile the palm wine and rice spirits flowed freely. I was
amazed at how elegant, gracious, and seductive she remained after partaking so heartily of all that food. Any
other of the palace women would have felt obliged to peck
and nibble. Biltine put so much youthful gusto into her appetite that it communicated itself to me, and for a time I
ate as greedily as she, but only for a time, for as the hours
passed and night edged toward dawn, Satan's sobbing returned to my heart and a new suspicion poisoned my
mind: could Biltine, knowing she would be sharing my
bed before sunrise, be trying to deaden her senses with
food and drink? Did she have to drink herself into a stupor
before she could bear intimacy with a black man?

Nubian slaves were clearing away the dirty dishes and
the leavings of the banquet when I noticed that Galeka
had vanished. Such discretion on his part—I felt sure that
Biltine had something to do with it—touched me and restored my self-assurance. I withdrew to perfume myself
and remove my royal trappings and jewels. When again I
approached the welter of furs and cushions on the palace
terrace, Biltine was lying there with her arms outstretched.
She looked at me with a smile. I lay down beside her, I
enlaced her, and soon I knew all the secrets of blondness.
But why was it that I could see none of her body without
discovering part of mine? My hand on her shoulder, my
head between her breasts, my legs between her legs, thigh
against thigh—it was ivory and pitch! No sooner had my

amorous exertions let up than I sank into gloomy meditations on the contrast.

And what of her? What did she feel? What did she
think? I was soon to find out. Suddenly she wrenched herself free from my embrace, ran to the terrace balustrade,
and leaned out over the gardens. I saw her heaving and
retching. When at last she came back, she was pale, with
hollow cheeks and sunken eyes. She lay down on her back,
meekly, like a statue on a sarcophagus.

"It must have been the antelope," she said simply. "The
antelope or the ewe's tail."

I wasn't fooled. I knew it was neither the antelope nor
the ewe that had made the woman I loved vomit with disgust. I arose and went to my apartments, overwhelmed
with grief.

So far I have said very little about Galeka, because Biltine filled all my thoughts. But now in my distress I turned
to the young man as an incarnation of herself, but one incapable of making me suffer, an inoffensive confidant.
Come to think of it, isn't that the true function of brothers
and brothers-in-law? I would have been disappointed if I
had sincerely expected him to divert my attention from
Biltine. For it soon became clear to me that he lived entirely in his sister's shadow, putting all his trust in her
judgments and her decisions. I was also surprised to learn
how little he seemed to miss his native Phoenicia. According to the story he told me, they were on their way from
Byblos, the city of their birth, to Sicily, where they had
relatives. There seems to be a Phoenician tradition that
young people should leave home in the hope that the haz-
ards of travel will make them rich. Their adventures had
begun on the eighth day, when their ship fell into the

hands of pirates. The market value of their youth and
beauty had saved their lives. The pirates had landed on a
beach near Alexandria, and a caravan had carried them
southward. On the way their owners had spared them for
the sake of their looks, and they had not suffered exces-
sively. The charm of children and small animals compen-
sates for their weakness, and protects them from their ene-
mies. A woman's beauty and a youth's freshness are no less
effective weapons. I have found that out to my sorrow. No
army could have invested me and reduced me as those two
slaves did. . . .

I couldn't resist asking a question that surprised and
amused him: Are all the inhabitants of Phoenicia so blond?
He smiled. Far from it, he told me. Some have black hair,
some dark brown, some light brown. There are redheads
too. Then he frowned, as though for the first time glimps-
ing a new and elusive truth. It seemed to him, come to
think of it, that the slaves were darker, yes, very dark, and
woolly-haired as well, and that among the free population
complexions grew lighter and hair blonder and straighter
as one rose in the social scale, so the upper middle class
vied with the aristocracy in blondness. And he laughed, as
though such words spoken by a blond slave to a black king
weren't punishable by impalement or crucifixion. In spite
of myself, I admired him for speaking so freely and seem-
ing to make so light of everything that had happened to
him. He had left Byblos rich and free for a visit to relatives, he had crossed deserts on foot with the rope of slavery around his neck, and here he was, the favorite of an
African king. Did he know that I could have toppled his
head with a snap of my fingers? But could I have?
Wouldn't that have meant losing Biltine? But wasn't she

lost to me already? O misery! "I am a slave but I am blond!" she might have sung.

At last I must resign myself to describing a scene I had with her. It will show, if there is any need to, how sad and lost I felt.

I have mentioned my custom of using censers to enhance the solemnity of the official ceremonies in which I appeared, vested in the most venerable attributes of royalty. I have also told you how I brought back a whole coffer full of little incense sticks from the great market of Nawarik. Self-styled free thinkers are sometimes so frivolous as to play games with things whose symbolic significance escapes them, and sometimes they pay rather dearly for their sins. I conceived the uninspired idea of using this incense to lend savor to the entertainments I arranged on some nights for Biltine, her brother, and myself. I swear that at first my only purpose was to perfume the air of my apartments, which was often close and charged with banquet odors. But, you see, incense is not so easily desacralized. Its vapor sifts the light and peoples it with impalpable silhouettes. Its fragrance lends itself to reverie, to meditation. Incense smoking on the coals suggests sacrifices, hecatombs. In short, whether we like it or not, incense makes for a religious atmosphere.

This we at first avoided by crude buffoonery. Probably drink had something to do with what happened. It occurred to Biltine that she and I might exchange colors, so after daubing her face with soot she plastered mine with kaolin, and we clowned for a good part of the night. Then, at the hour of anguish when the old day is dead and the new one is still far from dawning, the heart went out of our merriment and the smoke of the incense gave our

buffoonery the air of a dance of death. The whited black
and the blackened blond faced one another, and the third
accomplice, like the thurifer of some grotesque cult, solemnly swung a smoking censer at their feet.

I loved Biltine, and lovers are always using such words
as idolize, worship, adore. You have to forgive them, because they don't know. Since that night I've known, but to
teach me it took those two carnival figures swathed in
swirls of fragrant smoke. Never has Satan's sobbing
pierced my heart as it did that night. It was a long, silent
cry within me, calling me to something different, to some
distant horizon. Which does not mean, not at all, that I
despised Biltine, that I was turning away from her. Far
from it. I felt closer to her than ever before, but in a
different way, with a feeling of kinship in abjectness, a
burning pity, an ardent compassion that carried me toward
her and moved me to carry her away with me. Poor Biltine—in spite of her childish duplicity, so weak, so fragile
in the midst of this court that hated her.

Of this hatred I was soon to have terrible proof, and, as
might have been expected, it was Kallaha who brought it
to me.

Her long years of service and her office of overseer of
the harem gave her access to my apartments day and night.
One night, accompanied by a eunuch with a torch, she
burst in on my insomnia. She seemed excited, as though
barely able to contain an overpowering joy. But etiquette
forbade her to speak first, and I was in no hurry to face
the disaster which I knew to be inevitable.

I got up, put on a night denchiki, and rinsed my mouth
—without a glance at the matron, who was boiling with
impatience. At length I arranged my cushions, lay down
again, and said nonchalantly: "Well then, Kallaha, what

has been going on in the harem?" For obviously there
could be no question of my authorizing her to speak of
anything else. She burst out, "Your Phoenicians! They are
no more brother and sister than him and me!"

And she touched the eunuch's shoulder.

"What do you know about it?"

"If you don't believe me, come. You'll see if the games
they're playing are the games of a brother and sister!"

I was on my feet in an instant. So that was the story!
The sickening sadness that had filled me for weeks had
turned to murderous rage. I threw a cloak over my shoulders. Kallaha, taken aback by the violence of my reaction,
shrank in the direction of the door.

"All right, you old sow, here we go!"

The rest had the weightless speed of a nightmare. The
lovers surprised in each other's arms, the soldiers summoned, the boy dragged to the dungeons, Biltine—more
beautiful than ever in her suddenly blasted happiness, more
desirable than ever with her tears and long hair, which was
her only garment—Biltine thrown into a six-foot-by-six-
foot cell, Kallaha vanished, for she was artful and knew
from experience that it was best to keep away from me at
such times. And so I was terrifyingly alone, in the midst of
a night as black as my skin and the bottom of my soul. I
would probably have wept if I hadn't known how ill tears
befit a black man.

Were Biltine and Galeka brother and sister? There was
every reason to doubt it. I have already noted that the
physical resemblance between them, which at first seemed
obvious, became less so as their individual features began to
shine through their ethnic type. And the stratagem is only
too easily explained: by passing off her lover—or husband—
as her brother, the Phoenician woman shielded him from

my jealousy and gave him a share in the favors I heaped on
her. Prudence should have counseled them to keep their
distance from one another. Their failure to do so infuriated me; surrounded by spies as they were, how light
they must have made of defying me! Still, their frivolity,
their rashness amazes me and touches me in a way. But
enough of this brother-and-sister question. What do I care
whether they are really brother and sister or not? The
pharaohs of Upper Egypt—who are not so very far from
me in time or space—married their sisters to preserve the
purity of their race. In my eyes, the union of Biltine and
Galeka remains a union of two likes. Blond attracts blond;
they mingle . . . and banish black into outer darkness. To
my way of thinking, that's all there is to it.

In the days that followed I had to contend with the silent or disguised entreaties of my entourage to make short
shrift of the guilty pair. What do the lives of two dis-
graced slaves weigh in the hand of a king? But I was old
enough and wise enough to realize that the important thing
for me was not to do justice, or even to avenge myself, but
to heal the wound from which I was suffering. I would let
myself be guided by judicious egoism. Would the quick or
slowly agonizing death of one of the two Phoenicians—but
of which one?—or of both at once appease my grief? That
was all I wanted to know, and on that score I questioned
the knowledge of all those who were screeching hatred
around me.

Once more it was my astrologer Barka Maï who
brought me the most enlightened counsel.

I was pacing my terrace, taking a morose pleasure in the
thought that the blackness of my soul was empty, whereas
the blackness of the night sky sparkles with stars, when he
came to me with—so he said—an important piece of news.

"It will be tonight," he announced mysteriously.

I had forgotten our last meeting and didn't know what he was referring to.

"The comet," he reminded me, "the long-haired star. Late tonight it will be visible from this terrace."

The golden-haired star! Now I remembered that he had predicted this apparition before Biltine had come into my life. Dear Barka! His clairvoyance amazed me. But more important, he had suddenly given a celestial dimension to the wretched imposture of which I had been the victim. Assuredly I had been betrayed. But now my misfortune had a royal density and celestial repercussions! This was a great comfort to me. At last Satan's flute consented to fall silent.

"Excellent," I said. "We shall wait for it together."

Its coming was foreshadowed by an almost imperceptible flickering over the hills that frame the southern horizon—faint flashes of heat lightning, one might have thought. Barka sighted it first. He pointed his finger at a glow that I might have mistaken for a planet.

"That's it," he said. "It comes from the sources of the Nile and it's heading for the Delta."

"But," I objected, "Biltine, on the contrary, came from the northern Mediterranean and crossed the desert on her way here."

Barka affected surprise. "Who has said anything about Biltine?" he asked with a crafty smile.

"Didn't you tell me this long-haired star was blond?"

"Golden. I spoke of golden hair."

"Exactly. When Biltine unbound her hair and let it hang loose over her shoulders, or spread it out on her pillow, I who had known only the black, round, woolly heads of our women, would touch her hair, run it through

my fingers, and marvel that hunger and thirst for the yellow metal could be transfigured to the point of being
mistaken for the love of a woman. The same goes for the
smell. You know the adage that gold has no smell. It means
that a man can draw profit from the impurest sources—
from brothels or latrines—without imparting the slightest
odor to the royal treasury. That is convenient, but also unfortunate, for it means that the most sordid crimes are
effaced by the profit one can derive from them. More than
once I have overturned a coffer full of gold pieces, picked
up a handful, and held them up to my nose. Nothing! No
smell whatever. The hands and pockets through which
they had passed, the swindles, betrayals, and murders in
which they had been involved, had left no smell. Whereas
the gold of Biltine's hair! You know that little aromatic
grass that grows in hollows between rocks . . ."

"Really, Lord Gaspar, that woman holds too great a
place in your thoughts! But look at the blond comet now.
It's coming nearer, it's dancing in the black sky like a luminous almeh. Perhaps it's Biltine. But perhaps it's someone else at the same time, for there's more than one blond
thing on earth. Coming from the south, its capricious
course is directed northward. Follow it. Get away from
here. Travel is a sovereign remedy for the ailment that's
gnawing at you. 'A journey,' says the poet, 'is a series of
irrevocable disappearances.'[1] Go away! A disappearance is
sure to do you good."

The luminous almeh shook her hair over the palm
grove. Yes, she was beckoning me to follow her. And so it
was decided. I would entrust Biltine and her brother to my
first intendant, making it clear that on my return his life
would answer to me for theirs. I would follow the course
of the Nile toward the cold sea, traversed by ships bearing

golden-haired men and women. And Barka Maï would come with me. As his punishment and his reward.

The preparations for our departure had a healing effect, renewing my youth and my strength. As the poet[2] said: "Stagnant, lifeless water becomes brackish and muddy, while flowing, singing water remains pure and limpid. Similarly, the soul of a sedentary man is a vessel in which endlessly ruminated grievances ferment. From the soul of the traveler pours a pure stream of new ideas and unforeseen actions."

For the pleasure of it more than from any necessity, I personally supervised the organization of our caravan. It would be limited in size, I decided—no more than fifty camels—but men as well as beasts must be of the strongest, for the goal of our expedition was both distant and uncertain. On that score, I was repelled by the thought of leading my companions and slaves into the unknown without an explanation. I therefore spoke of an official visit to a great white king on the eastern shores of the sea, and more or less at random mentioned Herod, king of the Jews, whose capital is Jerusalem. My concern proved superfluous. They hardly listened to me. To those men, all reluctantly sedentarized nomads, a journey is its own justification. The destination hardly matters. I believe they understood only one thing, that we would be traveling a long way and would be gone a long time. That was enough for them; they were jubilant. Even Barka Maï seemed to make the best of a bad business. After all, he was neither too old nor too skeptical to hope that our expedition might bring him lessons and surprises.

For my exit from Meroë I was obliged to use the large royal palanquin of red wool embroidered with gold, surmounted by a wooden pole bearing green banners and topped with an ostrich plume. From the palace gate to the last palm tree—after that comes the desert—the people of Meroë cheered and wept for their departing king, to the accompaniment, since in our country nothing is done without music and dancing, of innumerable castanets, sistrums, cymbals, sambucas, and psalteries. My royal dignity doesn't allow me to issue from my capital with less display. But at the very first halting place I had them take down the pompous contraption in which I had suffocated all day, changed my mount, and settled myself on my touring saddle, consisting of a light frame covered with sheepskin.

In the evening I wished to celebrate, and to meditate upon, my first day of uprooting, and for that I had to be alone. My familiars had long resigned themselves to such escapades, and no one tried to follow me when I left the clump of sycamores and the *guelta* where we had pitched our camp. In the sudden coolness of the dying day, I enjoyed the supple, ambling gait of my she-camel. This gait—both right legs advance together, shifting the animal's full weight to the left, then both left legs, shifting the body's weight to the right—is peculiar to camels, lions, and elephants. It favors metaphysical speculation, whereas the diagonal motion of horses and dogs inspires only indigent thoughts and sordid calculations. O joy! How solitude, so hateful and humiliating in my palace, lifted me up in the desert!

I gave my mount her head, and she directed her gangling trot toward the setting sun—actually, she was following tracks which I didn't notice at first. Suddenly she stopped at an embankment surrounding a low well, from which emerged a palm trunk with notches cut in it. I leaned over and saw my reflection trembling in a black

mirror. The temptation was too great. I threw off my
clothes and with the help of the palm trunk climbed down
into the well. Up to my waist in the water, I felt the cool
eddies of an invisible spring on my ankles. I immersed myself to the chest, the neck, the eyes, in the exquisitely
caressing water. Over my head, in the round opening of
the well shaft, I saw a first star twinkling in a disk of phos-
phorescent sky. A breeze passed over the well, making a
sound like a giant flute. The earth and the night wind were
playing together, and by an unconscionable indiscretion I
had surprised their sweet, profound music.

The days that followed were filled with hours of
marching over fissured red lands bristling with thorn
bushes. From fields of boulders interspersed with yellow
grass to the sparkling salt of the sebkhas, we seemed to be
journeying through eternity, and few of us could have said
how long we had been on our way. Travel is that, too: a
way of making time pass at once more slowly—to the careless amble of our mounts—and much more quickly than in
a city, where varied occupations and visits create a com-
plex past, consisting of successive planes and of diversely
structured zones and perspectives.

In those days animals were at the heart of our existence,
and first of all our camels, without which we would have
been lost. We were alarmed by an outbreak of diarrhea,
brought on by too much rich grass. Green liquid humors
flowed between their lean thighs. One day we had to force
them to drink, because the only spring within a three days'
march, though clear, was bitter with native soda. Three
she-camels were wasting away, and there was nothing we
could do but kill them before they became living skeletons.
That provided the occasion for a feast in which I partici-
pated, more to show solidarity with my companions than

from inclination. In accordance with tradition, the marrow
bones were inserted in the stomach pouches, which were
then buried under the coals. When uncovered the next
day, they were full of a bloody broth that is prized by the
men of the desert. But our milk supply was appreciably reduced.

We were slowly approaching the Nile and our hearts
leapt when suddenly we saw it before us, immense and
blue, bordered by papyruses which rustled like silk when
the wind caressed their umbels. In a marshy cove a hippo-
potamus lay on its back with its short legs in the air; its
bowels were hanging out of a great gash in its belly. As we
approached, a naked little boy emerged from the slimy
cavern, a statue reddened with blood in which only the
eyes and teeth were white. Laughing gleefully, he offered
us entrails and chunks of meat.

Thebes. Wishing to mingle with the crowd in the old
Egyptian city, we crossed the river. That was a mistake.
As we journeyed northward, we had seen complexions
growing lighter. I tried to foresee the moment when we
blacks would become the exception, black against a white
background rather than white against a black background
—an inversion hard to imagine.

We hadn't come to that yet, but even so it gave me a
start to see blond heads on the waterfront. Could they be
Phoenicians? Yes, it was a mistake, because contact with
people reopened my wounds. Only the desert could soothe
my stricken heart. With relief I went back to the silence
of the left bank, where the two colossi of Memnon watch
over the tombs of kings and queens. For a long while I
walked beside the river, watching the sacred falcons fish;
they are the emblems of the god Horus, son of Osiris and
Isis and conqueror of Set. Magnificent birds. Their beaks

are too short to catch fish. They seize them in their claws.
They plummet like meteorites and just before they reach
the water their claws, as though released by a catch, leap
out at the submerged prey. For a moment the falcons graze
the surface of the water. Then with a great flapping of
wings they rise and, holding the fish in their claws, tear it
apart with their beaks. The Egyptians more than any other
people were struck by the divine simplicity of this bird's
body and its perfect attunement to the natural order.
Surely that suffices to justify a cult. Lord Horus, give me
the naïve strength and savage beauty of your emblematic
bird!

Lured by the river's calm, clear water, we pitched our
camp directly on the bank. Barka Maï hadn't been the last
to notice my drooping mouth and the sadness in my eyes.
He knew it was all up with the high spirits occasioned by
our departure. In silence we ate the big brown beans and
chopped onions, sautéed in oil and seasoned with caraway
seeds, which seem to be the national dish of that country.
Having no appetite, I found it especially insipid and noted
on that occasion how the food became more and more
tasteless as one traveled northward, the sole exception
being the grasshoppers pickled in vinegar that awaited us
in Judea. Then I sank into contemplation of the eddies and
whirlpools that mottled the lazy waters of the river.

"You are as sad as death," said Barka. "Stop gazing at
those sea-green eyes. Make for the Mountain of the Kings.
Seek counsel with the two colossi, who watch over the
tomb of Amenophis. Go, they are expecting you!"

There is no better way of being obeyed, even by a king,
than to command him to do what in his innermost heart he
wants to do. From far off I had seen those two admirable
giants placed side by side, and had instantly been seized

with a desire to put myself under their mighty protection. For those statues, which are as tall as ten men, emanate serenity—in part no doubt attributable to their posture: quietly seated, their hands resting on their tight-pressed knees. I circled the two statues, then I went into the city of the dead, whose guardians they are. Of the mortuary temple of Amenophis nothing remains but columns, capitals, stairways mysteriously stopped in mid-flight, enigmatic blocks of stone. But this chaos veils the ordered blackness of the tombs and steles. Beneath the disorder, which is still living and human, the clock of the gods ticks imperturbably. We know for sure that time is on its side and that before long the desert will have swallowed up these ruins. Yet the colossi watch. . . . I wished to do likewise and squatted down in my cloak at the foot of the northern colossus. For part of the night I seconded the stone giant's eternal vigil with my frail human night-light. Then I lost consciousness.

I was drawn from my sleep by the wailing of an infant. Or so at least I thought. A plaintive, childlike voice. Where did it come from? From above me, it seemed, from the sky perhaps, or perhaps from the little head bearing Memnon's headdress. But sometimes it was like a song, with accents of tenderness, runs and warblings of childlike delight—as though a baby were gurgling in response to its mother's caresses.

I arose. In the pale light of dawn the desert and the tombs seemed even more desolate than at nightfall. But in the east, on the far side of the Nile, a purple gash pierced the sky, and an orange light fell on the stone torso of my colossus. Then I remembered a legend I had heard but dismissed as implausible. Memnon was the son of Aurora and of Tithonus, king of Egypt, who sent him to succor the besieged city of Troy. There he was killed by Achilles. Every morning since then, Aurora has covered the statue of her son with tears of dew and with her loving rays. Then, in the warmth of his mother's caresses, the colossus comes to life and sings for joy. What I witnessed was this tender meeting, and it filled me with a strange exaltation.

For the second time I discovered that the only true remedy for unhappy love is grandeur. Unhappiness finds its nadir in vulgar grievances, petty grudges, and sour stomach. First it was the comet—Biltine's celestial avatar—which wrenched me from the listless gloom of my apartments and sent me out over desert trails. And that morning I saw a mother's grief raised to sublime heights, heard the filial effusions of the rising sun and the stone colossus with the baby's voice. And I was a king! How could I fail to understand that inspiring lesson? I blush with shame and rage when I think of the abjectness into which I had fallen, tormenting myself over the vomiting of a slave, wondering in my despair if it was brought on by the haunch of antelope, the ewe's tail, or my negritude!

When I urged my men to re-form the caravan and press on to the northwest, toward the Red Sea, they hardly recognized their sovereign, who only the day before had been bowed with grief.

From Thebes it took us two days to reach Koenopolis, where jars, amphoras, and goblets are made from clay mixed with esparto ash. This produces a porous substance which, thanks to constant evaporation, keeps water cool. Then we entered a mountainous region, where our progress was slow. We were obliged to sacrifice two young camels which, either because of overloading or of insufficient training, had crippled themselves on the rocky trails. For my men it was one more occasion to gorge themselves

on meat. After a laborious march of no less than ten days
through chasms surmounted by snow-covered mountains—
for us a totally unfamiliar landscape—we finally came out
on the coastal plain. With immense relief we caught sight
of the sea and soon found ourselves on beaches of salt sand,
over which the most ardent members of my retinue leaped
and ran, crying out like children in their enthusiasm. For
the sea, when we first glimpse it, always seems to hold
promise of escape, a promise, alas, which often proves
deceptive.

We called a halt in the port of Kosseir. Like most of the
Red Sea ports, Kosseir carries on the bulk of its maritime
trade with Elath, situated at the northern end of the gulf
between the Sinai Peninsula and the Arabian coast. Elath is
the ancient Ezion Geber of King Solomon, which drained
the gold, sandalwood, ivory, monkeys, peacocks, and
horses of the two continents, Africa and Asia. Nine days
of palavering were needed before we were able to charter
the barks needed to carry our men, beasts, and provisions.
Then we had to wait another five days because of a north
wind that made navigation impossible. Finally we managed
to hoist anchor and after sailing for a whole week along
steep, forbidding granite cliffs topped by imposing sum-
mits, we put into the harbor of Elath. That quiet passage
gave all of us a welcome rest, especially the camels which,
immobilized in the shade of the holds, renewed their
humps by eating and drinking their fill.

We had been told that the journey from Elath to
Jerusalem would take twenty days, and we would probably have completed it in that time if not for an encounter
two days short of Jerusalem, which delayed us but also
gave our expedition new meaning.

Ever since we landed, Barka Maï had been talking about

the unparalleled majesty of Hebron, the ancient city for which we were heading and which, so he claimed, would in itself have made our journey worthwhile. Hebron prided itself on being the oldest city in the world, and that is hardly surprising, for it was there that Adam and Eve took refuge when they were driven out of Paradise. What is more: one can still see the field where Yahweh took the clay that he molded to make the first man!

Gateway of the desert of Idumea, Hebron mounts guard over three verdant little hills, planted with olive, fig, and pomegranate trees. Its white houses are shut up tight. No sign of life emerges from them. Not an open window, not a stitch of laundry drying on a line, not a living soul in its narrow-staired streets, not even a dog. Such at least is the forbidding mask that the oldest city in the world presents to the stranger. That, too, was the picture painted by the messengers I had sent ahead to announce our arrival. But in Hebron they encountered something more than this void. According to their report, a caravan had arrived there only a few hours before and, put off by the inhospitality of the inhabitants, had proceeded to the east of the town and set up a camp which gave promise of being magnificent. I thereupon sent an official emissary to inquire into these strangers' intentions. He returned, visibly delighted with his mission. These people were the retinue of Balthasar IV, ruler of the Chaldean kingdom of Nippur, who bade us welcome and invited me to sup with him.

The first thing that struck me on approaching Balthasar's camp was the abundance of horses. We people of the far south travel only with camels. The horse perspires and urinates too freely to sustain the water shortage that is a permanent fact of our life. Yet it was to Egypt that King Solomon sent for the horses that drew his famous war chariots. With their rounded faces, their short but powerful limbs, their cruppers as round as pomegranates, King Balthasar's horses are of the famous Mt. Taurus breed, descended, if legend is to be believed, from Perseus' horse Pegasus.

The king of Nippur is an amiable old man, who on first blush seems to value nothing more than comfort and gracious living. So imposing is his retinue that one wouldn't for a moment think of asking him for what purpose he is traveling. The tapestries, the plate, the furs, the perfumes, all in the care of specially trained attendants, reply in unison: for pleasure, for joy, for happiness. We had no sooner arrived than young girls, whose physical type did not fail to impress me, bathed us, dressed our hair, and anointed us most expertly. I was told later on that they were all of the race of Queen Malvina, who hailed from remote and mysterious Hyrcania. It was there that the king, as a delicate homage to his wife, recruited the maidservants for the palace in Nippur. Their skin is exceedingly white and their abundant jet-black hair contrasts charmingly with their light-blue eyes. My unhappy adventure had made me attentive to such details, and I examined them closely as the girls were prettifying me. Once the first surprise had worn off, they lost some of their charm for me. A white skin and copious black hair are all very well, but I detected traces of dark down on their upper lips and forearms. Yes, I'm not at all sure these girls gain by closer scrutiny. All in all I prefer blondes or black women; at least their complexions harmonize with their pilosity.

Of course I took care not to ask Balthasar any indiscreet questions, just as he abstained from asking me where I was going and why. Cramped by courtesy, we played a strange game, each concealing the essential and drawing what he could from the other's affable but designedly uninformative remarks. The upshot was that I knew next to nothing about him at the end of our first interview and he was hardly better informed about me. Luckily, we were not alone, and our slaves and courtiers were not subject to the same rule of discretion. Thanks to the gossip of pantry, kitchen, and stable, which would be reported to us, we would know a good deal more the next day. One thing seemed certain: that the king of Nippur was a great connoisseur of art, an ardent collector of sculptures, paintings, and drawings. Maybe his aim in traveling was merely to see and acquire beautiful things. The splendor of his retinue suggested as much.

We were to meet again the next day in the cave of Machpelah, which harbors the tombs of Adam and Eve, of Abraham, Sarah, Isaac, Rebecca, Leah, and Jacob—a biblical family vault, as it were, lacking only the ashes of Yahweh himself to make it complete. If I speak lightly and irreverently of those venerable things, it is doubtless because I feel them to be remote from me. Legends live on our substance. They derive their truth from the complicity of our hearts. If we cannot recognize our own story in them, they are dead wood and dry straw.

It was very different with King Balthasar, who seemed deeply moved as we entered the maze of underground passages leading down to the tombs of the patriarchs. The darkness was relieved only by the smoke and the dancing torchlight, and all we could see of the tombs was vaguely delineated mounds. When Adam's tomb was pointed out to him, my companion bent over it for a long while, as though looking for something, a secret, a message, or at least, I suppose, some sign. On the way back, a shadow of disappointment marred the impassive beauty of his face. He looked with indifference at the magnificent terebinth, which was so enormous that ten men locking hands could not have girdled its trunk, and which, so it was said, dated back to the Garden of Eden. He had only a contemptuous glance for the waste ground grown to brambles, where, so they claim, Cain killed his brother Abel. But his curiosity revived at the sight of the freshly plowed field enclosed in hawthorn hedges, where Yahweh allegedly molded Adam before moving him to the Garden of Eden. Picking up a little of the earth from which the human statue was made and into which God breathed life, he thoughtfully sifted it through his fingers. Then, possibly addressing me, but more as though talking to himself, he uttered words which I have remembered despite their obscurity:

"One cannot meditate too much on the first lines of Genesis. *God made man in his image and likeness.* Why those two words? What difference is there between image and likeness? It must be that the likeness covers the whole being—body and soul—whereas the image is only a superficial and possibly deceptive mask. As long as the man remained as God made him, his divine soul transverberated his mask of flesh; he was as pure and simple as an ingot of gold. Thus image and likeness formed a single statement of man's origin. There would have been no need of two distinct words. But as soon as the man disobeyed and sinned, as soon as he tried to evade God's wrath with lies, he forfeited his likeness to his Creator, and there remained only his face, a small deceptive image, recalling as though in spite of itself, a remote, renounced, flouted, but not effaced origin. Now we see why the representation of man in painting and sculpture has been cursed: in producing *an image without a likeness,* these arts make themselves ac-

complices in an imposture. Fired with fanatical zeal, the
clergy persecute the figurative arts, destroying even the
sublimest works of the human genius. When we question
them, they say it will be thus as long as the image conceals
a profound and secret unlikeness. One day perhaps fallen
man will be redeemed and regenerated by a hero or savior.
Then his restored likeness will justify his image, then
painters and sculptors will be able to practice ·their art,
which will have recovered its sacred dimension. . . ."

As he was pursuing this meditation, I looked down at
the freshly plowed earth and with the words image and
likeness falling insistently on my ear, I searched that
ground for some trace of a human being, of Balthasar, of
Biltine, or possibly of myself. He fell into a thoughtful silence. I picked up a handful of earth and, holding it out to
the king, I said, "Tell me if you will, Lord Balthasar,
would you say that this earth from which Adam was
molded is white?"

"White? Certainly not!" he cried with a frankness that
made me smile. "If you want my impression, it looks black
to me. Though I also see a trace of brownish-red, which
reminds me that in Hebrew, 'Adam' means ocher-red."

He had said more than was needed to rejoice my heart.
I brought the handful of earth close to my own face.

"Black, brown, red, ocher, you say. Look and compare.
Mightn't Adam's face have been in the image—if not in the
likeness, for we are speaking of color—of your cousin, the
king of Meroë's face?"

"A black Adam? Why not? I hadn't thought of that,
but it's quite conceivable. Just a second, though! Eve was
made from Adam's flesh. So if Adam was black, she too
must have been black. How curious! Our mythology with
its immemorial imagery resists the assaults of our imagina-

tion and our reason. Adam, if you will; but when it comes
to Eve, I can only see her as white."

And I? Not only as white, but as blond, with Biltine's
impertinent nose and childlike mouth. . . . Then, drawing
me back to our great joint caravan, where horses were
rubbing shoulders with camels, Balthasar asked me a question which for him was only an amusing paradox, but for
me was fraught with incalculable meaning.

"Is it not conceivable," he asked, "that the aim of our
journey is the exaltation of negritude?"

BALTHASAR,
KING OF NIPPUR

Nothing could have delighted me more than our meeting at Hebron with the caravan of King Gaspar of Meroë. I am sorry not to have busied myself more with Black Africa and its civilizations, which must have immense riches to offer. Was it ignorance, lack of time, or too exclusive an interest in Greece? Something more, I believe. Black men put me off because, frankly, they raised a question I was incapable of answering, and I had no desire to wear myself out looking for an answer. I had a long road to travel before I could meet my African brother. By dint of growing older and thinking, I traveled that road without knowing it, and it led me to the edge of the plowed field near Hebron, where, so legend has it, Yahweh molded the first man. And there Gaspar, king of Meroë, was waiting for me. I have always been preoccupied with the myth of Adam, self-portrait of the Creator, for I have long felt that it embodied important truths which no one thus far had fathomed. In speaking to Gaspar, I let my tongue run away with me. I developed the idea of an opposition between the two words *image* and *likeness*—which have hitherto been regarded as a rhetorical tautology—and went on to suggest that this opposition might serve as a lever with which to prise open this too-familiar story and penetrate to its secret. It was then

that my black friend pointed out to me how closely the
clay of Hebron resembled his face in color. This of course
suggests that Adam may well have been the color of our
African friends. Without delay I applied this new key—a
black Adam—to the problems of the image and the likeness, which had long been with me. The result proved surprising . . . and promising.

For obviously the black man has greater affinity with
the image than does the white man. One need only observe
how much more becomingly the black man wears bright-
colored clothing and ornaments—especially jewelry, precious stones, and metals. The black man is more naturally
an idol than the white man. And what is an idol but an
image?

I was able to observe this gift for ornament at its fullest
in King Gaspar's companions, who present a fine display
of jewels and trinkets, and better still, of those incarnated
jewels and trinkets that are tattoo marks and scarifications.
I discussed the matter with Gaspar, who surprised me by
moving the question into the ethical domain with a simple
sentence.

"I take that into account in choosing my men," he said.
"I have never been betrayed by a tattooed man."

What a strange metaphor! Identifying tattooing with
fidelity!

What is a tattoo? It is a permanent amulet, a living
jewel that cannot be removed because it is consubstantial
with the body. It is the body made jewel and partaking of
the jewel's unchanging youth. I have been shown finely
drawn, lozenge-shaped scars on the inner side of a little
girl's thighs: they were "barriers" intended to protect her
virginity. The tattoo mounts guard on the threshold of her
sex organ. A tattooed body is purer and better preserved

than an untattooed body. As for the soul of a tattooed person, it partakes of the tattoo mark's indelibility, which, translated into the language of the soul, becomes the virtue of fidelity. If a tattooed man does not betray, it is because his body forbids it. He belongs irrevocably to the empire of signs, signals, and signatures. His skin is logos. The scribe and the orator have bodies as white and immaculate as virgin paper. With their hands and mouths they project signs—writing and spoken words—into space and time. The tattooed man, on the contrary, neither speaks nor writes: he *is* writing and speech. All the more so if he is black. This disposition of Africans to incarnate the sign in their own bodies attains its paroxysm in raised scarifications. I observed the bodies of some of Gaspar's companions: the signs inscribed in their flesh had acquired a third dimension. Painting had become bas-relief, sculpture. In their skin, which is especially thick and tumid, they make deep incisions, artificially prevent the lips of the wound from knitting, and provoke keloid swellings. These they treat with fire, razors, needles, and coloring matter—yellow ocher, henna, laterite, watermelon juice or green barley, and kaolin. Sometimes they go so far as to immerse a ball or sliver of oil-coated clay in the wound, where it remains after cicatrization. But I find greater elegance in the technique which consists in plaiting strips of skin and inserting the braid in a central scarification, to which it remains grafted.

The relation of these body arts to Adam and the Garden of Eden is obvious. The flesh is not reduced to the level of a medium, something to be painted or sculptured; it becomes a work, and is sanctified as such. Yes, it would not surprise me if the painted and sculptured bodies of Gaspar's companions resembled that of Adam in his origi-

nal innocence and his intimate bond with the Word of
God. Whereas our smooth, white, necessitous bodies cor-
respond to the punished, humiliated flesh, banished far
from God, which has been ours since the fall of man. . . .
   We were in Hebron for three days. It took us three
more to reach the gates of Jerusalem.

Miserly fathers, bountiful sons. Thanks to the unflagging
cupidity with which first my grandfather Belsussar and
then my father Belsarar exploited the meager resources of
the small principality of Nippur—a brilliant but trifling
splinter of the Babylonian Empire, whose disintegration
was precipitated by the death of Alexander—and because
in the sixty-five years of their reigns they avoided all occa-
sions for expenditure—such as wars, expeditions, and public works—I, Balthasar IV, their grandson and son, found
myself, on acceding to the throne, in possession of a treasury such as to warrant the highest ambitions. Mine had
nothing to do with conquest or display. The one passion of
my youth was the love of pure, simple beauty, which, I
believed—and still believe—would instill in me the sense of
justice and the political instinct I would need to govern
my people.
   I see no contradiction between the avarice of my fathers
and my artistic tastes, nor do I regard these tastes as a form
of prodigality. I have always been a passionate collector. In
my opinion the miser and the collector have much in common, and while there is always a possibility of antagonisms
between them, these can usually be resolved with no great
commotion. When I was a child, my grandfather sometimes took me with him to the strong room he had built in
the heart of the palace, where the treasures of the kingdom
slept in sepulchral peace. A narrow corridor, broken by

steep and angular little stairways, led to a block of granite
as big as a house, which could be moved only by a system
of chains and winches, the commands of which were situated in a distant room. That required a bit of an expedition, and then we were able to enter the holy of holies. A
narrow slit in the wall admitted a ray of sunlight, which
cut through the half-darkness like a luminous sword.
Bending his scrawny back, Belsussar moved the coffers
about with a vigor surprising at his age. I saw him bending
over mounds of turquoises, amethysts, hydrophanes, and
chalcedonies, rolling rough diamonds in the hollow of his
hand, holding rubies up to the light to appraise their water,
or pearls to enhance their orient. It took me years of
reflection to realize that my feeling of closeness to him at
such times rested on a misunderstanding, for it was the
beauty of those gems and nacres that filled me with jubila-
tion, whereas what he saw in them was a certain amount of
wealth, an abstract and therefore polyvalent symbol,
which could equally well stand for a piece of land, a ship,
or a dozen slaves. In short, while I immersed myself in the
contemplation of a precious object, my grandfather took it
as the starting point of a process of sublimation, culminating in a pure number.

My father lifted the ambiguity that made it possible for
a miser bending over a coffer of precious stones to be
taken for an art lover. This he accomplished by getting rid
of the treasure in the strong room as soon as he came to the
throne. At first he kept only gold pieces struck with
effigies, originating in the Mediterranean basin, the African
continent, or the confines of Asia. Preserving a last illusion,
I fell in love with those effigies, which appealed to my taste
for portraiture and in general for representations of persons living or dead. In my eyes, the face of a dead sover-

eign took on a divine dimension when engraved in gold or silver. But my illusion was shattered when even those coins vanished to make room for the abacuses and writing equipment of the Chaldean bankers with whom the king and his minister of finance regularly conferred. There is a troublingly paradoxical kinship between, on the one hand, acute avarice and the exorbitant wealth it secretes and, on the other, the extreme indigence fostered by the asceticism of the God-possessed mystic. In the miser as in the mystic, the appearance of poverty veils enormous unseen wealth, though the nature of this wealth is entirely different in the two cases.

My passionate vocation was far removed from such indigence and such wealth. I love tapestries, paintings, drawings and statues. I love everything that beautifies and ennobles our existence, and most of all those figurations of life which exhort us to rise above ourselves. I have little taste for the geometric designs of Smyrna tapestries or Babylonian ceramics, and architecture crushes me with its everlasting lessons in grandeur and arrogant eternity. I need flesh-and-blood creatures, sublimated by the artist's hand.

Soon I discovered an aspect of my esthetic vocation—travel—which further distinguished me from my fathers, whose stinginess condemned them to a sedentary existence. But rest assured, it was not the Trojan War or the conquest of Asia that drew me out of my native palace. I have put such provocative irony into these lines in spite of myself that I can't help laughing as I write. Yes, I must own, it was not with sword in hand but brandishing a butterfly net that I ventured out into the world. The palace of Nippur, I regret to say, is distinguished neither by rose gardens nor by orchards. It is a triumphant marriage of stone and sun—blinding cascades of light, falling on white terraces. Consequently I was delighted when sometimes in the early morning I caught sight, on the balustrade of my apartments, of a lovely mottled butterfly quivering to dry off the morning dew. I would watch it rise into the air, hesitate in its navigation, and finally fly away—always westward—with the strange angular movement of a creature whose wings are too large for proper flight.

This fragile visit was repeated now and then, but each time the visitor changed its livery. It could be yellow with shadows of black velvet, or reddish brown with a mauve eyespot, or simply as white as snow; and once it was tesselated gray and blue, like a piece of marquetry.

I was still a child, and in my eyes those butterflies, coming to me like messengers from another world, incarnated pure beauty, weightless and without market value, the exact opposite of what I was taught in Nippur. I sent for the chamberlain in charge of my material maintenance and bade him have made for me the instrument I required, namely, a bamboo pole, surmounted by a metal ring equipped with a light, wide-meshed net. After some trial and error—the materials used were almost always too heavy, lacking the necessary affinity with my prospective prey—I found myself in possession of a fairly serviceable butterfly net. Without waiting for the encouragement of a morning visit, I set out in the direction—eastward—whence my little travelers had come.

Never before had I left the royal precinct alone. To my surprise, no sentinel stood in the way of my escapade; everything seemed to conspire in its favor: an exquisitely soft breeze, the gently sloping plateau shaded by tamarisks, and here and there, of course, a spot flitting from flower to flower, as though to challenge me or recall me to my duty as a hunter of butterflies. As I made my way downward toward an affluent of the Tigris, the vegetation became richer. Having started at the end of a winter relieved by a sprinkling of crocuses, I seemed to be moving into the springtime, through fields of narcissuses, hyacinths, and daffodils. And strange to say, not only were there more and more butterflies, but they all seemed to be coming from the same place, clearly the goal of my expedition.

A cloud of insects, still at some distance, was the first indication of Maalek's farm. Centered on a well—which had no doubt determined the choice of location—a great, whitewashed cube offered no opening but a low door. Built onto it were two large, lightly built structures, roofed with crisscrossed palm fronds. From one of these roofs there rose an airy veil which spread out in all directions. One might have mistaken it for a cloud of blue smoke, but its motion, far from being passive like that of a cloud, was active, urgent, almost willful. It was a rising swarm of winged insects. By the time I reached the farmyard, I had picked up several identically gray, translucent butterflies, no doubt the laziest members of the migrant swarm.

A dog came running, putting a handful of chickens to flight with his barking. His anger may have been aroused by the strange instrument I was holding, for he persisted in his hostility until the master appeared. An imposingly tall, thin man in an ample, long-sleeved yellow tunic, he stepped out of one of the big palm huts. His clean-shaven face was that of an ascetic. He held out his hand, in greeting I thought, but it was to relieve me of my butterfly net, which he, like the dog, may have felt to be out of place on that particular farm.

I did not think it fitting to conceal my identity, and savoring in advance the slightly scandalized surprise I expected to provoke, I said without preamble, "I left the palace at Nippur this morning. I am Prince Balthasar, son of Belsarar and grandson of Belsussar."

He replied rather archly, with a gesture in the direction of the cloud of butterflies, which had ceased to rise from the roof and was dispersing over the trees, "Those are bluish Callicores. They pupate in clusters, and a mysterious instinct leads them to fly away all together. As late as yesterday, there was no indication that anything of the kind was imminent. Yet at some obscure signal each individual started gnawing the tip of its cocoon."

Meanwhile, he did not neglect the usual rites of hospitality. Drawing water from the well, he filled a cup and held it out to me. I drank gratefully, gaining awareness of my thirst as I slaked it. The long jaunt had made me thirsty and once I had drunk I felt my legs wobbling with fatigue. I knew he was aware of my fatigue but was deliberately ignoring it. This slightly mad young prince, who had sallied forth with that absurd contraption, deserved a little rough treatment.

"Come along," he commanded. "You've come to see them. They're waiting for you."

Without giving me time to ask who was waiting for me, he led me into the first palm hut.

"They" were there all right. Thousands, hundreds of thousands of them. The air was filled with the crackling and crunching sound they made in eating. There were tubs filled with leaves: fig, mulberry, eucalyptus and vine leaves, fennel, carrot, asparagus greens, and still other leaves that I could not identify. Each tub had its variety of leaf and each leaf its variety of caterpillar, some smooth-skinned, some hairy—like tiny brown, red, or black bears—soft or horny, decked in baroque ornaments—thorns,

spines, brushes, bulbs, wattles, or eyespots. But all
consisted of twelve articulated rings, culminating in a
round head with imposing jaws. The most frightening
were those whose form and color blended exactly with the
plant they lived on, so much so that it seemed at first sight
as though the leaves, seized with cannibalistic fury, were
devouring themselves.

Maalek watched me as, wide-eyed with curiosity and
amazement, I bent over one tub and then another, to fill
my soul with this astonishing spectacle.

"How delightful!" he said as though to himself. "I
watch you watching, I see you seeing, and through this
second sight, as it were, I give these essential things a new
clarity and freshness. I should receive young visitors here
more often. But so far you have seen only half the show.
Come. Through this door."

And he drew me into the second hut.

After feverish, voracious life, here was a spectacle of
death or rather sleep, but of a sleep that imitated death
with terrifying refinement. There was nothing to be seen
but a forest of dry twigs and branches, an artificial thicket
growing in tubs of sand. And this whole forest was covered with cocoons, strange, inedible fruit, wrapped in
silky, light-yellow envelopes, swollen with rather suspi-
cious-looking inner protuberances.

"You mustn't imagine they're sleeping," said Maalek,
guessing my thoughts. "A chrysalis doesn't hibernate. On
the contrary, it's hard at work; few people know how
much it accomplishes. Listen to this, little prince: the cat-
erpillars you just saw are living bodies, made up of organs,
like you and me. Stomach, eye, brain, and so forth, nothing is lacking. And now, look!"

He detached a cocoon from a branch, took it between

thumb and forefinger, and cut it in two with a scalpel. The dissected larva revealed a whitish substance, rather like the flesh of an avocado.

"You see, there's nothing, just an undifferentiated farinaceous mass. All the caterpillar's organs have melted. Nothing remains of the caterpillar with its complete physiological panoply! Simplified in the extreme, liquefied! That's what it takes to become a butterfly. For years now, in observing these minuscule mummies, I have been meditating on this absolute simplification that leads up to a magnificent metamorphosis. I keep looking for equivalents. Emotion, for example. Yes, emotion, fear if you like."

He sat down on a stool to be more at his ease and closer to me while speaking.

"Fear. . . . One fine April morning you're taking a walk in the castle park. Everything breathes peace and happiness. You relax, you abandon yourself to the smells, the blossoming boughs, the balmy breeze. But suddenly a wild beast appears, ready to pounce on you. You have to face it, to prepare to fight, a fight for life. You are seized with violent emotion. For a few seconds your thoughts seem to be in disarray, you haven't the strength to call for help, your arms and legs have ceased to obey you. That's what is known as fear. I should call it *simplification*. What the situation demands of you is a radical metamorphosis. The carefree stroller must become a fighter. This is impossible without a transitional phase, which liquefies you like the pupa in its cocoon. From this liquefaction must emerge a man ready for combat. Let's hope it won't be too late!"

He stood up and took a few steps in silence.

"Of course this theory of transitional simplification is much better illustrated in the political sphere. Ordinarily a country that changes its political regime—or merely its

sovereign—goes through a troubled period, when all the
organs of administration, justice, and defense seem to dissolve into anarchy. But that is just what is needed before
the new authority can be established.

"The metamorphosis that turns a caterpillar into a butterfly is obviously exemplary. I have often been tempted to
regard the butterfly as an animal flower which—respond-
ing to the mimicry that blends insect and leaf—hatches out
of a plant named caterpillar. The metamorphosis is exemplary because of its impressive success. Can you conceive of any more sublime transfiguration than that which
starts with a gray, crawling caterpillar and ends with a
butterfly? But you mustn't suppose that the example is always followed! I have spoken of popular revolutions. But
how often a tyrant is driven from power only to make
place for an even more sanguinary tyrant! And what of
children! Might one not liken the puberty which turns
them into adults to the metamorphosis of a butterfly into a
caterpillar?"

He then admitted me to a small room filled with a per-
vasive balsamic smell. It was there, he explained, that the
butterflies he wished to preserve were sacrificed and
pinned with wings outspread for all eternity. The moment
they issued from the cocoon—still moist, rumpled and
trembling—they were put into a little glass case, which was
then hermetically sealed. There one watched them awaken
to life and spread their wings in the sunlight. But before
they even attempted to fly, one asphyxiated them by intro-
ducing the burning tip of a myrrh-coated stick into the
cage. Maalek thought very highly of this resin, exuded by
an oriental shrub[3] and used by the Egyptians to embalm
their dead. He regarded it as the symbolic substance which
enabled putrescible flesh to attain the perennity of marble,

the perishable body the timelessness of a statue, and these frail butterflies the density of jewels. He gave me a block of it. I have kept it ever since and am hefting it in my left hand as I write these lines. I observe this reddish, rather oily substance, traversed with white streaks. It will leave my hand with the persistent smell of dark temples and faded flowers.

Afterward he took me to his living quarters. All I remember is the thousands of butterflies in flat crystal cases which covered the walls. He named them all to me in a fantastic litany: there were sphinxes, peacocks, noctuas, satyrs, and I can still see before me the Nacreous Giant, the Atalanta, the Chelonia, Urania, Heliconia, and Nymphalina. But more than any other variety, it was the Knight-Banneret that delighted me, not so much for its "spears," those fine, curved extensions of the lower wings, as with the escutcheon on the corselet, showing an often geometrical but sometimes distinctly figurative design, a head, yes, if you will, a death's head, but at the same time that of a living man, a portrait: my portrait, Maalek assured me, while pressing into my hand a Knight-Banneret Balthasar, as he solemnly baptized it, encased in a block of pink beryl.

The next day I returned to Nippur, having exchanged my butterfly net for the Knight-Banneret Balthasar, which I hugged under my tunic along with my block of myrrh—two objects which now, seen in the long perspective of the years, seem to mark the first turning points of my destiny. For this Knight-Banneret Balthasar—black with a moiré sheen, spotted with violet—which bore, sculptured and tattooed in the horn of its corselet a head, unquestionably human and more questionably my own, was for that very reason fated to be the first victim, followed by many

others, of our priests' fanatical hatred. With the impru-
dence of a child, I showed everyone my acquisition when I
got back to the palace, neither seeing nor wishing to see
how certain faces hardened when I boasted that the design
on the lovely Knight-Banneret's back was my own portrait. The interdiction of images in general and of portraits
in particular has remained an article of faith with the
Semitic peoples, who are obsessed with a horror—or perhaps one should say the temptation—of idolatry. Moreover,
a bust, portrait, or effigy of a member of a ruling family
suggests an attempt at self-deification, and that, in the eyes
of our clergy, is the worst of abominations.

Some time later, a hunting expedition took me away
from the palace for three days. On my return I found my
block of beryl with its precious contents pulverized on the
floor of my terrace, crushed with a stone, or possibly with
a club. I couldn't get anything out of my servants, who
cannot have failed to witness the "execution." I had come
up against the limits of royal power for the first time; it
was not to be the last.

Still, the enemy was not without name or face. The
high priest, a mild old man, whom I suspected of secret
skepticism, would not on his own initiative have destroyed
my treasure. But he was assisted by a young levite, the
vicar Sheddad, a rock-ribbed traditionalist and fanatical
iconoclast. First out of weakness and timidity, later out of
calculation, I was always careful to avoid a head-on clash
with him, but I soon identified him as an intransigent
enemy of what I loved best in all the world, my true
reason for living, namely, painting and sculpture. And
what is perhaps still graver, I never forgave him for destroying my beautiful butterfly, that Knight-Banneret
Balthasar which carried my portrait etched on its corselet,

and bore it up to the heavens. Woe betide him who wounds a child in what he holds most dear! Let him not hope that his crime will be judged as juvenile because its victim is a child!

In accordance with an old family tradition, dating back no doubt to the Hellenistic golden age, my father sent me to Greece. In advance I was so dazzled by Athens, the goal of my journey, that I was blind, as it were, to what I might have seen on the journey through Chaldea, Mesopotamia, and Phoenicia, and in Attalia and Rhodes, where we stopped in the course of the sea voyage to Piraeus. Of the wonders and novelties that passed before my eyes—it was my first time at sea—next to nothing remained in my memory, for, as we all know, youth is distinguished far more by ardent passions than by an open mind.

No matter! When I set foot on Greek soil, I might almost have knelt down and kissed it! I had no eyes for the ruin of that nation, fallen from its opulence to servitude and internecine strife. The temples laid waste, the pedestals without statues, the fallow fields, cities like Thebes and Argos reduced to the state of wretched villages—none of all that existed for my wonder-struck mind. The fact is that all the life which had drained from the provincial towns and villages had flowed into the two cities of Athens and Corinth. As far as I was concerned, the sacred host of the statues of Apollo would have sufficed to populate the whole country. The Propylaea, the Parthenon, the Erechtheion, the Errephoroi, so much grace allied with so much grandeur, so much sensuous life wedded to so much nobility, struck me with a happy sort of stupor, from which I have not yet recovered. I discovered what I had long been expecting, and my expectation was magnificently surpassed.

Yes, I have remained passionately faithful to the great
Hellenic revelation of my youth. After that, of course, I
matured and so did my vision. With the passing years I
acquired a certain perspective toward that world of marble
and porphyry, worshipped from dawn to dusk by the
great Apollonian orb. The conclusion which had painfully
forced itself upon me at the time of my first visit was that
I belonged heart and soul to my cherished Greece and that
destiny had made a dreadful mistake in bringing me into
the world elsewhere. Little by little, however, I perceived
and availed myself of what I shall call the *privilege of
banishment*. The very agony of my exile made me see the
land of Greece in a light which must have been unknown
to its inhabitants, and this taught me something, though it
did not console me. Meditating in my remote Chaldea, I
discovered the intimate tie between the plastic arts and
polytheism. So all-pervasive are the gods, goddesses, and
heroes of Greece that they hardly leave room for plain
human reality. In the mind of the Greek artist the opposition between the sacred and the profane was resolved quite
simply by ignorance of the profane. While monotheism
brings with it fear and hatred of images, in polytheism—
which presided over a golden age of painting and sculpture
—the gods appropriated all the arts.

Of course, I continued in my palace at Nippur to revere
faraway Greece, but I recognized the limits of its sublime
art. For it is neither good nor just nor true to confine art
to an Olympus from which man is excluded. To me the
most commonplace, but also the most passionate experience, has been the discovery of devastating beauty in the
profile of a humble African girl, the face of a beggar, or
the gesture of a child. Greek art knows only Zeus,
Phoebus, or Artemis, and refuses to see this hidden beauty

of the commonplace. At that point I turned to the Bible of the Jews, that charter of a fiercely exclusive monotheism. I read that God had created man in his image and likeness, so fashioning not only the first portrait but also the first self-portrait in the history of the world. I read that he had then commanded man to be fruitful and multiply, to fill the earth with his seed. After thus creating his own effigy, God wanted it reproduced ad infinitum and distributed throughout the earth.

This twofold action has been taken as a model by most sovereigns and tyrants, who make certain that their effigy will be distributed throughout their territories by having it struck on coins, which are destined not only to be reproduced in large numbers but also to circulate unceasingly from coffer to coffer, pocket to pocket, and hand to hand.

Then something incomprehensible happened, a break, a catastrophe, and the Bible, which began with a portraitist and self-portraitist God, suddenly took to pursuing the makers of images with its curse. That curse, which had its repercussions throughout the Orient, was the source of my misfortune, and I asked myself: Why, why, what has happened, and will it never cease?

My life was bound to take a new turn when the question of my taking a wife arose. The sentimental and erotic education of a prince is inevitably so incomplete as to be almost negligible. Why? Because everything is too easy for him. If a young man is poor, or even if he is merely a commoner, it costs him a struggle to satisfy his flesh and heart —a struggle with himself, with society, and as often as not with the object of his love. Such a struggle strengthens and feeds his desire. Whereas a prince has only to wave his hand or flick his eyelids, and a body that he has scarcely glimpsed will be wafted into his bed, even if it belongs to the wife of his grand vizier. This stultifying, debilitating facility cheats him out of the fierce joy of the chase and the subtle pleasure of seduction.

One day my father asked me in his fashion—which was especially offhand, playful, and indirect on this occasion because the subject was close to his heart—whether it had occurred to me that, like it or not, I would have to succeed him someday, and that the proprieties would then require me to have a wife worthy to be queen of Nippur. I was without political ambition, and for the reasons I have just gone into my sex organ made no demands of a nature to trouble my sleep. Nevertheless my father's question, to which I had found no answer, did not fail to preoccupy me, and perhaps it obscurely prepared me for my sufferings to come.

Some caravans from the headwaters of the Tigris had flooded the sooks of Nippur with their treasures of basketry, precious stones, drapery, nielloed bracelets, raw silk, hides, and wrought-gold torches. As soon as the market opened, I haunted the booths and shops with their piles of romantic bric-a-brac smelling of the Orient and of great desert spaces. At such times I was a sedentary traveler; exotic wares became my camels, ships, and flying carpets and carried me far away, beyond the horizon. That was how one day I found a mirror—or rather what had once been a mirror, for the backing of polished metal had been replaced or covered over by a picture painted with earth colors. It was the portrait of a pale, blue-eyed girl with abundant hair falling in undisciplined waves over her forehead and shoulders. Her unsmiling look contrasted with the extreme youth of her face and gave it an air of sullen sadness. Is it because I was holding the portrait by the handle of a mirror that I seemed to detect a certain family resemblance between that young girl and myself? We must have been about the same age; like me, she had dark hair and blue eyes. To judge by the caravan's point of departure, she had crossed the frozen Assyrian uplands before coming to me. I bought the mirror and took flight on the wings of my imagination. Where could this girl be now? Was she from Nineveh, from Ecbatana, from Rhagae? Or was she as far away from me in time as in space? Perhaps the portrait had been painted a century or two ago, and in that case its lovely model had been gathered to the dust of her ancestors. Far from depressing me, this supposition attached me all the more to the portrait, which thus took on greater value, an absolute value as it were, since it had lost all frame of reference. A strange reaction, which should have enlightened me about my true feelings.

My father sometimes paid me brief visits in my apartments. Preoccupied perhaps by the subject he had brought up, he went straight to the mirror-portrait and questioned me about it. Which naturally reminded me that he had advised me to look for a wife.

"It's the woman I love," I said. "I wish her to be the future queen of Nippur."

Then, of course, I had to admit that I had no idea of her name or where she came from or even of her age. The king shrugged his shoulders at my childishness and made for the door. But then he changed his mind and came back.

"Can I have it for three days?" he asked.

Though the thought of parting with my mirror-portrait was repugnant to me, I had to let him take it. But the pang in my heart showed me how strongly I felt about it.

Under the frivolous air he chose to assume, my father was a conscientious man, the soul of punctuality. Three days later he was back in my apartments with the mirror.

He put it down on the table, saying simply, "Well, her name is Malvina. She lives at the court of the satrap of Hyrcania, to whom she is distantly related. She is eighteen years old. Would you like me to ask for her hand for you?"

My father was deceived by my immense joy at recovering my treasure. To his mind, it was all settled. He had identified the girl so quickly by sending out a swarm of agents to question all caravaners coming from the north and northeast. He then sent a brilliant delegation to Samaria, where the satrap of Hyrcania had his residence. Three months later Malvina and I faced each other, both veiled in accordance with the Nippur marriage rite. We were man and wife before we had either seen each other's face or heard the sound of each other's voice.

I'm sure no one will be surprised when I say that in my eagerness to see how closely she resembled her portrait I was looking forward impatiently to the moment when Malvina would show her face. It seems only natural, don't you agree? But when you stop to think, you'll see that there's something incredible in all this. For a portrait is only an inert thing, made by a human hand, in the image of a living face. The portrait is supposed to resemble the face, not the other way around. But for me, the portrait was the beginning. Without the pressure of my father and the court I would never have dreamed of a Malvina from the shores of the Hyrcanian Sea.[4] The picture was enough for me. It was the picture I loved, and the feeling for the young girl could only be secondary, contingent on the resemblance I saw between her countenance and the beloved work of art. Is there a word for the strange perversion that possessed me? I've heard the word zoophile applied to a

wealthy woman who lived alone with a pack of greyhounds, to which she granted her ultimate favors. Ought I
to coin the word iconophile just for myself?

Life is made up of concessions and accommodations.
Malvina and I adjusted to a situation which, though based
on a misunderstanding, was not intolerable. The mirror-
portrait never left the wall of our bedroom. In a manner of
speaking, it watched over our conjugal frolics, and no one
—not even Malvina—could have imagined that my ardors
were addressed to the portrait through her intermediary.
Still, the passing years inexorably created a discrepancy
between portrait and model. Malvina blossomed out. What
had been childlike in her face and body when we were
married gave way to the majestic beauty of a matron and
future queen. We procreated. Each of her pregnancies
carried my wife further away from the unsmiling, melancholy portrait that continued to warm my heart.

My eldest daughter must have been seven when a little
scene took place, which no one noticed but which changed
my whole life. Miranda was cared for by a nurse and seldom ventured into her parents' bedroom. So one day when
we sent for her, she looked about in wide-eyed amazement. That day she approached the marriage bed and, raising her eyes, pointed a finger at the little portrait that
watched over it.

"Who's that?" she asked.

The moment she uttered those simple words, I recognized on her innocent pale face, lit by two blue eyes and
narrowed by the flow of her black curls—I recognized, I
say, the same look of sullen melancholy as in the painted
face at which she was pointing, as though the mirror, suddenly recovering its specular property, were reflecting the

little girl's face. A deep and exquisite emotion brought tears to my eyes. I took down the portrait, stood the child between my knees, and held it up to her sweet, fresh face.

"Look closely," I said. "You asked me who it is. Look closely, it's someone you know."

She kept an obstinate silence, a silence cruel and insulting to her mother, whom she simply refused to recognize in the youthful portrait.

"All right. I'll tell you. It's you. You as you'll be when you're bigger. Take it away with you. It's a present. Put it over your bed. Look at it every morning and say: 'Good morning, Miranda.' And each day, you'll see, you'll look more and more like it."

I held the portrait up to her eyes and, obediently, with childlike gravity, she said: "Good morning, Miranda." Then she put the picture under her arm and ran away.

The very next day I informed Malvina that we would keep separate rooms from then on. My father's death and our coronation soon eclipsed that dreary epilogue to our married life.

This block of myrrh that Maalek gave me years ago, this substance endowed, so he said, with the power to make temporal things eternal, that is, to convert men and butterflies from their putrescible to an indestructible state—I run my fingers over it and examine it as though trying to read the future in it. You see, my whole life has been an exchange between these two poles: time and eternity. In Greece I found eternity, incarnated in a divine sunlit tribe, immobile in its grace, itself a statue of the god Apollo. My marriage thrust me back into the heaviness of time, where everything changes and grows older. I saw the youthful Malvina's identity with the ravishing portrait I loved un-

dermined from year to year by the onslaughts of time.
Now I know that I shall not find light and peace again
until I see ephemeral, heartrending human truth merge
with the divine grandeur of eternity to form a single
image. But has anyone dreamed of a more unlikely marriage?

The affairs of the kingdom kept me in Nippur for several years. Then, when I had settled the worst of the inter-
nal and external difficulties bequeathed by my father, and
when above all I had come to realize that the first virtue of
a sovereign consists in knowing how to surround himself
with capable, upright men, and to put his trust in them, I
was in a position to set out on various expeditions with the
real and avowed aim of discovering and possibly acquiring
the art treasures of neighboring countries. When I say that
a sovereign must be capable of trusting the ministers he
himself has appointed, I should add that there is no point
in tempting the devil and that certain precautions must be
taken. In this connection, I made good use of page boys—
those young men of noble family, whose fathers send them
to court to serve the king and acquire knowledge and
friendships that will prove useful in later life. When I
traveled, I never left a man in a strategic post without taking at least one of his sons with me on my expedition. In
that way I provided myself with a brilliant escort of
young men, who enlivened our journey and broadened
their knowledge through contact with foreign things and
people. Furthermore, they functioned as hostages, so
shielding their fathers from all seditious temptation. This
institution proved successful and took on a life of its own.
Ceding to an inclination frequent in young men, my pages
—among whom my own sons were, of course, included—
organized a kind of secret society and chose the narcissus

as its emblem. I must own that I liked this naïvely provocative way of avowing their self-love. Shared experiences, a
certain remoteness from Nippur society due to our frequent trips, a grain of contempt for the sedentary citizens
of the capital mired in their habits and prejudices, contributed to make my Narcissi a revolutionary political nucleus.
I shall expect great things of them on the day when I retire
from power along with the men of my generation.

One of my first journeys was, of course, to Greece. I
wanted my young companions to be dazzled as I had been
twenty years before, and it was with joyful enthusiasm
that we embarked on a Phoenician ship at Sidon. Was it
because the years had altered my vision or because I had
my pages with me? I didn't find the Greece of my youth,
but I did discover another. Energetic and eager for human
contact, the Narcissi were soon admitted to the gatherings
of the Athenian youth, whose society at the time was open
and easily accessible. With a rapidity that amazed me they
learned to speak like young Athenians, copied their dress,
and took to frequenting their baths, gymnasiums, and theaters. Sometimes I found it hard to distinguish my own
among the throngs of ephebes in the steam rooms and
palaestras. I was proud to see them cutting such a good
figure and pleased to think how they would enrich the life
of the Nippur stay-at-homes. I was even glad to see how
wholeheartedly they adopted a certain form of love—
which may be termed a specialty of the Greeks, not because they practice it—the practice, after all, is universal—
but because they do it so lightly and openly—for it seemed
to provide a happy, gratuitous, and inoffensive diversion
from the dreary fetters of conjugal heterosexuality.

But the athletes, actors, masters at arms, and masseurs
were not the only people in that city which had dazzled

the world with its genius. I myself spent delightful eve-
nings under leafy porticoes, drinking white wine from
Thasos and conversing with infinitely cultivated, subtle,
and skeptical men and women, who were curious about
everything, the finest hosts in the world. Yet I soon saw
that there was little to be expected from these consum-
mately civilized people, who with their cold hearts,
superficial minds, and sterile imaginations created a feeling
of near emptiness. My first visit to Greece had shown me
only gods. On my second visit I saw men. Unfortunately,
the two were unrelated. Centuries earlier, the peasants, soldiers, and thinkers who made up the population may have
been superhuman, Olympian, living on familiar terms with
demi-gods, fauns, and satyrs, with Castor, Pollux, and
Herakles, with giants and centaurs. In those days there
were great men whose voices we still hear, resounding
over the centuries, Homer, Hesiod, Pindar, Aeschylus,
Sophocles, Euripides. The people I met then were not
their direct descendants or even the descendants of their
descendants. The Greece of my first journey was a sublime image. That image, I discovered on my second visit,
was a mask with no face under it.

But what was that to us! The ship that carried us back
was laden with busts, torsos, bas-reliefs and ceramics. If
only I could have disassembled a whole temple and carried
it away in pieces! In any event, it was during that first expedition that we conceived the idea of a *Balthasareum*, a
royal foundation where my collections and the art treasures acquired by the Crown would be exhibited. Each
new expedition enriched it, and from year to year the
collection of Punic mosaics, Egyptian sarcophagi, Persian
miniatures, Cypriot tapestries, and even of Indian idols
with the trunks of elephants was expanded under the su-

pervision of specialists. This museum—rather eclectic, I admit—was my pride, the justification not only of my travels but of my whole life. After acquiring a new marvel, I would wake up at night and laugh for joy, already visualizing it on display in its proper place in the Balthasareum. Falling in love with the work, my Narcissi became experts in mirabilia of all kinds, which they would ferret out and bring back to me with youthful enthusiasm. I had hopes, of course, that one or another of them would some day benefit by the admirable artistic education I was giving them and take up the engraver's stylus, the painter's brush, or the sculptor's chisel. Because true creation must be contagious, and masterpieces are fully themselves only when they foster other masterpieces. Thus I encouraged the gropings of a boy in our group; his name was Assur and he was of Babylonian descent. But apart from the hostility of our clergy, I could see that he was hampered by the contradiction I have already mentioned between the frozen, hieratic art we encountered and the simple, spontaneous manifestations of life, which overwhelmed him with joy and admiration. His quest was mine, only more ardent, more anxious, because of his youth and his ambition.

And then came the catastrophe, the black crime of that black night, the autumnal equinox that transported me directly from the eternal youth in which I had shut myself up with my Narcissi and my marvels, to an embittered, reclusive old age. In a few hours my hair turned white, my back bent, my eyes clouded, my ears began to fail me, my legs grew heavy, and my member shriveled.

We were in Susa, searching the ruins of Darius I's Apadana for what the Achaemenid dynasty had to offer us. The harvest was good, but of sinister augury. Especially the painted vases we dug up spoke to us only of suffering, ruin, and death. There are signs that cannot be misread. We had just emerged from a tomb containing skulls encrusted with chrysoprase, an ill-omened stone if ever there was one, when we saw a black horse winged with dust approaching us from the west. So ravaged was the rider's face by five days at a frantic gallop and, alas, by the terrible news he was bringing that we had difficulty in recognizing him as the young brother of one of my Narcissi. The Balthasareum was no more. Rioters from the poorest quarters of the town had taken it by storm. The faithful servants who tried to guard the doors had been massacred. Nothing was left of our treasures. What could not be carried away had been smashed with clubs. To judge by the shouts and banners of the mob, their fury was religious. They had risen to destroy an edifice and institution which offended against the cult of the true God, with its interdiction of idols and images.

In other words, the crime was signed. I knew the slum dwellers of my capital. They don't care a fig for the cult of the true God, but they are most amenable to slogans backed up by gifts of money and drink. Obviously the vicar Sheddad had fomented this allegedly popular uprising. But, of course, he had managed to hide his hand. My worst enemy had struck me without showing his face. To punish him would have exposed me as a tyrant, and under the influence of the clergy the whole population would have cursed me. The ringleaders and those convicted of mortally wounding the Balthasareum guards were caught and sold as slaves. After that, myself mortally wounded, I shut myself up in my palace.

It was then that I first heard talk of a comet. Coming from the southwest, so it was said, it was heading northward. My astrologers—all Chaldeans—were thoroughly

wrought up and wrangled from morning to night. What
could it mean? Calamity—on that they were all agreed.
Plague, drought, earthquake, the accession of a bloodthirsty tyrant—all these were announced by extraordinary
meteors. My astrologers vied with one another in pessi-
mistic interpretations. The ebony gloom in which I was
plunged provoked me to contradict them. To their great
consternation, I argued that the present situation was so
bad that a great change could only be for the better. Consequently the comet was a good omen. . . . But it was
when the comet finally appeared in the sky of Nippur that
my interpretations raised the stupefaction of my dunce-
caps to its zenith. Here I must tell you that according to
my reckoning the sack of the Balthasareum occurred exactly fifty years after the loss of my beautiful butterfly,
the Knight-Banneret, which had fallen victim to the same
stupid fanaticism. In my bitterness, I identified the glorious
insect bearing my effigy on its back with the palace in
which I had invested the better part of my life. And now
that this tremulous, capricious star had appeared over our
heads, I calmly announced that this was a supernatural
butterfly, a butterfly angel, bearing, sculptured on its
corselet, the portrait of a sovereign. And I informed all
who would listen that a benign revolution was imminent
and would take place in the west. None of my learned
sky-searchers dared contradict me, some even tried to
curry favor by backing me up, so much so that in the end
I began to believe what I had originally said for the sake of
argument. This was what gave me the idea of setting out
on one more expedition, of countering my melancholy by
following this fiery butterfly, just as years ago I set out
with my butterfly net and discovered Maalek's magic
farm.

The Narcissi had been deep in gloom since the sack of
the Balthasareum. Their spirits revived as they selected the
horses and provisions necessary for an expedition to the far
west. In those days my memory of Maalek and his butterflies was rekindled, and wherever I went the block of
myrrh he had given me went along. To my mind, this fragrant, translucent object gave promise of a solution to the
painful contradiction that was tearing me apart. In the
view and custom of the ancient Egyptians, it was myrrh
that conferred eternity on corruptible flesh. Taking to unknown roads at an age when most men would think of
withdrawing into their memories, I was not, like certain
others, looking for a new route to the sea, the sources of
the Nile, or the Pillars of Herakles. The object of my
quest was an intermediary between the impersonal and in-
temporal gold mask of the Greek gods and . . . my little
Miranda's face with its childlike gravity.

From Nippur to Hebron you must count a hundred
days' march, including the detour to the south that is necessary if you don't wish to put across the Dead Sea in
boats. Every night we saw the fiery butterfly fluttering in
the west, and by day I felt the vigor of my youth flowing
back into my body and soul. Our journey was an unbro-
ken celebration, becoming more radiant from day to day.
We were only two days from Hebron when the riders we
had sent out as scouts informed me that a camel caravan
led by black men, apparently coming from Egypt and
probably from Nubia, would soon cross our path but that
their intentions seemed peaceful. We had been camping
for twenty-four hours at the gates of Hebron when an emissary from the king of Meroë approached the guardians of
my tent.

MELCHIOR, PRINCE OF PALMYRA

I am a king but I am poor. Legend, perhaps, will make me the king who came to worship the Savior with gifts of gold. That would be a bitter and rather delectable irony, though consonant with the truth in a way. Other kings have retinues, servants, horses, tents, fine plate. That's as it should be. A king doesn't travel without a proper retinue. I, however, am alone, except for an old man who never leaves my side. My old preceptor, who saved my life, is my companion, but at his age he needs my help more than I need his services. We have walked all the way from Palmyra, like tramps, with no other baggage than bundles slung over our shoulders. We have crossed rivers and forests, deserts and steppes. To enter Damascus, we outfitted ourselves with the headgear and sacks of itinerant peddlers. To enter Jerusalem, with the staffs and skullcaps of pilgrims. For there was reason to fear not only the Palmyrans sent in pursuit of us but also the sedentary population of the regions we passed through, with their hatred of poor but otherwise nondescript travelers.

We had come from Palmyra, Tadmor in Hebrew, the city of palm trees, the pink city, built by King Solomon after his conquest of Hamath-Zoba. It is my native city. It is my city. In leaving it, I took only one treasure, but to my mind it was both a family memento and a token of my

rank. This was a gold coin struck with the effigy of my father, King Theodenos, sewn into the hem of my coat. For
I am the rightful heir to the throne of Palmyra, the legal
sovereign since the death, under highly suspicious circumstances, of the king, my father.

The king had long been childless, and his younger
brother Atmar, prince of Hamath on the Orontes, who
had wives and children to spare, regarded himself as the
heir presumptive. So, at least, I inferred from his persistent
hostility to me. My birth was a cruel blow to his ambition
and the fact is that he never resigned himself to it. In the
course of expeditions on the right bank of the Euphrates,
my father had met and loved a simple Bedouin woman.
When he heard she was expecting a child, he was overjoyed as well as surprised. He at once repudiated Queen
Euphorbia and enthroned the newcomer, who accommo-
dated herself with inborn dignity to her sudden move from
a Bedouin tent to the palace in Palmyra. I have learned
since then that my uncle, in terms as insulting to my father
as to my mother, expressed doubts about my origin. The
result was a break between the two brothers. Some time
later Atmar met with a rebuff when he made advances to
Queen Euphorbia and invited her to come and live in
Hamath, where, so he claimed, he had a palace all ready
for her. He hoped no doubt to find in her a natural ally,
who would supply him with information that he could use
against his brother. But with irreproachable dignity the
erstwhile queen went into retirement, resolutely shutting
her door to all plotters. For spies and conspirators, not to
speak of mere opportunists, kept shuttling back and forth
between Hamath and Palmyra. My father knew all that.
After a rather dubious hunting accident that nearly cost
me my life at the age of fourteen, he contented himself

with keeping me well guarded. About his own life he worried a good deal less. There, of course, he was mistaken. But we shall never know for sure whether the wine of Riblah, a half-full goblet of which fell from his hand when he collapsed as though struck to the heart, was responsible for his death. When I arrived on the scene, it was too late to retrieve the wine that had spilled on the floor, and the jar it had been in was mysteriously empty. But almost instantly, courtiers whom I had thought loyally devoted to the throne, or else remote from the business of politics and indifferent to honors, let fall their masks, revealing themselves to be ardent partisans of Prince Atmar, opposed to my accession.

I gave the necessary orders for my father's funeral. The next day I was to be solemnly presented to the twenty members of the Crown Council and officially confirmed as heir to the throne. Late in the night, exhausted by my grief and the many things I had had to attend to, I lay down for a short rest. In the first light of dawn Baktiar, my old preceptor, who had always been a second father to me, burst into my room and said I would have to get up and escape without delay. The news he brought exceeded my blackest imaginings. The queen, my mother, had been abducted. The conspirators were trying to make her sign a confession to the effect that I was the consequence of an affair she had been having with a Bedouin of her tribe, threatening to kill me if she declined. Undoubtedly the Council, two-thirds of whose members had been suborned, would declare me unfit and give the crown to my uncle. Only by escaping could I free the queen from her cruel dilemma. Then the conspirators would have to release her, and I would be safe, though reduced to the most dire poverty and deprived of the very right to bear my name.

We fled through the underground passages connecting the palace with the necropolis. In passing I stopped, almost in spite of myself, to salute my ancestors and meditate for a moment beside the vault that had been made ready for my father in accordance with orders that I myself had given a few hours before. To mislead our pursuers, we took what might have seemed the least likely direction. Instead of heading for Assyria in the east, where we would have been given asylum—but we would certainly have been overtaken before reaching the Euphrates—we started westward in the direction of Hamath, the residence of my worst enemy. And true enough, two days later, lying hidden on a rocky slope, I had occasion to see my uncle Atmar's cavalcade passing on their way to Palmyra. Knowing in advance what the decision of the Council would be, he hadn't even waited to receive it before starting out. His precipitation brought the magnitude of his treachery home to me.

We lived by begging. If those terrible trials enriched me in a way, it was by teaching me to know my own people from a new angle—the exact opposite of what it had been before. I had presided now and then over the distribution of food to the paupers of Palmyra. With the thoughtlessness of my age, I was only too glad to assume the easy and seemingly flattering role of the generous benefactor who, moved by compassion for the misery of his people, comes to them with his bounty. And now I was a beggar, knocking at doors and holding out my cap to passersby. An admirable and beneficial inversion! At first I was plagued by the thought of the abominable injustice I had suffered; I couldn't help thinking that the rich man I was imploring for food was by right my subject, that by right I could have sent him to the mines or had his head cut off with a mere snap of my fingers. My black thoughts must have communicated themselves to my face. Some of the passersby, made inattentive by contempt, gave me a pittance or rebuffed me without looking at me. Others, repelled by my looks, pushed me aside in silence or with a word of reproach: "You have a very proud look for a beggar"; or "I don't give to dogs that bite." And some went so far as to vouchsafe a rather cynical bit of advice: "If you're so proud, why don't you take instead of begging?" or "At your age and with that look in your eyes, you'd do better on the highways than at the gates of temples!" I came to see that the combination of royalty and indigence is better suited to a bandit than to a beggar, but that king, bandit, and beggar have this in common: living outside the usual workaday world, they acquire nothing by toil or exchange. These reflections, added to the memory of the recent coup d'état by which I lost everything, opened my eyes to the precariousness of all three conditions and led me to hope that someday there would dawn a social order with no room for kings, bandits, or beggars.

Jerusalem and our visit to King Herod the Great would give my thoughts new food and a new direction.

Since my father's death, I had the impression that time was passing with abnormal rapidity, with sudden leaps, cataclysmic changes, shattering revelations. One of these revelations was the discovery of Jerusalem. We had crossed the hills of Samaria in the company of a Jew of strict orthodox observance, whom only the fear of bandits and wild animals could have impelled to join up with unclean foreigners like us. He kept mumbling prayers—an excellent pretext for neither talking nor listening to anyone else.

Suddenly, at the top of a bald hill, he stopped still and spread his arms to prevent us from going on ahead of him.

Then, after a long silence, he cried out in a kind of ecstasy: "Holy! Holy! Holy! The holy city!"

There was Jerusalem before our eyes, at the foot of Mt.
Scopus, the hill where we were standing. This was my first
sight of a larger, mightier city than my native Palmyra.
But what a difference between the pink-and-green palm
grove I came from and King Herod's metropolis! We
were looking down on a maze of terraces, cubes, and walls,
all crowded into a ring of ramparts interspersed with
crenellations as hostile as the teeth of a trap. The entire
city, crisscrossed with somber alleys and stairways, was
bathed in a uniformly gray light, and from it, along with
sparse wisps of smoke, there arose a dismal rumbling, mingled with the cries of children and the barking of dogs,
and that rumbling also had a grayness about it. The jumble
of houses large and small was bordered on the east by a
spot of pale green, the Mount of Olives, and further on by
the arid, mournful-looking Valley of Jehoshaphat; in the
west by the bare hill of Golgotha; and in the distance before us by the Valley of Hinnom, that chasm six hundred
feet below the city, with its confusion of tombs and caves.

As we drew nearer, we were able to distinguish three
massive buildings whose walls and towers seemed to crush
the swarm of small houses round about. The first was
Herod's palace, a glowering fortress of rough-hewn stone;
the second was the older and less ostentatious palace of the
Hasmonaeans; while the last and easternmost was the still
unfinished third temple of the Hebrews, a prodigious
edifice, Cyclopean, Babylonian, grandiose in its majesty, a
veritable holy city in the midst of the profane city, with
colonnades, porticoes, courts, and monumental stairways
rising by stages to the holy of holies, the summit of Yahweh's kingdom.

We entered the city through the Gate of Benjamin and were instantly caught up in an unusually animated crowd. Baktiar asked what the excitement was all about. It wasn't a holiday, or a declaration of war, or the announcement of a betrothal in the royal family. No, it seemed that two royal visitors had arrived, one from the south, the other from Chaldea, they had joined forces in Hebron, they were soon to be received by Herod, and in the meantime they and their retinues had occupied all the inns and other available quarters in Jerusalem.

This news filled me with consternation. From my earliest childhood I had been taught to admire and fear King Herod. For thirty years the entire Orient had resounded with his crimes and accomplishments, the cries of his victims and the blaring of his victorious trumpets. For one threatened on all sides, with no other defense than his obscurity, it seemed the height of folly to venture within the tyrant's reach. My father had always watched his step with his dangerous neighbor. No one could accuse him of showing friendliness or hostility toward the King of the Jews. But what of my uncle Atmar? Had he acted without Herod's knowledge, judging that he would accept the fait accompli? Or had he, before moving, assured himself of Herod's benevolent neutrality? Never had it occurred to me to take refuge in Jerusalem and appeal to Herod for help and asylum. At best he would have made me pay too dearly for the slightest service rendered. At worst he would have handed me over to the usurper in exchange for some little thing he wanted.

Consequently, when Baktiar told me about the two foreign kings and their retinues, my first thought was to keep away from all this diplomatic bustle. Regretfully, to be sure, because Herod's grandiose and awe-inspiring reputa-

tion and what I had already heard about the royal travelers
from the ends of Fertile Arabia suggested that their meeting would be an event of incomparable splendor. I made a
show of sensible indifference and even spoke of saving our
skins by leaving the city in all haste, but my old preceptor
read my face like an open book and knew how unhappy it
made me to miss so magnificent an occasion.

We spent the first night at a third-rate caravansary that
sheltered more beasts than men—the men were there to
wait on the beasts. Though I slept heavily, I was not unaware of Baktiar's absence of several hours. He reappeared
with the pink of dawn. Dear Baktiar! He had expended
treasures of ingenuity to solve the dilemma he had seen
weighing on me. It was all arranged. I would attend the
audience of the kings. But hidden under a borrowed identity. That way Herod wouldn't get the idea of making use
of me. My old teacher had found a distant cousin in the
retinue of Balthasar, king of Nippur in eastern Arabia.
Through his good offices the king had granted Baktiar an
audience, and Baktiar had explained our situation. Thanks
to my youth, it was decided, I could reasonably pass for a
young prince entrusted to the king's protection as a page
boy. It seems that's a custom with them. If my father had
thought of it I might have enjoyed a useful stay at the
court of Nippur. In so large and brilliant a retinue I could
easily pass unobserved, especially in the page's costume
that Baktiar had brought me from the king. All in all, Baktiar had the impression that the old king took a certain
pleasure in our little game. He had the reputation of a
playful man, a friend of letters and the arts, and his retinue, it was said with a degree of malice, comprised more
jugglers and actors than diplomats and priests.

My age and misfortunes had put me in a solemn frame

of mind, hardly calculated to make me understand or love
Balthasar. Young people often find fault with the frivolity
of their elders. But Balthasar's kindness and generosity,
and above all the infinite charm he put into everything he
said and did, soon dispelled my misgivings. In next to no
time I saw myself dressed in silk and purple, and welcomed into a group of gilded youth, radiating the animal
beauty that comes of immemorial wealth. Happiness trans-
mitted from generation to generation produces an aristocracy made up of innocence, gratuitous impulse, and spontaneous acceptance of all life's gifts, but also of a secret
hardness, which is frightening when you first notice it, but
adds enormously to its charm. Those young men seemed
to form an exclusive social group. Since its emblem was the
narcissus, they came to be known at court as the Narcissi.
Some of them enjoyed special prestige because they had
been educated in Rome, but the ultimate distinction was to
have lived in Athens—despite the present decadence of
Hellas—to speak Greek and to sacrifice to the gods of
Olympus. At first I thought them utterly frivolous and
was rather scandalized to discover their very serious com-
mitment—of whose provocative character they hardly
seemed aware—to what I regarded as unconscionably futile
pursuits, namely, music, poetry, and the theater, not to
mention contests of strength and beauty.

Most of them were my age. Their manifest happiness
made me think they were much younger. Their friendliness and especially their discretion concerning my origins
made it clear that they had been given instructions. We
were sumptuously lodged in the east wing of the palace.
From the three terraces, disposed like the steps of an enormous stairway, one could look out over the rolling hills of
Judea to the white houses of Bethany and further still to

the steel-blue surface of the Dead Sea deep down in its hollow. On the lowest terrace we had at our disposal a hanging garden planted with red-blossoming carob trees, pink-spiked tamarisks, scarlet-clustering laurels, and varieties unknown to me, from remote regions of Africa and Asia.

I had more than one occasion to speak to the aged king of Nippur alone, while his Narcissi were out exploring the problematic resources of the town. He questioned me with kindness and curiosity about my childhood and youth, and concerning the manners and customs of Palmyra. He was surprised at the simplicity, not to say crudeness of our ways, and seemed—his reasoning escaped me at first—to regard them as the undoubted source of my misfortune. Could he really have supposed that greater refinement would have protected our court from my uncle's designs? Little by little, I came to understand that in his view the cult of the beautiful—beauty in language, the quest of beautiful objects—if practiced at the summit of society would be reflected at lower levels in virtues which, though inevitably less noble, were essential to the preservation of the kingdom, to wit, courage, loyalty, honesty, and disinterestedness. Unfortunately, a fanatical obscurantism had given rise among his neighbors and in his own kingdom to an iconoclastic fury that transformed these virtues into vices. He believed that if he had been able—as he ardently wished—to surround himself with a group of poets, sculptors, painters, and dramatists, the light that went out from them would have benefited the humblest navvy or cowherd in the kingdom. But every project of this would-be patron of the arts was thwarted by the vigilance of a clergy fiercely hostile to all images. He hoped that as his Narcissi gained in authority they would develop into an aristocratic body strong enough to counterbalance the traditionalist element in his capital. But the game was far from won. Rome and Athens were far away, and in between, a barrier to their influence, lay the fierce and hostile kingdom of Judea. I seemed to gather that in the course of a riot fomented by the high priest Sheddad during one of the king's absences, the king's collections of art treasures had been destroyed. I believe this crime, which obviously caused him great suffering, had a good deal to do with his present journey.

I made friends with one of the king's companions, a young Babylonian artist, whom he seems to love even more than his own sons. Assur has magical hands. We were sitting under a tree, chatting. He picks up a lump of earth and takes it between his fingers. Absently, without even looking at it, he kneads it. And a figurine appears, as though of its own accord. It's a sleeping cat, rolled up in a ball, a lotus blossom, or a woman squatting, with her knees pressed against her chin. When we're together, I always watch his hands to surprise the miracle. Assur has neither the responsibilities nor the philosophy of King Balthasar. He draws, paints, and sculptures as a bee makes its honey. He's not mute, though, far from it. But when he talks about his art, it's always in connection with a specific work; it's the work that seems to dictate his words.

One day I saw him finishing the portrait of a woman. She was neither young nor beautiful nor rich. But there was something radiant in her eyes, her faint smile, her whole face.

"Yesterday," Assur said to me, "I went to the Prophet's Fountain, the one fed by a wretched Persian wheel. The flow is meager and intermittent, so each time it starts up there's a good deal of pushing and shoving. At the back of

the crowd a feeble old man was waiting with a tin cup
trembling in his hand, and there wasn't a chance that he'd
ever be able to fill it. But then this woman, who had just
filled an amphora with great difficulty, went over and
shared her water with him.

"It was nothing. An infinitesimal gesture of friendship
among the desperately poor—people among whom sublime
and abominable deeds are done every day. What was un-
forgettable was the woman's expression from the moment
when she caught sight of the old man to the time when she
gave him his water and left him. I carried that face away
with me in my memory, and then, concentrating to keep it
alive in me as long as possible, I did this drawing. What is
it? A fugitive glimmer of love in a harsh existence. A moment of grace in a pitiless world. That rare and precious
moment when, as Balthasar puts it, the likeness sustains and
justifies the image."

He fell silent, as though to let his obscure words sink in.
Then, giving me his drawing, he added, "You see, Melchior, I've visited the monuments of Egyptian architecture
and of Greek statuary. The artists who created those masterpieces were surely inspired by the gods, they must have
been demigods themselves. Their world was bathed in the
light of eternity and one can't enter into it without feeling
somehow dead. There's no place for our hungry, feverish
carcasses in Giza or on the Acropolis. And I'm convinced
that if these carcasses were always what they are now, no
artist would have been justified in celebrating them, except
out of perversity. Yet once in a blue moon, there's . . .
something like this"—he took back his drawing—"a ray of
light, a suggestion of grace, a glimmer of eternity, buried
in flesh, inseparable from the flesh and transverberating the
flesh. And you see, up until now no artist has thought of

recreating this glimmer to the best of his powers. I realize
that what I'm after is quite a revolution. I sometimes wonder if a more profound revolution is even conceivable.
That's why I'm so patient, because I understand what resistance and persecution artists have to contend with.
There's very little hope of winning out. But it's that bit of
hope that I live for."

It was ten days before we laid eyes on King Herod, but
we had felt his oppressive presence ever since our arrival.
Despite the vastness of the palace and the throngs of courtiers and servants, we never for a moment forgot that we
were in the lion's den, that he was near us, breathing the
same air as we did, that we breathed his hot breath day and
night. Now and then we would see men running, cries
would ring out, doors turn on their hinges, soldiers would
assemble to the sound of the trumpet: the invisible monster
had moved and his movement reverberated in great waves
that would reach the ends of his kingdom. Despite the
comfort, our stay would have been unbearable if we had
not been sustained by an avid curiosity, inflamed by the
stories we had heard and continued to hear about his past
and present.

Herod the Great was then in the seventy-fourth year of
his life and the thirty-seventh year of a reign marked from
the first by violence of every kind, including murder. A
main source of trouble was that the King of the Jews—the
greatest they have ever had—is not a Jew and has always
been rejected by a section of his people, the most influen-
tial and most stubbornly intolerant. His family hailed from
Idumea, the mountainous southern province recently con-
quered and incorporated into the kingdom of Judea by
Hyrcanus I. In the eyes of the Jerusalem Jews, the Idu-

means, those sons of Esau forcibly converted to Judaism, remained barbarians, barely civilized, barely circumcised, still under suspicion of paganism. That one of them should raise himself to the throne of Jerusalem was sheer blasphemy, an intolerable provocation. Herod had won the throne of David and Solomon by currying favor with the Romans, whose creature he was, and by marrying Mariamne, granddaughter of Hyrcanus II and the last-born descendant of the Maccabees. Though at first providential for the Idumean, this alliance soon became a heavy burden to him, for his parents-in-law, his wife, and even his children, all of nobler lineage than himself, never ceased to regard him as an adventurer. With Herod all conflicts ended in a bloodbath. He drowned his ineradicable inferiority—which Mariamne was always ready to bring home to him—in a series of murders and executions, which left him sole master of the kingdom but detested by his own people, who had remained faithful to the Maccabean dynasty.

Herod made no attempt to spare the sensibilities of the Jewish integrists. In the course of travels throughout the Mediterranean world, he had acquired cosmopolitan, universalist opinions on everything under the sun. He sent his sons to study in Rome. He loved the arts, games, and festivities. He was determined to make Jerusalem a great modern city. He built a theater, which he dedicated to Augustus. He laid out parks, built fountains, columbaria, canals, a hippodrome. The Jews spat on the sacrilegious innovations. They accused their king of bringing back the customs introduced by Antiochus Epiphanes—of execrated memory—which it had taken them a century of strictest vigilance to uproot. Herod was unruffled. He subsidized temples, baths, and triumphal avenues indiscriminately in

Ascalon, Rhodes, Athens, Sparta, Damascus, Antioch, Berytus, Nicopolis, Acre, Sidon, Tyre, and Byblos. Everywhere he caused the name of Caesar to be incised. He revived the Olympic games and outraged the Jews by magnificently restoring the cities of Samaria, destroyed by the Maccabees, and Caesarea, which replaced Jerusalem as the seat of the Roman governors of Palestine. And carrying mockery to an extreme, he paid his actors, gladiators, and athletes in Jewish currency, those effigyless coins with the words "Herod King" on one side and a horn of plenty on the other.

This last symbol, however, is not undeserved, for much as the traditionalists of Jerusalem execrated Herod, he is honored by the enriched bourgeoisie, whose sons, reared in the Graeco-Roman style, frequent the gymnasiums financed by the crown and display themselves in the nude with reconstituted foreskins.[5] But Herod's openmindedness is most appreciated by the rural Jews and those of foreign countries. The Jewish communities of Rome benefit by his excellent relations with the Emperor, and in the provinces of Palestine his reign has been a period of unprecedented prosperity. The hills and valleys of Judea are grazed by enormous flocks of sheep, which in winter get the benefit of a Roman innovation: the use of lucerne as fodder. Barley, wheat, and grapes thrive in the red soil of Palestine. Figs, olives, and pomegranates give a rich yield with little expenditure of labor. At Herod's accession the roads swarmed with homeless, uprooted peasants. Herod set them up on his own estates as tenant farmers. Thus the lowlands around Jericho were artificially irrigated and converted into model farms. King Solomon had made a specialty of exporting arms and war chariots. Herod proved an astute businessman, developing a brisk trade in the salt of Sodom, the asphalt of the Dead Sea, the copper of Cyprus, the precious woods of Lebanon, the pottery of Bethel, balm from the balsam forests which he rented from Queen Cleopatra and of which Augustus made him a present after her death. As a result of Herod's total submission to the emperor, there are no Roman soldiers to be seen in Judea. Though he is forbidden to wage even a defensive war, a rule which he scrupulously observes, he maintains an army of Gallic, German, and Thracian mercenaries and a brilliant personal guard, traditionally recruited in Galatia. He is not allowed to use these soldiers outside his borders, but unfortunately he finds plenty for them to do inside the kingdom and even in his own family.

But the great undertaking of Herod's reign and his chief bond with the Jewish people has been the building of the temple. There had been two temples in Jerusalem. The first, built by Solomon, was pillaged by Nebuchadnezzar, then completely destroyed a few years later. The second, a less imposing structure, was dear to the Jews despite its poverty and decrepitude, because it commemorated the return from exile and symbolized the rebirth of Israel. This is the one Herod found on his accession and later decided to tear down and rebuild. At first, as one might expect, the Jews were hostile to the project. They felt sure that after destroying the old temple Herod would renege on his promise to rebuild it. But he somehow appeased their fears, and in the end they decided that his purpose in undertaking this huge project was to atone for his crimes, a pious illusion that the king was careful not to dispel.

Huge indeed. No less than eighteen thousand workmen were engaged in it, and though the new temple was consecrated less than ten years after the work had begun, it is far from completed even now. And since it's right next door to the palace, we see the comings and goings of the workmen and hear the clatter they make. The presence of this Cyclopean construction project next door seems to fit in with the prevailing atmosphere of terror and cruelty. Hammer blows mingle with the sound of whips, the oaths of the workmen with the groans of the tortured, and when we see a corpse being carried away, we never know if someone has been executed or if a workman has been crushed by a block of granite. Seldom, I think, have grandeur and ferocity been so closely linked.

Herod seems to have made a point of honor of disarming the distrust of the Jews. To make sure that the holy precincts of the temple would not be profaned, he had priests trained in stonecutting and masonry, and they worked without removing their vestments. Not for a single day were divine services interrupted, for nothing was ever demolished until construction was far enough advanced. The new building is of grandiose proportions. I won't attempt to describe its splendors in detail. Still, I would like to mention the "court of the pagans," a vast rectangular esplanade five hundred cubits[6] in width, where people can walk and chat or stop at the merchants' stalls to browse or buy. It's something like the Agora in Athens or the Forum in Rome. Anyone who wants to can seek shelter from the rain or sun under the cedar-roofed porticoes which surround the court, as long as his shoes are clean, he isn't armed with so much as a stick, and he refrains from spitting on the floor. The actual temple is in the center, a building with several levels, the highest of which is the Holy of Holies, which it's forbidden to enter on pain of death. Its door of solid metal is edged by golden vines, each cluster of which is the size of a man. Over this door hangs a curtain of Babylonian cloth, showing a chart of

the heavens embroidered with hyacinths, fine linen, scarlet
and purple, symbols of fire, earth, air, and water. In conclusion I must say a word about the roof, which is framed
in a balustrade of white marble fretwork and consists of
gold slabs, bristling with shiny spikes to keep the birds
away.

Yes, the new temple is a sublime marvel, which makes
Herod the Great at least the equal of King Solomon. You
can imagine how the sight of so much splendor, so much
power, and so much grandiose horror as well, bewildered a
poor dethroned prince and what a tempest it aroused in
my heart.

Still, my emotion was infinitely greater when on the
tenth day we were informed that by order of the king the
Grand Chamberlain had invited us to a dinner to be given
that same night in the large throne room. We had no
doubt that Herod would be present, though the invitation
said nothing of the kind. It was as though the tyrant had
wished to cloak himself in mystery up to the last moment.

I must own that when I entered the hall I neither saw
nor recognized Herod. I thought he would appear later;
that, to give his entrance its full effect, he would be the
last to arrive. But, as I have since learned, that would have
been contrary to the Jewish laws of hospitality, which
require a host to be present to receive his guests. It is true
that the king, lying on an ebony divan piled with cushions,
was engaged in an apparently confidential conversation
with a white-haired old man reclining by his side, whose
pure and noble features contrasted strikingly with the
king's ravaged, grimacing mask. I was later told that this
was the celebrated Menahem, the Essenian necromancer
and interpreter of dreams, whom Herod has consulted regularly ever since Menahem—Herod was then a boy of

fifteen—struck him on the back and called him King of the Jews. But at first I had no suspicion of Herod's presence; I saw only the forest of flaming torches reflected a thousand times over in the silver platters, crystal pitchers, gold dishes, and goblets of chalcedony.

While swarms of servants busied themselves around the low tables and divans, the majordomo hurried to meet Balthasar and Gaspar, who had arrived at the head of a procession in which their respective retinues, the one black, the other white, were mingled but still as recognizable as two tightly plaited cords of different colors. The two kings took the places of honor on either side of the large couch where Herod and Menahem were conversing, while I installed myself as best I could between, but slightly to the rear of, my preceptor Baktiar and young Assur. An open space in the shape of a horseshoe separated the tables from a large bay window, through which we could see a corner of Jerusalem, mysterious in the darkness. We were served aromatic wine and golden scarabs roasted in salt. Amidst the hubbub of voices and the clatter of dishes, three female harpists provided a harmonious musical background. A large yellow dog turned up from somewhere, provoking confusion and laughter until a slave led him away. I caught sight of a small curly-headed man, no longer young, with round, rosy cheeks. He had on a white tunic dotted with flowers and he was carrying a lute under his arm. With a low bow he approached Herod's couch. Herod interrupted his conversation, listened to the man for a moment and said, "Yes, but later." This was Sangali, the oriental storyteller from the Malabar coast, a master of the *mashal*. Yes, there would be time for speech later on, but now we were going to eat. The doors opened wide to admit carts laden with steaming kettles and platters. It was the custom to make everything available to the guests at once. There were plaice livers mixed with lamprey milt, peacock and pheasant brains, eyes of mouflon and young camels' tongues, ibises stuffed with ginger, and above all an enormous stew consisting of mares' vulvas and bulls' genitals bathed in a brown sauce. Hooked fingers reached out on bare arms. Jaws opened and closed, fangs sank in, Adam's apples bobbed with the effort of chewing. At a gesture from the majordomo, the three harpists, who were still at their ethereal chords, stopped playing when the servants brought in a large steel frame holding a dozen revolving spits. The birds on the spits were dripping with fat; their flesh was white and coarse-grained. Herod had broken off his conversation and was smiling into his sparse beard. The servants placed the spits on platters and split the birds in two with sharp knives. They were stuffed with black, cone-shaped mushrooms.

"My friends," Herod cried out. "I invite you to partake of this delicate, historic and symbolic dish, which I do not hesitate to term the national dish of the kingdom of Herod the Great. It was invented under the pressure of necessity some thirty years ago, shortly after the war I waged, at the instigation of Queen Cleopatra, against Malchus, king of Arabia. In the space of a few minutes an earthquake turned Judea into a heap of ruins, killing thirty thousand people and immense quantities of cattle. A catastrophe that benefited only the vultures and the Arabs. The tremor spared my army, which was bivouacking in open country. Nevertheless I immediately sent Malchus a peace mission, arguing that in such a situation there were better things to do than fight. But Malchus, wishing on the contrary to take advantage of the situation, murdered my emissaries and attacked me without delay. Disgraceful conduct. It was I who had saved him from slavery at the hands of Cleopatra. To obtain peace, I had paid two hundred talents and committed myself to paying as much again, without its costing Malchus so much as a denier. But there you have it. Thinking the earthquake had rendered me helpless, he flung his troops against me. I didn't wait for him. I crossed the Jordan and fell on him like a thunderbolt. In three battles I cut his army to pieces. Naturally I refused to negotiate or listen to any talk of ransoming prisoners. I wanted and obtained an unconditional surrender.

"It was under those glorious and dramatic circumstances that my cooks, at the end of their resources, one day served me a roasted bird stuffed with mushrooms. That bird was a vulture and the mushrooms were death trumpets. I had a good laugh. I tasted. Delicious! I made my intendants promise to serve me Malchus himself next time, even though we are forbidden to eat pig!"

The guests roared with laughter at Herod's joke. Herod joined in, a servant held out a half vulture and Herod seized it with both hands. The guests all did likewise. Wine was poured into goblets. For several minutes the only sound to be heard was the cracking of bones. Later on, platters of honey cakes, baskets filled with pomegranates, grapes, figs, and mangoes were passed around. Then the king, his voice rising above the tumult, sent for the oriental storyteller who had spoken to him at the start of the banquet. He was brought in. His air of frail innocence contrasted with the bestial, sated faces around him. The simplicity of the man seemed to provoke Herod's cruelty.

"Sangali," he said, "you will tell us a story. But watch

your tongue, be sure you don't unwittingly disclose any secrets. I warn you: You are risking your two ears. By your right ear I command you . . ."

He paused, evidently wondering what he was going to command. And then he unleashed a storm of laughter by completing his sentence: ". . . to make me laugh. And by your left ear I command you to tell me a story about a king, yes, a wise king, worried over the problem of succession. That's it: a king has grown old, he doesn't know who will succeed him, and he is deeply worried. If you speak of anything else or if you don't make me laugh, you will leave here with your ears cropped, like Hyrcanus II, whose nephew Antigonus mutilated him with his own teeth to prevent him from becoming high priest."

After a silence, Sangali said, without a trace of fear in his voice: "The name of the king whose story you wish to hear was Goldbeard."

"Goldbeard it shall be!" cried Herod. "We shall all listen to the story of Goldbeard and his succession. Because, my friends, you must know that nothing interests me so much at the present time as questions of succession."

KING GOLDBEARD, OR THE PROBLEM OF SUCCESSION

Once upon a time, in the city of Shamur, which is situated in Fertile Arabia, there was a king named Nabunassar III, who was famous for his ringleted, flowing, golden beard, for which reason he was surnamed Goldbeard. He took excellent care of it, going so far as to shut it up at night in a silken case. There it remained until morning, when it was entrusted to the expert hands of a beard dresser, a trade practiced exclusively by women at the time. For barbers, you should know, wield razors and massacre beards, whereas beard dressers operate exclusively with comb, curling iron, and vaporizer, and are not authorized to cut so much as a single hair.

Nabunassar Goldbeard, who as a young man had let his beard grow—more out of negligence than by design—and hardly given it a thought, began with the passing years to attach an almost magical significance to that appendage. He was not far from regarding it as the symbol of his kingship, if not as the embodiment of his power. He never wearied of admiring his golden beard in the mirror, meanwhile caressing it affectionately with his ring-laden fingers.

The people of Shamur loved their king. But he had been reigning for over half a century. Urgent reforms were constantly being postponed by ministers who, like their king, basked in indolent contentment. The Council had taken to meeting only once a month. Through the doors of the council chamber, the attendants would hear sentences—always the same—punctuated by long silences:

"Something should be done."

"Yes, but undue haste must be avoided."

"The situation must be allowed to ripen."

"There is no greater statesman than time."

"Only one thing is urgent: to wait."

The members would congratulate one another as they left the council chamber, but no decision was ever taken.

One of the king's main occupations, after the midday meal—which was traditionally long, slow, and heavy—was a deep siesta, which would continue until late in the afternoon. He took it—the detail is important—in the open, on a terrace shaded by twining aristolochia.

For several months Goldbeard had not enjoyed his usual peace of mind. It should not be supposed that the remonstrances of his councillors or the murmurs of his people had upset him. No. His anxiety had a higher, deeper, in a word, nobler cause: for the first time, King Nabunassar III, while admiring himself in the mirror that his beard dresser held out to him after her ministrations, had discovered a white hair mingled with the golden flow of his beard.

This white hair plunged him into abysmal meditations. Well, well, he thought, so I'm growing old. Of course it was to be expected, but now the fact is at hand, as undeniable as this hair. What is to be done? What is not to be done? For white hair or not, I have no son to succeed me. Twice married, but neither of the two queens who successively shared my bed was capable of giving me an heir. This calls for a decision. But undue haste must be avoided. I ought to have an heir. Yes, perhaps I should adopt a child. But one who resembles me, who resembles me enormously. In short, a younger me, much younger. The situation must be allowed to ripen. There's no greater statesman than time. Only one thing is urgent: to wait.

While unwittingly repeating the familiar sayings of his ministers, he fell asleep dreaming of a little Nabunassar IV, who resembled him like a twin brother.

But one day he was suddenly startled out of his siesta by a rather sharp stinging sensation. Instinctively he raised his hand to his chin, because that was where the sensation was. Nothing. No blood. He struck a gong. He sent for his beard dresser. Ordered her to bring him the big mirror. Looked himself over. A vague foreboding had not deceived him: his white hair had vanished. Taking advantage of his slumbers, a sacrilegious hand had dared to violate the integrity of his pilose appendage.

Had the hair really been plucked out, or was it concealed by the density of his beard? The question arose, because the following morning, when the beard dresser had done her work and held up the mirror to the king, there it was, incontestable in its whiteness, as conspicuous as a vein of silver in a copper mine.

That day Nabunassar lay down to his traditional siesta in a troubled state of mind; the problem of his succession and the mystery of his beard were confusedly mingled in his thoughts. He was far from suspecting that those two questions were one and would find their solution together. . . .

Well then. King Nabunassar III had barely dozed off when he was startled out of his sleep by a twinge in the chin. He jumped, called for help, demanded his mirror: once again the white hair had vanished!

The next morning it was back again. But this time the

king was not deceived by appearances. One might go so far as to say that he took a long stride toward the truth. For it did not escape him that the hair, which the day before had been on the lower left of his chin, was now on the upper right—not far below his nose. Since hairs do not move about, he was forced to conclude that this was a *different* hair, which had turned white during the night, for it is well known that hairs turn white under cover of darkness.

While getting ready for his siesta that day, the king knew what was going to happen. And no sooner had he closed his eyes than he opened them again in response to a stinging sensation in the place where he had located the last white hair. He did not send for the mirror, for this time he had no doubt that someone had plucked his hair.

But who? Who?

The same thing happened day after day. Every time the king lay down under the aristolochia, he resolved not to doze off. He pretended to sleep, leaving just enough space between his eyelids for a scowling glance to filter through. But when you pretend to sleep, there's always a chance that you'll really fall asleep. And that is just what happened. When the twinge came, he was sound asleep, and it was all over before he opened his eyes.

But no beard is inexhaustible. Every night one of his golden hairs was transformed into a white hair, which was plucked out the following afternoon. The beard dresser didn't dare say anything, but the king saw her face grow drawn with anguish as his beard became thinner and thinner. He looked at himself in the mirror, caressed what was left of his golden beard, and noted the lines of his chin, which became more and more apparent through the sparseness of his fleece. Strange to say, he was not dis-

pleased with the metamorphosis. Through the dwindling
mask of the majestic old man, he saw reappearing—more
pronounced, to be sure—the features of the beardless
youth he once had been. At the same time the question of
his succession became less urgent in his eyes.

When he had only a dozen hairs left on his chin, he
thought seriously of dismissing his hoary-headed ministers
and taking the reins of government into his own hands. It
was then that events took a new turn.

Could it have been because his denuded cheeks and chin
became more sensitive to drafts? Now, on occasion, he was
awakened from his siesta by a faint cool breeze that set in a
fraction of a second before the morning's white hair
vanished. And one day he saw! What did he see? A beautiful white bird—as white as the white beard he would
never have—which fled as fast as its wings could carry it,
bearing in its beak the white hair it had just plucked. That
explained everything: this bird wanted a nest the color of
its plumage and had found nothing whiter than certain
hairs of the royal beard.

Nabunassar was delighted with his discovery but
burned with desire to know more. And he knew he would
have to hurry, for on his chin there remained only a single
hair, which was as white as snow, and when that was gone
the beautiful bird would have no occasion to show itself.
Great was the king's emotion as he lay down under the
aristolochia for his siesta! Once again he would have to
feign sleep without succumbing to it. But the particularly
rich and succulent noonday meal he had eaten that day invited him to take a truly royal siesta. Nabunassar struggled
heroically against the torpor that invaded him in delicious
waves. To keep awake, he squinted at the long white hair,
which started from his chin and undulated in the warm

light. My word, he dropped off for just an instant, the merest instant, and he was awakened by the quick caress of a wing on his cheek and a stinging sensation on his chin. He thrust out his hand and touched something soft and throbbing, but his fingers closed on emptiness, and when he opened his eyes, all he saw was the white bird's black shadow against the red sun. The bird had flown away and would never come back, for in its beak it was carrying the last hair of the king's beard.

The king awoke in a rage and was on the point of summoning his archers and ordering them to bring him the bird dead or alive. But that was only the brutal, unthinking reaction of an exasperated king. And then he saw something white gliding slowly through the air. It was a feather, a snow-white feather, which he had no doubt pulled from the bird in grabbing hold of it. The feather fell gently to the floor, and then the king witnessed a phenomenon that interested him enormously: After remaining motionless for a moment, the feather pivoted on its axis and turned its tip in the direction of. . . . Yes, that little feather turned like the magnetic needle of a compass, but instead of pointing north, it pointed in the direction the bird had fled in.

The king bent down, picked up the feather, and balanced it on the palm of his hand. Whereupon the feather turned and came to rest at south-southwest, the direction the bird had taken in flying away.

That was a sign, an invitation. Still holding the feather balanced on his palm, Nabunassar ran down the palace stairway, making no reply to the obeisances of the courtiers and servants he passed on his way.

But when he reached the street no one seemed to recog-

nize him. None of the passersby would have dreamed that
this beardless man, dressed only in baggy trousers and a
short jacket, who was running down the street with a little
white feather balanced on the palm of his hand, could be
his sovereign majesty Nabunassar III. Was it because such
behavior seemed incompatible with the dignity of a king?
Or could it have been something else, an unprecedented air
of youthfulness, that made him unrecognizable? This, as it
happened, was a question of vital importance, but Nabunassar didn't ask it. He was too busy keeping the feather
on his palm and following where it pointed.

King Nabunassar—or should I already say the former
King Nabunassar III?—ran a long time. He left Shamur,
crossed cultivated fields, passed through a forest, climbed
up and down a mountain range, crossed a bridge over a big
river, forded a little river, then traversed a desert and another mountain range. He ran and ran, without great fatigue, which was most surprising for a corpulent old man,
softened by a life of indolence.

At last he stopped in a small wood, at the foot of a large
oak tree, for the white feather was rising vertically toward
its crown. At the very top, in the fork of the last branch,
he saw a pile of twigs, and on this nest—for a nest, of
course, it was—he saw the beautiful white bird, which was
trembling with fear.

Nabu leaped into the air, seized the lowest branch,
swung himself up on it, rose to his feet, and repeated the
operation with the second branch. And so he climbed, as
light and nimble as a squirrel.

He soon reached the fork. The white bird fled in terror.
There, wreathed in twigs, lay a white nest. Nabunassar
had no difficulty in recognizing the hairs of his beard,

carefully interlaced. And in the middle of this white nest he saw an egg, a beautiful egg as golden as King Goldbeard's onetime beard.

Nabu removed the nest from the fork and started climbing down, but, holding his fragile burden in one hand, it wasn't easy. More than once he thought he would drop it, and when he was still nearly forty feet from the ground he almost lost his balance and fell, but at last he set foot on the mossy forest floor.

He had been walking for some minutes in what he thought was the direction of the city when he met an extraordinary figure. It was a pair of boots with a big belly over it and over that a gamekeeper's hat—in short, a forest giant. The giant shouted in a voice of thunder, "Ho ho, little boy! Have I caught you stealing eggs in the king's forest?"

Little boy? How could anyone call him a little boy? Suddenly Nabu realized that he had indeed become very small, slender, and agile. That explained how he had been able to run for hours and climb trees. And now he had no difficulty in escaping into a thicket, where the gamekeeper, hampered by his size and the roundness of his belly, could not follow him.

The road into Shamur leads past the graveyard. There little Nabu found his way barred by a brilliant crowd surrounding a splendid hearse drawn by six black horses, magnificent beasts adorned with black plumes and caparisoned with silver tears.

Several times he inquired who was being buried, but the people shrugged their shoulders and declined to answer, as though his question were just too stupid. He noticed only that the hearse was emblazoned with an "N" surmounted by a crown. Finally he took refuge in a mortuary chapel at the other end of the cemetery, set his nest down beside him, and, at the end of his strength, fell asleep on a tombstone.

The sun was high in the sky when he again started out for Shamur. To his surprise, the great gate was closed, and that was most unusual at midday. Some important or distinguished visitor must be expected, he thought, for it was only under exceptional circumstances that the great gate was closed and then solemnly reopened. Curious and undecided, he was standing outside the high portal, still holding the white nest in his hands, when suddenly the golden egg it contained split open and a little white bird came out. And in a clear, intelligible voice the little white bird sang, "Long live the King! Long live our new king Nabunassar IV!"

Slowly the heavy gate turned on its hinges and opened wide. A red carpet had been laid from the gate to the steps of the palace. Jubilant crowds had gathered to the right and left of it, and as the child passed through with the nest all the people took up the bird's cry: "Long live the King! Long live our new king Nabunassar IV!"

The reign of Nabunassar IV was long, peaceful, and prosperous. Though two queens, one after the other, shared his bed, neither provided an heir to the throne. But remembering how he had once run off into the forest in pursuit of a white, beard-stealing bird, the king didn't worry about his succession. Until the day when, with the passage of the years, that memory began to fade from his mind. It was then that, little by little, a beautiful golden beard began to cover his chin and cheeks.

HEROD
THE GREAT

Herod had laughed several times while listening to the little story, and his docile courtiers had laughed with him. The atmosphere was relaxed and Sangali's mind was at rest concerning his ears. He bowed down to the ground, and each time a purse full of gold fell at his feet he strummed a chord on his lute in token of thanks. As he left the hall a broad smile illumined his childlike face.

But laughter didn't agree with Herod. That sort of spasm was too much for a body racked with nightmares and disease. Convulsed with pain, he clutched the triclinium and bent over the paved floor. In vain his courtiers gathered around him. Irresistibly, conjectures invaded their minds. What if the despot were to die? What a chaotic problem of succession he would leave behind him, he with his ten wives and his children in all four corners of the earth. . . . Succession . . . that was the subject that the king himself had imposed on Sangali. Proof enough that it was always on his mind. And there he lay with his mouth open and his eyes shut, retching. His whole body heaved. He vomited up a mixture recalling the main dishes of the banquet. No one dreamed of slipping a basin under his mouth. That would have been to outrage the majesty of the royal vomit. Nor was it permissible to avert one's eyes. He raised a livid face, covered with green splotches

and bathed in sweat. He wanted to speak. With a gesture
he bade his courtiers gather in a semicircle around his
couch. He emitted an inarticulate sound. He tried again.
At length words emerged from the gurgling sludge that
flowed from his mouth.

"I am a king," he said, "but I'm dying. I'm alone and
desperate. You see how it is: I can't keep my food down.
My ravaged stomach rejects everything my mouth sends
it. But at the same time I'm hungry. I'm starving! There
must be some stew left, a half vulture, some cucumbers
with citron, or one of those dormice fattened with lard
that Jews use to cheat the Mosaic law? Oh God! Bring me
something to eat!"

Terrified servants came running with baskets full of
cakes, dishes piled high, platters dripping with gravy.

"And if it were only my stomach," Herod went on.
"But my entrails burn like hellfire! When I squat down to
empty my guts, I drop a puddle of blood and pus crawling
with worms. The only life I have left is a bellow of pain.
But I cling to it with a frenzy, because there's no one to
take my place. This kingdom of Judea, which I have made,
which I have carried on my shoulders for nigh on forty
years, to which I have given prosperity thanks to an era of
peace unprecedented in the history of mankind, this Jewish nation, bursting with talent but execrated by other peoples for its arrogance, its intolerance, and the cruelty of its
laws, this land that I've covered with palaces, temples,
fortresses, and villas—alas, I see plainly that all this, these
people, these things, are doomed to lamentable disaster for
want of a sovereign endowed with my strength and my
genius. God will not give the Jews a second Herod!"

For a long while he was silent. His head hung so low
that nothing could be seen but his tiara with its threefold

garland of gold. And when he raised his head, all were horror-stricken to see his face bathed in tears.

"Gaspar of Meroë, and you Balthasar of Nippur, and you, too, young Melchior, hiding in a page boy's livery behind King Balthasar—it's to you I speak, for you alone are worthy to hear me in the midst of this court, where I see only traitorous generals, prevaricating ministers, corrupted counselors, and intriguing courtiers. Why all this corruption around me? This gilded rabble may have been honorable long ago, or in any event no better or worse than the rest of humanity. But, you see, power corrupts. It's I, the all-powerful Herod who, in spite of myself, in spite of them, have made traitors of all these men! Because my power is immense. For forty years I have worked feverishly to increase and perfect it. My police are everywhere, and sometimes at night I myself in disguise visit the city's taverns and brothels to hear what's being said there. All of you here: I see through you as if you were made of glass. Balthasar, I know all about the sacking of the Balthasareum. If you want a list of the guilty parties, I have one ready for you. You showed deplorable weakness at the time. Good God, you should have struck, struck with redoubled force. Instead, you let your hair turn white.

"You're fond of sculpture, painting, and drawing. So am I. You're mad about Greek art. So am I. You've come up against the stupid fanaticism of an iconoclastic clergy. So have I. But let me tell you about the Eagle on the Temple.

"This third temple of Israel, by far the largest and most beautiful, is the crowning achievement of my life. At the cost of enormous sacrifice, I completed a task to which none of my Hasmonaean predecessors was equal. I had every reason to expect the unmingled gratitude of my people, and especially of the Pharisees and the clergy. On the

pediment of the great gate of the temple I caused my ar-
chitects to place a golden eagle with a wingspread of six
cubits. Why this emblem? Because in twenty passages in
Scripture it appears as the symbol of power, generosity,
and fidelity. And also because it's the emblem of Rome.
Biblical tradition and Roman majesty—those two pillars of
civilization—were here glorified, and posterity will not be
able to deny that a conjunction between them has been the
goal of my entire policy. Not to mention the circumstances—in short, the whole thing was unforgivable. I was
desperately sick, in agonies of pain. My doctors had sent
me to the hot sulfur springs in Jericho. One day, no one
knows why, the rumor of my death spread in Jerusalem.
Two Pharisee doctors, Judas and Mattathias, gathered
their disciples and harangued them. This emblem, repre-
senting the Greek Zeus and symbolizing the Roman presence, must be destroyed, they said, because it violated the
Second Commandment. At high noon, while the Court of
the Gentiles was swarming with people, some young men
climbed up on the temple roof. With the help of ropes
they lowered themselves to the level of the pediment and
shattered the golden eagle with ax blows. They regretted
it soon enough, because Herod the Great wasn't dead at
all, far from it! The temple guards and soldiers sprang into
action. The profaners and those who had incited them
were arrested. In all some forty men. I had them brought
to Jericho and there I questioned them. The trial was held
in the big theater of that city. I was there, borne on a litter. The judges delivered their sentence. The two doctors
were publicly burned alive, the profaners beheaded.

"You see, Balthasar, when a king is an art lover, that's
how he has to defend his masterpieces.

"As for you, Gaspar, I know more than you do about

your Biltine and that rascal who's with her. Every time
you took your lovely blonde in your arms, one of my
agents was hiding behind the drapes or under your royal
bed, and the very next morning he would send me a report. Your negligence, if that can be, is even more criminal
than Balthasar's. Good God! This slave girl cuckolds you,
defies you, makes you a general laughingstock, and you let
her live! You loved her white skin, you say? In that case,
you should have stripped it off. I can send you specialists
who have a wonderful way of flaying prisoners; they roll
up the skin on hazel rods!

"And you, Melchior, how very naïve you are, thinking
you could sneak into my capital, my palace, my dining hall
under a false identity. What sort of caravansary do you
take this for? Get this through your head: Not the
slightest detail of your flight from Palmyra with your
preceptor escaped my spies, no part of your journey, not
one of your conversations with travelers—every last one of
them was in my pay. I could easily have warned you that
your uncle Atmar was plotting a coup for the day after
the king your father's death. I did nothing of the kind.
Why? Because the laws of morality and justice don't
apply to questions of power. How do I know that your
uncle—who, I agree, is generally regarded as a traitor and
murderer—won't be a better ruler, better for his people
and above all a better ally to King Herod, than you would
have been? He wanted to have you killed. He was right.
The existence abroad of the legal heir to the throne he oc-
cupies is an intolerable state of affairs. To be perfectly
frank with you, he disappointed me by letting you escape.
What a blunder to make at the very start! Never mind!
I've decided not to meddle in this business, and I won't.
You may come and go as you please in Judea. Officially I

will not see through your disguise; as far as I'm concerned you're one of King Balthasar's Narcissi. Otherwise, I have only this to say to you who have lost a throne and are dreaming of getting it back: Keep your eyes and ears open. Learn the terrible law of power by my example. What law? Let me explain. Consider the eventuality I just mentioned: I notify your father King Theodenos and you yourself that Prince Atmar has arranged to have you murdered as soon as the king dies. My revelation may or may not be true. You can't—do you hear me, *can't?*—stop to verify it. That's a luxury you and your father cannot afford. You have to do something, and quickly. What? Strike first. Have Atmar murdered. That's the law of power: When in doubt, strike first. I have always observed that law—scrupulously. A terrible law; it has created a ghostly void around me. The consequences—if you care to look back over my life—have been twofold. Of all the kings of the Orient I am the richest; I've lived the longest and I've done the most for my people. On the other hand, I'm the unhappiest man in the whole world, the most betrayed friend, the most flouted husband, the most defied father, and the most hated despot in history."

He fell silent for a moment, and when he spoke again it was in an almost inaudible voice, which obliged the company to prick up their ears.

"The being I've loved most in the world was named Mariamne. I'm not referring to the daughter of Simon the High Priest, whom I took as my third wife for no other reason than that she, too, was called Mariamne. No, I'm speaking of the first and only woman in my life. I was young and passionate. All my undertakings thus far had been successful. When tragedy struck, I had just resolved

to my advantage the most diabolically intricate imbroglio
I've ever known.

"Thirteen years after the assassination of Julius Caesar,
the rivalry between Octavius and Mark Antony for mas-
tery of the world culminated in a fight to the death. My
reason favored Octavius, who was master of Rome. But
my geographical position as the neighbor and ally of
Cleopatra, queen of Egypt, threw me into Antony's arms.
I had raised an army and was flying to his help against Octavius, when Cleopatra, alarmed at the prospect of my
growing too great in the estimation of Antony, whose
favor she was intent on monopolizing, stopped me and
forced me to turn instead against my old enemy, Malchus,
king of the Arabs. By intriguing against me, she saved me.
For on the second of September[7] Octavius crushed Antony near Actium on the coast of Greece. All was lost for
Antony, Cleopatra, and their allies—and would have been
for me if I had been able to fight on Antony's side as I had
wanted to. My only hope was to turn my coat, and that
called for delicate maneuvering. I started by helping the
Roman governor of Syria to put down an army of gladiators, who were devoted to Antony and were trying to join
forces with him in Egypt, whither he had fled. Then I
went to see Octavius on Rhodes, where he happened to be
at the time. I made no attempt to deceive him. On the contrary, I represented myself as Antony's faithful friend,
who had done everything possible to help him, supplying
him with money, provisions, troops, and above all advice,
good advice: not only to drop Cleopatra, who was leading
him to his ruin, but better still to have her murdered. But
alas, blinded by his passion, Antony had refused to listen.
Then I laid my royal diadem at the feet of Octavius, and

said: 'You have every right to treat me as an enemy, to
depose me and put me to death. I shall accept your decision without a murmur. But if you so desire, you can accept my friendship, and then I shall be as lucidly faithful
to you as I was to Antony.'

"I have never played for higher stakes. Stupefied at my
audacity, the future Augustus took a moment to make up
his mind. My fate hung in the balance—would it be triumph or ignominious death? Octavius picked up my diadem, set it on my head, and said: 'Continue to be a king
and become my friend, since you value friendship so
highly. To seal our alliance, I will give you Cleopatra's
guard of four hundred Gauls for your own.' A short time
later, we learned that Mark Antony and the Queen of
Egypt had taken their lives rather than be exhibited in Octavius' triumph.

"I had every reason to suppose my future assured after so
startling a swing of fortune. Not at all. I was to pay for
my success with the worst of domestic misfortunes.

"The main cause was undoubtedly my love for
Mariamne. That was the black sun that illumines the
whole tragedy. In going to see Octavius, I knew I was
risking my freedom and my life; I knew I had little chance
of coming away alive. I left four women behind me: my
mother Cypros, my sister Salome, Queen Mariamne, and
her mother Alexandra. They were divided between two
bitterly hostile clans: the Idumeans, of whom I was one,
and the survivors of the Hasmonaean dynasty. The four
women had to be prevented from tearing each other to
pieces in my absence. So before setting out for Rhodes, I
sent Mariamne to the fortress of Alexandrion with her
mother, and shut up my mother, Salome, my three sons,
and my two daughters in the fortress of Masada. Then I

gave Soemos, the military governor of Alexandrion, the secret order to put Mariamne to death if he received news of
my own demise. This extreme measure was dictated by my
heart as well as my reason. On the one hand, the thought
of my beloved Mariamne surviving me and possibly marrying another man was more than I could bear. On the
other hand, with me dead, nothing would prevent the Hasmonaean clan, with Mariamne at its head, from retaking
power and holding on to it at any cost.

"On my return from Rhodes, radiant with my success, I
assembled all these fine people in Jerusalem, convinced that
my political good fortune would bring about a general
reconciliation. Nothing less was needed. From the first I
encountered faces grimacing with hatred. My sister
Salome was carrying a black cloud of insinuations and
devastating disclosures about with her, and only waiting
for an opportunity to send them raining down on
Mariamne's head. Mariamne treated me with contempt;
the long separation and the dangers I had been through
had exacerbated my love for her, but she refused to let me
come near her. She kept after me with niggling references
to the death of her grandfather Hyrcanus—an old story,
and, besides, my hand had been forced. Little by little the
mystery was cleared up, and I found out what had happened in my absence. Thinking my death as good as certain, those women had set up their intrigues accordingly.
And in this they were not alone. To curry favor with
Mariamne, whom he regarded as the future regent,
Soemos, the governor of Alexandrion, had informed her of
my order to execute her in the event of my death. In such
a situation I had to put my house in order. Soemos's head
was the first to roll in the sawdust. That was only the beginning. My first cupbearer asked me for a secret audi-

ence. He appeared before me with a flagon of aromatic wine. Mariamne had told him it was a love philter and promised a large reward if he would get me to drink it without my knowledge. In a quandary, he had confided in my sister Salome, who had advised him to tell me all. I sent for one of the Gallic slaves and made him drink some of the wine. He fell stone dead. I summoned Mariamne, who swore that she had never heard of any philter and that the whole thing was a machination of Salome, who was determined to ruin her. Since that seemed likely enough and I wanted, if possible, to spare Mariamne, I asked myself: Which of the two women should I strike? Of course, I had the possibility of putting the cupbearer properly to the torture, and then he would spit out the whole truth. At that point events took a dramatic turn. My mother-in-law, Alexandra, who had kept her peace until then, suddenly launched an open attack on her daughter. Not only did she confirm the attempt to poison me, she also opened a second affair by claiming that Mariamne had been the mistress of Soemos and that she had promised him a leading political position after my death. To save Mariamne, I might have shut that fury up for good. Unfortunately the scandal had gone too far. All Jerusalem was talking of nothing else. A trial was inevitable. I convened a jury of twelve sages, and she appeared before them. Her courage and dignity were admirable. To the end she refused to defend herself. The unanimous verdict was death. It came as no surprise to Mariamne. She died without a word.

"I had her body laid in an open sarcophagus, filled with transparent honey, and kept it in my apartments for seven years. From day to day I watched her beloved flesh dissolve in the liquid gold. There was no limit to my grief. I had never loved her so much, and today, thirty years later,

I love her no less, in spite of other marriages and separations, in spite of all the things that have happened. It's for your benefit, Gaspar, that I speak of this tragedy that wrecked my life. When you hear the howling that still echoes through the vaults of this palace, it's I, Herod the Great, shouting the name of Mariamne at the walls of my room. My grief was so savage that my servants fled in terror. When I managed to catch one of them, I made him call Mariamne with me, as though two voices had twice as much chance of bringing her back. It came almost as a relief when a cholera epidemic broke out among the lower and middle classes of Jerusalem. That calamity, it seemed to me, made the Jews share my misery. People were dropping like flies all around me, and I was obliged to leave Jerusalem. Rather than retire to one of my palaces in Idumea or Samaria, I gave orders to set up a camp in the desert, in the great depression of Ghor, a harsh, barren region, stinking of sulfur and asphalt, a landscape in keeping with my ravaged heart. There I spent weeks in a state of prostration, from which I was roused only by excruciating headaches. Even so, my instinct had guided me well, for evil combats evil. The furnace of Ghor acted on my grief as a hot iron acts on a festering wound. I revived from my torpor. Just in time to learn that my mother-in-law, Alexandra, whom I had imprudently left in Jerusalem, was plotting to gain control of the two fortresses that rise above the city, the Antonia near the temple, and the Eastern Tower in the center of the city proper. I let that fury, whom I held largely responsible for the death of Mariamne, wade knee-deep in her machinations; then, suddenly appearing on the scene, I confounded her. Her corpse soon joined others of her dynasty.

"But I hadn't seen the last of the Hasmonaean clan. I

still had two sons by Mariamne, Alexander and Aristobulus. After their mother's death, to get them away from the miasmas of Jerusalem, I had sent them to be educated at the imperial court. They were seventeen and eighteen when I received alarming reports about their conduct in Rome. It seems they were planning to avenge the supposed injustice of their mother's death—for which they held me entirely responsible—and were intriguing to that effect with Augustus. Years had passed since my misfortune, and it still left me no peace. I was nearly sixty; I had a hard life behind me, I could boast of glowing political triumphs, but I had paid for them with cruel misfortunes. I seriously thought of abdicating, or retiring for good to my native Idumea. But once again my vocation for kingship won out. I went to Rome and brought my sons back with me. I established them near me and took good care to marry them. To Alexander I gave Glaphyra, the daughter of Archelaus, king of Cappadocia, and to Aristobulus Berenice, my sister Salome's daughter. Before I knew it, they were all intriguing like mad. Glaphyra and Berenice declared war on each other. Glaphyra persuaded her father Archelaus to plot against me in Rome. Berenice allied herself with her mother Salome, who did everything in her power to compromise Alexander in my eyes. And out of fidelity to his mother's memory, Aristobulus sided with his brother. To add to the confusion, I had the unfortunate idea of bringing my first wife Doris and her son Antipater, who had been living in exile since my marriage to Mariamne, to Jerusalem. They flung themselves into the thick of the melee, and Doris knew no rest until she had recovered her old place in my bed.

"I was utterly sickened, and didn't know what to do. Up until then my domestic broils had always ended in bloodbaths, and I was determined not to let that happen again. The only way out, I finally decided, would be to submit the whole problem, and in particular my quarrel with my sons, to a higher authority. And who could that be but Augustus—especially since all the plotting seemed to center on Rome.

"I outfitted a galley and, taking Alexander and Aristobulus with me, set out for Rome, where we joined Antipater, who was studying there. The emperor, on the other hand, was not there, and concerning his whereabouts we obtained only the vaguest information. With my three sons I set out on a haggard search from island to island and port to port. We ended up in Aquileia at the north end of the Adriatic, where Augustus had a dream palace. He had gone there for a rest, and I'd be lying if I told you he was pleased to have this family that he'd been hearing only too much about come barging in on him. Still, he consented to listen to us. The debate that followed was stormy and confused; it went on for the better part of the day. As often as not, all four of us spoke at once and so violently it almost looked as if we would come to blows. Augustus had an amazing gift of hiding his boredom and indifference under a mask of sculptural immobility, that could be mistaken for attention. In the end, though, this incredible outpouring of domestic venom astonished him and even aroused his interest; it was like a battle of snakes or wood lice. After several hours, when we were all growing hoarse, he finally broke his silence, ordered us to be still, and announced that after carefully weighing our arguments he was going to hand down his verdict.

" 'I, Augustus, Emperor,' he said solemnly, 'command you to be reconciled and to live on terms of friendship from now on.'

"That was the imperial decision, and we had to be satisfied with it. Pretty thin, considering the expedition we had just put ourselves through. But then, what a weird idea of mine, expecting an arbiter to settle our family quarrels. All the same, I couldn't resign myself to leaving with nothing to show for my trouble. I could see that Augustus wanted desperately to get rid of us. When his exasperation seemed to have reached a proper pitch, I put in a word about the copper mines he owned on the island of Cyprus. Hadn't he once said something about letting me exploit them? A pure invention on my part, but for Augustus it was a chance to get rid of us and he jumped at it. Yes, yes, he agreed, he would let me exploit the mines, but that was the end of the audience. We took our leave. At least, I wasn't coming away empty-handed.

"A ruler has to be able to make something of every trifle. Augustus had given me a twig, and with that twig I made a great bonfire in Jerusalem. Standing before my jubilant people, I announced that the problem of my succession had at last been settled. My three sons, Alexander, Aristobulus, and Antipater—whom I presented to the crowd—would share the throne, Antipater, the eldest, presiding over a kind of triumvirate. I added that I myself, with God's help, felt capable of handling the real power for a long time to come, while allowing my sons the prerogatives of royal pomp and a court of their own.

"Capable, perhaps . . . but was that what I wanted? Never had I so fervently longed to get away from it all. Once I had thrown a purple mantle over the family anthill, I left for Greece, hoping that its splendors would cleanse me and give me new strength. The Olympic Games had long been neglected and were in danger of dying out. I reorganized them, establishing athletic associations and

awards to secure their future, and for that year I served as
president of the jury. The sight of those young men bur-
geoning in the sun buoyed my heart. Oh, to be a youth of
sixteen with a flat belly and long thighs and nothing in the
world to worry about but throwing the discus or running
the marathon. . . . Of one thing I'm certain: if there is a
paradise, it's Greek and oval-shaped, like an Olympic sta-
dium. . . .

"Then my beautiful holiday was over; my royal trade,
with its grandeur and filth, took me back again. That was
when the new temple was consecrated with unparalleled
pomp. After that I went to Caesarea to complete the
works project I had begun and preside at the inauguration
of the new harbor. Originally the place had been no more
than a wretched anchorage; it owed its importance to its
situation halfway between Dora and Joppa. Coasting vessels would drop anchor there when the southwest wind
was raging. I created an artificial harbor by sinking stone
blocks fifty feet long, ten feet wide and nine feet high in
twenty fathoms of water. When they reached the surface,
they formed a foundation on which I built a dike two hundred feet wide, with towers at regular intervals. The finest
of the towers I named Drusium, after Caesar's stepson.
The entrance to the harbor faced north, because in this
part of the world Boreas is the fair-weather wind. On both
sides of the opening stand colossi, like tutelary deities, and
on the hill overlooking the city a temple dedicated to
Caesar sheltered a statue of the emperor inspired by the
Olympian Zeus. How beautiful was my Caesarea, with its
stairways, squares, and fountains all of white stone. I was
putting the finishing touches to the harbor warehouses,
when screams of indignation reached me from Alexander
and Aristobulus in Jerusalem. It seemed that my latest fa-

vorite was wearing the dresses of their mother Mariamne.
There were also complaints from my sister Salome, who
was at daggers drawn with Alexander's wife Glaphyra.
But there was worse trouble with Salome; she had formed
an alliance with our brother Pheroras. Pheroras was er-
ratic, unbalanced. I had made him governor of Trans-
jordania to get him out of the way, but he never missed an
opportunity to defy me. He even had the audacity to
marry a slave girl of his own choosing rather than the
princess of the blood I had picked for him.

"Every year at the height of the summer drought the
Jerusalem water supply threatened to fail. I built new
aqueducts parallel to the existing ones that brought water
from King Solomon's Ponds along the Hebron and Bethlehem road. And inside the city I built new reservoirs and
cisterns to provide better storage of rain water. In that
same period the unprecedented prosperity of the country
was reflected in the quality of our silver coinage, whose
lead content was reduced from twenty-seven to thirteen
percent, undoubtedly the finest monetary alloy in the
whole Mediterranean world.

"Yes, I had ample grounds for satisfaction, but they
hardly made up for the irritation provoked by what my
police—who sent me daily reports—had to tell me about the
ferment at court. For a while it was rumored that I had
taken Glaphyra, my son Alexander's young wife, as my
mistress. Then this same Alexander claimed that his aunt
Salome—who was over sixty—slipped into his bed at night
and forced him to commit incest. Then came the affair of
the eunuchs. There were three of them, in charge of my
table, my cellar, and my wardrobe. The three of them
shared my antechamber at night. The presence so close to
me of these Orientals had always scandalized the Pharisees,

who insinuated that their services went beyond my table and my wardrobe. A report came to me that Alexander had won them to his designs by persuading them that my reign would soon be at an end and that despite the provisions I had made, he alone would succeed me on the throne. What made this so serious was that these servants came into close contact with me and enjoyed my fullest confidence. If someone was trying to corrupt them, he could only be harboring the darkest designs. My police went into action. Tyrants—and that's one of their worst misfortunes—are often unable to temper the zeal of the men to whom they entrust their security. For weeks Alexander was held in solitary confinement; the palace echoed with the groans of his familiars, who were being questioned by my executioners. Once again, however, I managed to restore a precarious peace in my house. In this I was helped by Archelaus, king of Cappadocia, who hastened to Jerusalem, alarmed at the danger threatening his daughter and his son-in-law. With remarkable astuteness, he showered them with curses and demanded exemplary punishment for them. I let him talk, glad to have him play the indispensable part of prosecutor and reserving for myself the role, so unusual for me, of advocate for the defense, pleading for clemency. Alexander's confessions helped us: the young man put all the blame on his uncle Pheroras and his aunt Salome. Pheroras chose to plead guilty, and this he did forthwith with all his natural extravagance. Clothed in black rags, his head covered with ashes, he flung himself weeping at our feet, accusing himself of all the sins in the world. With this Alexander was amply exculpated. All I had to do now was dissuade Archelaus from taking his daughter back to Cappadocia with him, as he wished, allegedly because she had made

herself unworthy to be my daughter-in-law, but in reality
to save her from what was obviously a hornet's nest. I escorted him as far as Antioch and sent him on his way with
gifts: a purse containing seventy talents, a golden throne
encrusted with precious stones, a concubine by the name
of Pannychis, and the three eunuchs who had been at the
bottom of the whole affair and whom, much as it grieved
me, I could not keep on in my intimate service.

"Those wishing to justify the conduct of princes often
invoke a kind of higher logic—unrelated, if not radically
opposed, to that of common mortals—which they call
reason of state. Perhaps I myself am not really a statesman,
for I can't see or hear those two words together without
laughing into my scraggly beard. Reason of state! Yet it's
true that the name of Eumenides—the Benevolent Ones—is
given to the Erinyes or Furies, those daughters of the earth
with snakes entwined in their hair, who go about punish-
ing crime, with a dagger in one hand and a lighted torch in
the other. This kind of thing is known in rhetoric as antiphrasis. And it's no doubt for purposes of antiphrasis that
people speak of reason of state when what they mean is
obviously *madness* of state. The sanguinary frenzy that has
possessed my unfortunate family for half a century is a
good example of this sort of god-inspired unreason.

"Taking advantage of a brief respite, I set myself to
solving the troubling question of Trachonitis and Batanaea.
These provinces, situated in the northeast of the kingdom
between Lebanon and Anti-Lebanon, were a favorite refuge of smugglers and armed bands, a source of constant
complaint for the inhabitants of Damascus. I came to the
conclusion that military expeditions would be ineffectual
until the region was colonized by a sedentary and indus-

trious population. To Batanaea I sent Jews from Babylonia, and in Trachonitis I established three thousand Idumeans. To protect the colonists I built a number of citadels
and fortified villages. A promise of tax exemption brought
in a steady flow of immigrants. Fallow lands were soon
transformed into green fields. The trade routes between
Arabia and Damascus, Babylonia and Palestine took on
new life, and the Crown benefited very considerably from
the resulting tolls and customs duties.

"But then an unexpected and unwanted visitor awakened all the old demons of the court. Eurycles, tyrant of
Sparta as his father had been before him, owed his fortune
to the decisive assistance he had given Octavius in the battle
of Actium. The emperor had shown his gratitude by grant-
ing him Roman citizenship and confirming him as sovereign
of Sparta. One day he turned up in Jerusalem, smiling,
affable, laden with sumptuous gifts, determined to become
the friend and confidant of all the clans. The scarcely ex-
tinguished fires of our hatred were rekindled, for Eurycles
was at pains to pass on to one group what he had heard
from the others, not without magnifying and deforming it.
After reminding Alexander that he, Eurycles, had always
been the friend of King Archelaus, which made him a kind
of father to Alexander, he expressed his astonishment that
the young man, son-in-law to the king and a Hasmonaean
on his mother's side, should accept the tutelage of his half-
brother Antipater, whose mother was a commoner. Then
he would put Antipater on his guard against the undying
hatred of his half-brothers. Finally, he informed me of a
plan allegedly conceived by Alexander: to have me murdered and then escape, first to his father-in-law in Cappadocia, then to Rome in the hope of inclining Augustus

in his favor. By the time the Spartan tyrant, covered with
presents and caresses, reembarked for Lacaedemonia, my
whole house was seething like a witch's caldron.

"There was no avoiding it; I had to have Alexander and
his familiars questioned. The results were damning. Two
of my cavalry officers confessed that Alexander had given
them a large sum of money to murder me. In addition, a
letter from Alexander to the commandant of the Alexandrion fortress was intercepted. It revealed that Alexander intended, after committing his crime, to take refuge
in Alexandria along with his brother. Questioned sepa-
rately, the two brothers confessed to their plan of going to
Rome via Cappadocia, but they consistently denied any intention of killing me first. They had probably agreed on
this version in advance. But my sister Salome ruined her
nephews irretrievably by showing me a letter from Aristobulus, in which he warned her to fear the worst from
me, since, so he said, I had accused her of betraying the secrets of the court to my personal enemy, the Arab king
Syllaeus, whom she was longing to marry.

"A trial for high treason could no longer be avoided.
First I sent two messengers to Rome. On the way, they
stopped in Cappadocia and took the testimony of Archelaus, who owned that he was expecting the visit of his
son-in-law Aristobulus, but insisted that he knew nothing
of any plan to continue on to Rome and still less of a plot
against me. As for Augustus, he informed me in writing
that, though opposed in principle to a death sentence, he
granted me full freedom to judge and condemn the guilty
parties. He advised me, however, to hold the trial outside
of my kingdom, in Berytus, for example, where there was
a large Roman colony, and to let Archelaus testify.
Berytus? Why not? The change of venue struck me as ju-

dicious, because of the sympathies the Hasmonaeans still enjoyed in Jerusalem. On the other hand, I could hardly cite
the king of Cappadocia as a witness, because he was
seriously implicated in the plot.

"It was known to me that the governors Saturninus and
Pedanius, who presided over the courts, had received instructions from Augustus. The tribunal also included the
procurator Volumnius, my brother Pheroras, my sister
Salome, and in place of Archelaus some members of the
Syrian aristocracy. To avoid a scandal, I had decided that
the two defendants should not be present. I had placed
them under guard at Platanaea, a town in the vicinity of
Sidon.

"I spoke first. After picturing the misery of a betrayed
king and flouted father, I described my constant efforts to
reform my diabolical family, the favors I had showered on
the Hasmonaeans, and the outrages with which they had
rewarded me. The source of all this evil was their birth,
which, not without a semblance of reason, they judged su-
perior to my own. But did that mean that I should put up
with their affronts? Did it mean that I should let them
conspire against the security of the kingdom and against
my own life? I concluded by saying that in my heart and
conscience I thought Alexander and Aristobulus deserving
of the death penalty, that I felt sure the tribunal would be
of the same opinion, but that such a verdict pronounced
against my own progeny would be for me a bitter victory.

"Then Saturninus spoke. He condemned the two young
men, but not to death, because, as he said, he himself was
the father of three children—who were present in the
court—and could not bring himself to sentence another
man's progeny. It would be hard to conceive of a more
inept defense. But it made no difference. Duly instructed

by the emperor, the other Roman followed Saturninus in rejecting the death sentence—they and no one else. As at the end of a gladiatorial combat, I saw all thumbs turned down. Volumnius the procurator, the Syrian princes, the courtiers from Jerusalem, and, it goes without saying, Pheroras and Salome, the lot of them motivated by stupidity, hatred, or calculation—none of which precludes the others—voted for death.

"Sickened with grief and disgust, I had my sons taken to Tyre, and there I embarked with them for Caesarea. They had been condemned. It was within my power to pardon them. These were—and still are—two men within me; the merciless ruler, who obeys only the laws of power: To take power, to keep it, to wield it are all one and the same act, which cannot be performed in innocence. And side by side with him, a weak, credulous, emotional, frightened man, who was still hoping against all reason that his children would be saved. He pretended to be unaware of his double, of his fierce will to power, his merciless severity. Off the coast of Judea, within sight of the green slopes of Mt. Carmel, the ship isolated us from the world and its happenings. I decided to have my sons brought up on deck. It was the father who summoned them. The moment they stepped out of the hatchway, I knew it was the king who would receive them. To tell you the truth, I hardly recognized them in the black chlamys of the condemned, with their shaved heads and the marks of the interrogations they had undergone. The judicial machine had done its work. The metamorphosis was irreversible: Two radiant, carefree aristocrats had perished and in their place stood two conspirators and would-be parricides, whose plot had foundered. The glow of youth and happiness had given way to the mask of convicted crime. I hadn't a single word to say to them. I looked at them, they looked at me, and a wall of silence arose between us. Finally I ordered the centurion who was guarding them: 'Take them away!' They went back down to the hold and I never saw them again.

"From Caesarea I had them taken to Sebaste, where the executioner was waiting. They were strangled and their bodies rest in the citadel of Alexandrion beside that of Alexander, their maternal grandfather. Their funeral oration, like their lives, was a hideous mockery. It was spoken by the Emperor Augustus when he heard of their execution: 'At Herod's court it's better to be a pig than a prince. At least they respect the law against eating pork.'

"The death of his two half-brothers left Antipater in sole possession of the field. I expected him to change, to settle down, to develop his gifts. He could no longer doubt that he would be king. He was already sharing the throne with me, and after me he was the most powerful man in the kingdom. Was it the same old story, the approach of power that corrupted him? With horror I watched the disintegration of the man in whom I had placed all my hopes.

"The first alarm was connected with my grandchildren. The severity I had shown toward Alexander and Aristobulus had changed to tenderness for their orphaned children. Glaphyra had borne Alexander two sons: Tigranes and Alexander. Berenice had given Aristobulus three sons: Herod, Agrippa, and Aristobulus, and two daughters, Herodias and Mariamne. That made seven grandchildren, including five boys, all patently of Hasmonaean blood. What was my horror when my police alerted me to Antipater's fear and hatred of Mariamne's descendants. He referred to them as a 'nest of vipers' and told anyone who would listen that he would never be able to reign with such a threat hanging over him. I saw that the abominable curse, which has weighed on the alliance between Idumeans and Hasmonaeans for half a century, would be perpetuated after me.

"That wasn't all. When he spoke of 'making a clean sweep,' he was obviously thinking primarily of me. He was quoted as saying: 'I shall never reign! Look, I already have gray hairs, and he dyes his!' Even my illnesses exasperated him; it drove him half mad to see me revive when I had been given up for dead. Since the death of his brothers, he had become careless; he spoke his mind too freely, and from day to day the blackness of his heart became plainer to me. While the storm was gathering over the heads of Alexander and Aristobulus, Antipater had kept his peace, apparently observing a benevolent neutrality toward his half-brothers. His conduct couldn't have been more diplomatic. But now I discovered that he had secretly done everything in his power to ruin them. It was he who had pulled the strings and set the traps in which they were to perish. My resentment against him soon surpassed all bounds.

"It was reported to me that he had formed a sort of coterie with my brother Pheroras and various women, including his mother Doris, his own wife and Pheroras' wife, and that they met secretly at midnight banquets. My sister Salome told me these things. I decided to disperse this precious crew. I assigned Pheroras to residence at Peraea, the capital of his tetrarchy. As for Antipater, I sent him to Rome on a mission to represent me at Caesar's trial of the Arabian minister Syllaeus—the one Salome had wanted to marry—who was accused of complicity in the murder of his king, Aretas IV. The delegation that accompanied Antipater was larded with men in my pay, instructed to in-

form me of everything he did and said. A short time after
his arrival in Peraea, Pheroras fell sick, so sick that I was
persuaded to go there if I wanted to see him alive. I
went—as you can imagine—not so much for reasons of
brotherly compassion as to throw light on a situation that
struck me as suspicious. Pheroras died in my arms, swear-
ing that he had been poisoned. That seemed unlikely. Who
had an interest in doing away with him? Certainly not his
wife, a former slave, who in losing him lost everything.
Nevertheless, it was she who let the cat out of the bag. In
the course of the midnight meetings organized unbe-
knownst to me by Antipater and Pheroras, they had decided to bring in a female poisoner from Arabia, equipped
to do away with me and the children of Alexander and
Aristobulus. When Antipater and Pheroras had separated,
Pheroras had kept the phial of poison in the intention of
using it while Antipater was at Rome, where he would be
beyond all suspicion. I told Pheroras' wife to go and get
the poison. She pretended to obey, but instead tried to kill
herself by jumping off one of the terraces. She was
brought to me in a desperate condition. The phial of
poison had been found in the meantime; it was half empty.
The poor woman told me she herself had emptied it into
the fire at the bidding of Pheroras, who, touched by my
visit, had decided not to murder me. Herod is not a man to
be taken in by edifying fairy tales. The one thing this rig-
marole made clear to me was Antipater's guilt. Which was
definitely established when I intercepted a letter he had
written to Pheroras from Rome, asking if the 'deal had
gone through' and enclosing a dose of poison 'in case of
need.' I arranged that no word of Pheroras' death or of
my presence at Peraea should reach him.

"He returned unsuspecting to Jerusalem, whither I had

preceded him, and covered me with caresses while telling
me about the successful outcome of the trial. Syllaeus had
been confounded and condemned. I repulsed him, flung his
uncle's death in his face, and told him how the whole plot
had been discovered. He fell at my feet and swore he was
innocent of everything. I packed him off to prison. Then,
as always happens when the betrayal of my familiars steeps
me in bitterness, illness laid me low. I couldn't tell you
how long my prostration lasted. I was in no condition to
pay the slightest attention to the investigation being carried on at my request by Quintilius Varus, the Roman
governor of Syria. One day a basket of fruit was brought
to me. The only thing I saw was the silver knife, the kind
used for splitting mangoes and peeling pineapples. I han-
dled it for a moment, taking pleasure in the tapering blade,
the handle that fitted so cozily into the palm of my hand,
and the happy balance between the two. Really a beautiful
thing, graceful, elegant, perfectly adapted to its function.
What function? Peeling apples? Ridiculous. Ending the
lives of desperate kings! With one stroke I plunged the
blade into my chest. Blood spurted. A veil fell over my
eyes.

"When I recovered consciousness, the first thing I saw
was the face of my cousin Ahab bending over me. I knew
I had failed. But my brief absence had sufficed to create
havoc. Antipater was trying to bribe his prison guards. It
was written that I wouldn't die without toppling some
more heads. The first to roll was that of Antipater, my eldest son, whom I had chosen to reign after me.

"That was the day before you arrived. I no longer had
an heir, but at least my scouts brought me word of a
strange and solemn procession of visitors. True, that

wouldn't have meant much to me if Menahem, my necromancer, hadn't drawn my attention to a capricious new
star that was passing through our sky, the very same star
that led you here—you, Gaspar, and you, Balthasar. In it
Gaspar recognized the golden hair of his Phoenician slave
and Balthasar saw the Knight-Banneret butterfly of his
childhood. Permit me, too, to give this planet a face in
keeping with my character. The story Sangali told us is in-
structive. In my opinion the wandering star can only be
the white bird with the golden egg that King Nabunassar
pursued in his quest for an heir. The old King of the Jews
is dying. The king is dead. The little King of the Jews has
been born. Long live our little king!

"Gaspar, Melchior, Balthasar, listen to me! I appoint
you all plenipotentiaries of the kingdom of Judea. I am too
feeble, too frail, to run after the fiery bird that holds the
secret of my succession. Even carried in a litter, I
wouldn't survive such an expedition. Menahem has drawn
my attention to a prophecy of Micah, according to which
the Savior of the Jewish people will be born in Bethlehem—
the place of King David's birth.

"Go! Find this Heir and bow down to Him in my name.
Then come and tell me all about it. Whatever you do,
don't fail to come back . . ."

The old king broke off and buried his face in his hands.
When he uncovered it, it was hideously disfigured.

"Don't get the idea of betraying me! I believe I've described certain episodes of my life clearly enough this evening! Oh, I'm used to being betrayed. But now you know.
When I'm betrayed, I strike—I strike hard and quickly,
without pity. I command you . . . no, I conjure you, I beg
you: make sure that for once, just this once, on the brink

of the grave, I am not betrayed. Give me this last alms: an act of fidelity, of good faith. Then I shall not be in utter despair on entering the other world."

They set out. They passed through the deep valley of Gihon, climbed the steep slopes of the Mountain of Evil Counsel. In passing they paid their respects to the tomb of Rachel. The star in the icy firmament bristled with needles of light. They followed it at a sidereal pace. Each had a secret and a gait of his own. One rocked with his camel's ambling walk and in the black sky saw only the face and the hair of the woman he loved. One, whose trotting mare cut diagonal tracks in the sand, gazed at the horizon and saw only the quivering wings of a glittering butterfly. One went on foot because he had lost everything, and dreamed of an impossible kingdom of heaven. The ears of all three were still ringing with a story full of screams and horrors, the great King Herod's story of a long and prosperous reign, blessed by the peasants and artisans.

Is that then power? Melchior wondered—that noxious magma of torture and incest? Is that the price one must pay to be a great king, whose name will go down in history?

Is that then love? Gaspar wondered. Herod loved only one woman, Mariamne, with a total, absolute, indestructible—but alas, unreciprocated—love! Because Mariamne the Hasmonaean was not of the same race as Herod the Idumean, disaster struck the accursed pair, and repeated itself with monotonous ferocity in every generation of their progeny. Shuddering, the black Gaspar measured the gulf that separated him from Biltine, the blond Phoenician woman.

Is that then the love of art? Balthasar wondered, his eyes

fixed on the celestial Knight-Banneret with its quivering wings of flame. In his mind two rebellions were confounded: the one in Nippur that destroyed the Balthasareum and the other in Jerusalem that toppled the golden eagle from the temple. But while Herod opposed the rebels in his manner, with a massacre, he, Balthasar, had given in. The Balthasareum had been neither avenged nor rebuilt, for the old king of Nippur harbored a doubt. If a whole religious tradition condemned the beauty of Greek statuary, of Roman painting, of Punic mosaics and Etruscan miniatures, might there not truly be a curse in such beauty? And he thought of his young friend, Assur the Babylonian, who was trying to find ways to celebrate the humble human realities. But how can one exalt what nature condemns to the mockery of transience?

And all three, each in his own way, tried to imagine the little King of the Jews, in search of whom Herod had bidden them follow his white bird. But then confusion blurred their thoughts, for this Heir to the Kingdom combined incompatible attributes: greatness and littleness, power and innocence, riches and poverty.

On they went. They would go and see. They would open their eyes and hearts to unknown truths, listen to words such as had never been spoken before. On they went, borne by a tenderly jubilant intimation that a new era might be opening before them.

THE ASS
AND THE OX

The Ox

The ass is a poet, a literary sort, a chatterbox. The ox, for his part, says nothing. He is meditative, taciturn, a ruminant. He says nothing, but he thinks plenty. He reflects and he remembers. His head is as heavy and massive as a boulder, and it has age-old images knocking about in it. The most venerable of these images comes from ancient Egypt. It is the image of the Bull Apis: born of a virgin heifer impregnated by a thunderbolt; bearing a crescent on his forehead and a vulture on his back. A scarab is hidden under his tongue. He is fed in a temple. You can hardly expect an ox with all that behind him to be impressed by a god born in a stable to a maiden and the Holy Ghost!

He remembers. He sees himself as a young bull. At the center of the harvest procession in honor of the goddess Cybele, he strides forward wreathed in clusters of grapes, escorted by grape-harvesting girls and paunchy, flushed silenuses.

He remembers. Black autumn fields. The slow labor of the earth, laid open by the plowshare. The work mate that shared his yoke. The steaming warm stable.

He dreams of the cow. The mother animal par excellence. The softness of her womb. The gentle thrusts of the baby calf's head inside this living, generous horn of plenty. The clustered pink teats, the spurting milk.

The ox knows he is all that, and he knows it is incumbent on his reassuring, immovable bulk to watch over the labor of the Virgin and the birth of the Child.

The Ass's Story

Don't let my white hair fool you, says the ass. I was once jet black, with just a light-colored star on my forehead, obviously a sign of my predestination. The star is still there, but you can't see it anymore, because my whole coat has gone white. It's like the stars of the night sky, that fade in the pale of dawn. Old age has given the whole of me the color of the star on my forehead, and there again I like to see a sign, the mark of a kind of blessing.

Because I'm old, very old. I must be almost forty, which is amazing for an ass. It wouldn't surprise me if I were the dean of asses. That, too, would be a sign.

They call me Kadi Shuya. That calls for an explanation. Even in my childhood my masters noticed an air of wisdom that distinguished me from other asses. They were impressed by the serious, subtle look in my eyes. That's why they called me Kadi, because everyone knows that in our country a kadi is both a judge and a priest, in other words, somebody remarkable for two kinds of wisdom. True, I was still an ass, the humblest and most ill-treated of animals, and they couldn't very well give me a venerable name like Kadi without downgrading it by tacking on something ridiculous. This was Shuya, which means small, insignificant, contemptible. So that made me Kadi Shuya,

the no-account Kadi, whose masters sometimes called him
Kadi but more often Shuya, according to their humor at
the time. . . .

I'm a poor man's ass. For years I affected to be pleased
about it, because I had a rich man's ass as a neighbor and
confidant. My master was a small farmer. There was a
beautiful estate right next to his field. A Jerusalem merchant used to spend the hottest weeks of summer there
with his family. His ass was called Yawul, a magnificent
animal, nearly twice as big and fat as me; his coat was a
solid gray, as fine as silk. It was something to see him go
out harnessed in red leather and green velvet, with his tap-
estry saddle and his big copper stirrups, his jiggling pom-
pons and tinkling little bells. I pretended to find this carnival outfit ridiculous. I remembered the sufferings they had
put him through in his childhood to make him into a luxury mount. I'd seen him streaming with blood after his
master's initials and emblem were cut into his flesh with a
razor. I'd seen the tips of his ears cruelly sewn together to
make them stand up straight like horns instead of drooping
pathetically to the right and left like mine, and his legs
squeezed into tight bands to make them slenderer and
straighter than ordinary asses' legs. That's what humans
are like: they manage to inflict more pain on the creatures
they love and take pride in than on ones they hate or de-
spise.

But Yawul had compensations that were not to be
sneezed at, and there was a secret envy mixed with the
commiseration I felt entitled to show him. For one thing,
he ate barley and oats every day in a spanking clean stall.
And best of all, those mares! You won't quite get the point
of this unless you know how insufferably arrogant horses
are about asses. The fact is, they don't look at us at all; as

far as they're concerned, we don't exist any more than
mice or cockroaches. And the mares are the worst of all,
haughty, unapproachable . . . great ladies! Yes, to mount a
mare is an ass's dream—that's his idea of revenge on that
big ninny of a stallion. But how is an ass to compete with a
horse on his own ground? Well, fate has more than one
card up its sleeve, and it has given certain members of the
asinine nation the most amazing and amusing privilege.
The key to that privilege is the mule. What is a mule? A
mule is a sober, safe and surefooted mount (to these adjec-
tives in "s" I might add "silent," "scrupulous," and "studi-
ous," but I try to keep my weakness for alliteration under
control). The mule is the king of sandy trails, slippery
slopes, and fords. Calm, imperturbable, indefatigable,
he . . .

And what is the secret of all these virtues? The secret is
that he is spared the tumult of love and the trials of
procreation. The mule doesn't bear children. To make a
little mule, you need a daddy ass and a mummy mare.
That's why some asses—and Yawul was one of them—are
selected as fathers-of-mules (the most prestigious of titles
in our community) and given mares for wives.

I'm not oversexed, and if I have any ambitions, they're
not in that direction. But I must confess that there were
mornings when the sight of Yawul, exhausted and drunk
with pleasure, staggering back from his equestrian exploits,
made me doubt the justice of life. It's true that life didn't
spoil me. Constantly beaten, insulted, loaded with burdens
heavier than I was, fed on thistles—where, I ask you, did
humans get the idea that asses dote on thistles? Couldn't
they give us clover or grain just once, to let us relish the
difference!—and in the end, the dread of crows, when we
drop with exhaustion and wait by the roadside for merci-

ful death to come and put an end to our sufferings! Yes,
the dread of crows, because we know that when our last
hour comes there's a big difference between vultures and
crows. Vultures, you see, attack only corpses. As long as
there's a breath of life left in you, there's no need to worry
about vultures; somehow they know what's what, and wait
at a respectful distance. But crows are devils; they pounce
before you're half dead and eat you alive, beginning with
the eyes. . . .

I had to tell you all this, because otherwise you
wouldn't understand my state of mind that winter's day,
when I arrived in Bethlehem—that's a small town in Judea
—with my master. The whole province was in a turmoil,
because the Emperor had ordered a census of the population, and everybody and his family had to go back to the
place they came from to register. Bethlehem is hardly
more than a big village perched on the top of a hill, the
sides of which are terraced and covered with little gardens
with dry-stone retaining walls. In the spring and at normal
times it's probably a nice enough place to live in, but at the
onset of winter and with all this census bustle, I certainly
missed my stable at Djela, our home village. My master
and mistress had been lucky enough to find a place for
themselves and their two children in a big inn that was
humming like a beehive. Alongside of the main building
there was a kind of barn where they probably stored provisions. In between there was a narrow passage, leading
nowhere, with a sort of thatched roof made by throwing
armfuls of reeds on top of some crossbeams. Under this
precarious shelter some feeding troughs had been set up
and the ground had been strewn with litter for the beasts
belonging to the guests at the inn. That was where they
tethered me, next to an ox who had just been unharnessed

from a cart. I don't mind telling you that I've always had a
horror of oxen. I admit they haven't an ounce of malice in
them, but unfortunately my master's brother-in-law owns
one. At plowing time the two brothers-in-law help each
other out, and that means harnessing us to the plow together, though it's expressly forbidden by law.[8] That is a
very wise law, because, take it from me, nothing could be
ghastlier than working in that sort of team. The ox has his
pace—which is slow—and his rhythm—which is steady. He
pulls with his neck. The ass—like the horse—pulls with his
crupper. He works spasmodically, in fits and starts. To
team him up with an ox is to put a ball and chain on his
legs, to curtail his energy—which he hasn't got so much of
to begin with.

But that night there was no question of plowing. Travelers turned away from the inn had invaded the barn. I
strongly suspected that they wouldn't leave us in peace for
long. And pretty soon, true enough, a man and a woman
slipped into our improvised stable. The man was an old
fellow, some kind of artisan. He had kicked up a big fuss,
telling everyone who would listen that if he had to register
in Bethlehem for the census, it was because his family tree
—twenty-seven generations no less—went back to King
David, who himself had been born in Bethlehem. Everybody laughed in his face. He'd have had more chance of
finding lodging if he had mentioned the condition of his
very young wife, who seemed dead tired and very preg-
nant besides. Taking straw from the floor and hay from
the feeding troughs, he put together a kind of pallet between the ox and me, and laid the young woman down on
it.

Little by little, everybody found his place and the noise
died down. Now and then the young woman moaned

softly and that's how we found out that her husband's name was Joseph. He comforted her as best he could, and that's how we found out that her name was Mary. I don't know how many hours passed, because I must have slept. When I woke up, I had a feeling that a big change had taken place, not only in our passageway, but everywhere, even, so it seemed, in the sky, glittering tatters of which shone through our miserable roof. The great silence of the longest night of the year had fallen on the earth, and it seemed as though, for fear of breaking the silence, the earth had stopped the flow of its waters and the heavens were holding their breath. Not a bird in the trees. Not a fox in the fields. Not a mole in the grass. The eagles and the wolves, whatever had beak or claw, watched and waited, with hunger in their bellies and their eyes fixed on the darkness. Even the glowworms and fireflies masked their light. Time had given way to a sacred eternity.

Then suddenly, in less than an instant, something enormous happened. An irrepressible thrill of joy traversed heaven and earth. A rustling of innumerable wings made it plain that swarms of angelic messengers were rushing in all directions. The thatch over our heads was lit up by the dazzling train of a comet. We heard the crystalline laughter of the brooks and the majestic laughter of the rivers. In the desert of Judea swirls of sand tickled the flanks of the dunes. An ovation rose from the terebinth forests and mingled with the muffled applause of the hoot owls. All nature exulted.

What had happened? Hardly anything. A faint cry had been heard, coming from the dark, warm pallet, a cry that could not have come from a man or a woman. It was the soft wailing of a newborn babe. Just then, a column of light came to rest in the middle of the stable: the Archan-

gel Gabriel, Jesus's guardian angel, had arrived. The moment he got there, he took charge, so to speak. At the same
time, the door opened, and one of the maids from the inn
came in, supporting a basin of warm water on her hip.
Without hesitation she knelt down and bathed the child.
Then she rubbed it with salt to toughen the skin, swaddled
it, and handed it to Joseph, who set it down on his knees,
in token of paternal recognition.

You have to hand it to Gabriel, his efficiency was remarkable. Meaning no disrespect to an archangel, I have to
tell you that for the past year he hadn't let any grass grow
under his feet. He was the one who announced to Mary
that she would be the mother of the Messiah. He was the
one who set the kindly old Joseph's suspicions to rest. And
it was he, later on, who would dissuade the Three Kings
from making their report to Herod, and organize the little
family's flight into Egypt. But that's getting ahead of my
story. Just then he was playing the majordomo, the master
of joyous ceremonies in that lowly place, which he
transfigured, pretty much the way the sun turns the rain
into a rainbow. In his very own person he went about
waking the shepherds in the country nearby. At first, as
you might expect, he gave them quite a turn. But then,
laughing to reassure them, he announced the big news, and
summoned them to the stable. Stable? That seemed
strange, but it also put those simple folk at their ease.

When they started pouring in, Gabriel arranged them in
a semicircle and helped them to come forward, one by
one, kneel on one knee, pay their respects, and proffer
their good wishes. And saying those few words was no
joke for those silent men, who as a rule speak only to their
dogs or the moon. Stepping up to the crib, they set down
the products of their toil, clotted milk, small goat's cheeses,

butter made from ewe's milk, olives from Galgala, syca-
more figs, and dates from Jericho, but neither meat nor
fish. They spoke of their humble sufferings, epidemics,
vermin, and animal pests. Gabriel blessed them in the name
of the Child, and promised them help and protection.

Neither meat nor fish, I said. But one of the last shepherds stepped forward with a little ram, barely four
months old, wrapped around his neck. He knelt down,
deposited his burden on the straw, then raised himself to
his full height. The country people recognized Silas the
Samaritan, a shepherd, to be sure, but also a kind of hermit, reputed among the simple folk for his wisdom. He
lived all alone with his dogs and his beasts, in a mountain
cave near Hebron. Everyone knew that he wouldn't come
down from his wilderness for nothing, and when the
archangel signaled him to speak, they all listened.

"My lord," he began, "some people say I withdrew to
the mountains because I hated men. That's not true. It
wasn't hatred of mankind but love of animals that made
me a hermit. But when someone loves animals, he has to
protect them from the wickedness and greed of men. It's
true, I'm not the usual kind of husbandman. I neither sell
nor kill my beasts. They give me their milk. I make it into
cream, butter, and cheese. I sell nothing. I use these gifts
according to my needs and give the rest—the greater part—
to the poor. If tonight I've obeyed the angel, who woke
me and showed me the star, it's because of the rebellion in
my heart, not only against the ways of my society, but
worse, against the rites of my religion. Unfortunately, this
thing goes back a long way, almost to the beginning of
time, and it would take a great revolution to bring about a
change. Has the revolution happened tonight? That's what
I've come to ask you."

"It has happened tonight," Gabriel assured him.

"I'll start with Abraham's sacrifice. To test Abraham, God commanded him to offer Isaac, his only son, as a burnt offering. Abraham obeyed. He took the child and climbed a mountain in the land of Moriah. The child was puzzled: They had brought wood, they had brought the fire and the knife, but where was the lamb for the burnt offering? Wood, fire, knife . . . there, my lord, are the accursed stigmata of man's destiny!"

"There will be more," said Gabriel gloomily, thinking of the nails, the hammer, and the crown of thorns.

"Then Abraham built an altar, laid the wood in order, and bound Isaac and laid him on the altar upon the wood. And he set his knife on the child's white throat."

"But then," Gabriel interrupted, "an angel came and stayed his arm. That was me."

"Yes, of course, good angel," said Silas. "But Isaac never recovered from the fright of seeing his own father holding a knife at his throat. The blue flash of the knife blasted his eyes; his eyesight was poor as long as he lived, and at the end he went stone blind. That's why his son Jacob was able to deceive him and pass for his brother Esau. But that's not what bothers me. Why couldn't you content yourself with stopping the child-killing? Did blood have to flow? You, Gabriel, supplied Abraham with a young ram, which was killed and offered up as a burnt offering. Couldn't God do without a death that morning?"

"I admit that Abraham's sacrifice was a failed revolution," said Gabriel. "We'll do better next time."

"Actually," said Silas, "we can go further back in sacred history and trace Yahweh's secret passion to its source. Remember Cain and Abel. The two brothers were at their devotions. Each offered up products of his labor. Cain was

a tiller of the soil, he offered up fruits and grain, while
Abel, who was a shepherd, offered up lambs and their fat.
What happened? Yahweh turned away from Cain's offering and welcomed Abel's. Why? For what reason? I can
see only one: It was because Yahweh hates vegetables and
loves meat! Yes, the God we worship is hopelessly carniv-
orous!

"And we honor Him as such. Consider the temple at
Jerusalem in its splendor and majesty, that sanctuary of
the radiant divinity. Did you know that on some days it's
drenched in steaming fresh blood like a slaughterhouse?
The sacrificial altar is a huge block of rough-hewn stone,
with hornlike protuberances at the corners and traversed
with runnels to evacuate the blood of the victims. On the
occasion of certain festivals the priests transform themselves into butchers and massacre whole herds of beasts.
Oxen, rams, he-goats, even whole flocks of doves are
shaken by the spasms of their death agony. They are dis-
membered on marble tables, and the entrails are thrown
into a brazier. The whole city is infested with smoke.
Some days, when the wind is from the north, the stench
spreads as far as my mountain and my beasts are seized
with panic."

"Silas the Samaritan," said Gabriel, "you have done well
to come here tonight to watch over the Child and worship
him. The complaints of your animal-loving heart will be
heard. I've said that Abraham's sacrifice was a failed revolution. Soon the Father will sacrifice the Son again. And I
swear to you that this time no angel will stay His hand. All
over the world from now on, even on the smallest of is-
lands, and at every hour of the day till the end of time, the
blood of the Son will flow on altars for the salvation of
mankind. This little child you see sleeping in the straw—

the ox and the ass do well to warm Him with their breath, for He is in truth a lamb. From now on there will be no other sacrificial lamb, because He is the Lamb of God, who alone will be sacrificed in *saecula saeculorum*.

"Go in peace, Silas. As a symbol of life you may take with you the young ram you have brought. More fortunate than Abraham's, he will testify in your herd that from now on the blood of animals will no longer be shed on God's altars."

After this angelic speech there was a thoughtful pause that seemed to make a space around the terrible and magnificent event the angel had announced. Each in his own way and according to his powers tried to imagine what the new times would be like. But then a terrible jangling of chains and rusty pulleys was heard, accompanied by a burst of grotesque, ungainly, sobbing laughter. That was me, that was the thunderous bray of the ass in the manger. Yes, what would you expect, my patience was at an end. This couldn't go on. We'd been forgotten again; I'd listened attentively to everything that had been said, and I hadn't heard one word about asses.

Everybody laughed—Joseph, Mary, Gabriel, the shepherds, Silas the hermit, the ox, who hadn't understood one thing—and even the Child, who flailed merrily about with His four little limbs in His straw crib.

"Don't let it worry you," said Gabriel. "The asses will not be forgotten. Obviously you don't have to worry about sacrifices. Within memory of priest no one has ever seen an ass offered up on an altar. That would be too much honor for you poor humble donkeys. And yet great is your merit, beaten, starved, crushed under the weight of your burdens. But don't imagine that your miseries escape the eye of an archangel. For instance, Kadi Shuya, I dis-

tinctly see a deep, festering little wound behind your left
ear. Day after day your master prods it with his goad. He
thinks the pain will revive your flagging vigor. Ah, poor
martyr, every time he does it, I suffer with you."

The archangel pointed a luminous finger at my right ear
and instantly the deep, festering little wound that had not
escaped him closed. What's more, the skin that covered it
was now so hard and thick that no goad would ever make
a dent in it. Then and there I tossed my mane with enthusiasm and let out a triumphant bray.

"Yes, you humble and friendly companions of man's
labor," Gabriel went on, "you will have your reward and
your triumph in the great story that's starting tonight.

"One day, a Sunday—which will be known as Palm
Sunday—the Apostles will find a she-ass and her colt in the
village of Bethany near the Mount of Olives. They will
loose them and throw a cloak on the back of the foal—
which no one will yet have mounted—and Jesus will ride
it. And Jesus will make His solemn entry into Jerusalem,
through the Golden Gate, the finest of the city's gates.
The people will rejoice and acclaim the Nazarene prophet
with cries of Hosannah to the Son of David! And the foal
will tread a carpet of palm branches and flowers that the
people will have laid over the paving stones. And the
mother ass will trot in the rear of the procession, braying
to all and sundry: 'That's my foal! That's my foal!' for
never will a mother ass have been so proud."

So for the first time in history someone had given a
thought to us asses, someone had stopped to think about
our sufferings of today and joys of tomorrow. But before
that could happen an archangel had to come all the way
down from heaven. Suddenly I didn't feel alone anymore,
I'd been adopted by the great Christmas family. I was no

longer the outcast whom no one understood. What a beautiful night we could all have spent together in the warmth of our sacred poverty! How late we would have slept next morning! And what a fine breakfast we'd have had!

Too bad! The rich always have to butt in. The rich are insatiable, they want to own everything, even poverty. Who could ever have imagined that this wretched family, camping between an ox and an ass, would attract a king? Did I say a king? No, three kings, authentic sovereigns, from the Orient, what's more! And really, what an outrageous display of servants, animals, canopies. . . .

The shepherds had gone home. Once again silence enveloped that incomparable night. And suddenly the village streets were full of tumult. A clanking of bridles and stirrups and weapons; purple and gold glittered in the torchlight; shouts and commands rang out in barbarous languages. And most marvelous of all: the astonishing silhouettes of animals from the ends of the earth, falcons from the Nile, greyhounds, green parrots, magnificent horses, camels from the far south. Why not elephants while they were about it?

At first a lot of us went out and looked. Curiosity. There had never been such a show in a Palestinian village. You have to hand it to them—when it came to stealing our Christmas, the rich spared no expense. But in the end too much is enough. We went back inside and barricaded ourselves and some beat it across the hills and fields. Because, you see, unimportant people like us can expect no good of the great. Better steer clear of them. For a farthing dropped here and there, how many whippings fall to the lot of the beggar or ass who crosses a prince's path!

That's the way it looked to my master. Awakened by the ruckus, he gathered up his family and belongings, and I saw him elbowing his way into our improvised stable. My master knows his own mind, but he's a man of few words. Without so much as opening his mouth, he untied me and we left that noisy village before the kings marched in.

TAOR, PRINCE OF MANGALORE

The Age of Sugar

Siri Akbar had that ambiguous—half cajoling, half ironic—smile on his face as he handed Prince Taor a casket of sandalwood inlaid with ivory.

"Here, my Lord, is the Occident's latest gift to you. To reach you, it has traveled for three months."

Taor took the casket, hefted it, examined it, and raised it to his nostrils.

"It's light," he said, "but it smells good."

Then he turned it about in his hands and observed that the lid was secured with a large wax seal.

"Open it," he said, handing it to Siri.

The young man tapped the seal several times with the hilt of his sword. It cracked and crumbled into dust. There was no difficulty in raising the lid. The little box returned to the prince's hands. There was next to nothing inside: a square compartment holding a cube of some soft, sea-green substance, coated with white powder. Taor picked it up delicately between thumb and forefinger, held it up against the light, then raised it to his nose.

"It smells of sandalwood, that's from the box, of course; the powder is powdered sugar; the green color suggests pistachio. Why don't I taste it?"

"That would be risky," said Siri. "Have a slave try it first."

Taor shrugged his shoulders.

"There wouldn't be anything left of it."

Thereupon he opened his mouth and popped the little delicacy into it. He closed his eyes and waited. After a while his jaws moved slowly. He couldn't talk, but the movements of his hands expressed surprise and pleasure.

"It's pistachio all right," he said finally.

"They call it *rahat loukoum*,"* Siri explained. "In their language that means 'happiness of the throat.' So this must be pistachio *rahat loukoum*."

Now Prince Taor Malek prized nothing more highly than the confectioner's art, and of all the ingredients used by his confectioners and pastry cooks, his preference went to pistachio nuts. He had gone so far as to plant an orchard of pistachio trees, which he tended with loving care.

Pistachio was definitely there, incorporated into the soft, cloudy-green, sugar-coated cube. Incorporated? No, exalted, enhanced! This mysterious *rahat loukoum*—since that was its name—from the land of the setting sun represented the highest degree of the pistachio cult; in it the pistachio had been made to transcend itself; in short, it was *suprême* of pistachio. . . .

Taor's candid features betrayed intense emotion.

"I should have shown it to my chief pastry cook! Perhaps he could have . . ."

"I doubt it," said Siri, still smiling. "It's a delicacy quite unlike anything they make here. Absolutely new."

"You're right," the prince agreed forlornly. "But why," he asked, "have they only sent me one? Did they want to

---

* Though older than Turkey or the Turks, this delicacy is known in English-speaking countries as Turkish delight.

—Tr.

drive me to distraction?" And he pouted like a child on the brink of tears.

"Don't despair," said Siri, suddenly grown serious. "We could piece together what little we know about this casket and its contents, and send a messenger to the Occident, with orders to bring back the recipe for pistachio *rahat loukoum*."

"Yes, of course. Why not?" cried Taor with enthusiasm. "But let's not just send for the recipe! Why wouldn't they bring back a whole shipment of . . . what do you call it?"

"Pistachio *rahat loukoum*."

"Exactly. Find a reliable man. No. Two reliable men. Give them silver, gold, letters of recommendation, whatever they need. But how long is this going to take?"

"They can't set out before the winter monsoon, and they'll have to wait for the summer monsoon before they can come back. If all goes well, we can expect them in fourteen months."

"Fourteen months!" cried Taor in horror. "It would make more sense for us to take the trip ourselves."

Taor was all of twenty, but the principality of Mangalore, situated on the Malabar Coast in southwestern India, had been governed by his mother since the death of Maharaja Taor Malar. And Maharani Taor Mamore's taste for power seemed to grow in proportion as her once radiant beauty faded, so that her main concern in life was to keep the prince as far as possible from the business of government, which she was determined to concentrate in her own hands. To this end, she had provided her son with a companion, whose parents were her creatures and who was only too glad to perform the duties she had assigned him. On the pretext of satisfying the young prince's every whim and of furthering his happiness, Siri Akbar encouraged him in utterly frivolous inclinations, all of a nature to exacerbate his laziness, his sensuality, and, above all, the immoderate taste for sweets that he had shown since early childhood. Siri Akbar was a cold, intelligent young man, an ambitious slave; in all his thoughts and actions he was motivated by the hope of acquiring his freedom and rising rapidly at court. But it would be unfair to see pure duplicity in his subservience to the maharani and his demoralizing devotion to Taor. He was not devoid of sincerity and of a certain naïveté. In his own way he was fond of the maharani and her son, and, seeing no incompatibility between the maharani's will to power, the prince's gourmandise, and his own ambition, he was able, or so he thought, to further all three at once. It must be said that the mental processes of the people of Mangalore were exceedingly simplified by their isolation, wedged in as they were between sea and desert. This also explains why at the time when our story begins Prince Taor had never left his kingdom and had seldom ventured outside the palace gardens.

Siri, however, with a view to satisfying his master's curiosity and gourmandise, had formed commercial ties with foreign parts. It was he who had bought this casket containing a single piece of *rahat loukoum* from some Arab navigators, and before they embarked on their return voyage he had obtained passage on their ship for two agents charged with elucidating the mystery of the little Levantine sweetmeat.

Months passed. The northeast monsoon which had carried the agents westward gave way to the southwest monsoon which brought them back. They reported at once to the palace. Alas, they brought neither *rahat loukoum* nor recipe. In vain they had traversed Chaldea, Assyria, and Mesopotamia. Perhaps they should have continued west to Phrygia and northward to Bithynia or southward to Egypt. Their dependency on the monsoons had obliged them to make a difficult choice. Prolonging their search would have taken them past the only season when the winds favored the return voyage to the Malabar Coast and would have delayed them a whole year. Possibly they would have kept Prince Taor waiting that long if they had nothing to show for their pains. But such was not the case. Far from it, for they had had strange encounters in the arid lowlands of Judea and the desolate mountains of Naphtali. Those formerly uninhabited regions were now swarming with hermits, stylites and solitary prophets, dressed in camel's hide and armed only with shepherd's staffs. Emerging from their caves, their eyes flashing through a mane of tangled head hair and beard, they would harangue the traveler, proclaiming the end of the world. Or, appearing on the shores of lakes or rivers, they would offer to bathe him to cleanse him of his sins.

Taor couldn't make head or tail of all this. He had listened with only half an ear and was growing impatient. What did these desert savages have to do with *rahat loukoum* and the recipe for it?

That was the whole point, said the agents. Some of these people were predicting the imminent invention of a transcendent food, so substantial that it would stanch the appetite for all time, so delicious that if you tasted of it just once you wouldn't want to eat anything else to the end of your days. Was it pistachio *rahat loukoum?* No, probably not, for the Divine Confectioner who was expected to invent this delicacy hadn't been born yet. The people of Judea were expecting him any minute, and on the strength of certain sacred writings, some thought he would be born in Bethlehem, a village some two days' march to the south of the capital, where King David had first seen the light.

It seemed to Taor that his informants were losing themselves in the sands of religious speculation. Too much talk, too much conjecture; he demanded concrete proof, material evidence, something one could see, touch, or better still, eat.

Whereupon the two men exchanged looks of connivance, rummaged in their sack, and produced an earthenware pot of imposing size but rather rustic workmanship.

"This," said one of the agents, "is the staple food of those hermits dressed like bears, who claim to be the precursors of the Divine Confectioner. It is an original and tasty mixture, possibly a foretaste, as it were, of the announced and expected divine food."

Taor took hold of the pot, hefted it, and raised it to his nostrils.

"It's heavy, but it smells bad," he concluded, handing it to Siri.

The crude wooden disk that stopped the opening tilted under the pressure of Siri's sword point.

"Bring me a spoon," the prince ordered.

He withdrew the spoon from the pot, coated with a viscous, golden substance. Suspended in the substance were numbers of small angular creatures.

"It's honey," he observed.

"That's right," one of the agents confirmed. "Wild

honey. It's found in the middle of the desert, in stony hollows and dried-out stumps. The bees feed on the acacia forests, which for a short period in the springtime are one great mass of fragrant white flowers."

"Shrimps," said Taor.

"Shrimps if you will," the agent conceded, "but sand shrimps. They are large insects that fly in dense swarms, destroying everything in their path. To the peasants they are an unspeakable plague, but the nomads regard them as a delicacy and welcome their arrival as heavenly manna. They are called grasshoppers."

"Hmmm," the prince concluded. "Grasshoppers preserved in wild honey." Then he put the spoon into his mouth.

The general silence that ensued was compounded of expectancy and degustation. At length Prince Taor delivered his verdict.

"It's more original than tasty, more startling than succulent. This honey combines a curious harshness with its basic sweetness. As to the shrimps—or grasshoppers—they are crisp and give the honey a surprising nuance of saltiness."

Another silence while he tasted a second spoonful.

"Sincerity obliges me, who detests salt, to state this stupefying truth: salty sweetness is sweeter than sweet sweetness. What a paradox! I must hear that from someone else's lips. Repeat the sentence if you please."

The prince's familiars knew his little eccentricities and gladly inclined to them. In perfect unison they repeated: "Salty sweetness is sweeter than sweet sweetness."

"What a paradox!" Taor said again. "Such marvels are found only in the Occident. Siri, what would you say to an expedition to those remote and barbarous regions? We would bring back the secret of *rahat loukoum* and a few others while we're about it."

"My Lord, I am your slave!" Siri replied with all the irony that he managed to put into his protestations of the most unconditional devotion.

What was his surprise a few days later to learn that the prince had asked his mother for an audience—his only way of seeing her—and submitted a plan for a journey. And Siri felt utterly overwhelmed, if not tricked and betrayed, when immediately after the interview his master informed him that Maharani Mamore had approved his undertaking and promised to supply him with five ships and their crews, five elephants and their drivers, a bookkeeper and treasurer by the name of Draoma, and a treasury of talents, shekels, bekas, minas, and gerahs, coins in currency throughout Anterior Asia. His whole world, the product of ten years' patient intrigues, was crumbling beneath his feet. How could he have foreseen that the pistachio *rahat loukoum* he had given the prince to taste would conspire with the maharani's desire to get rid of her son at all costs and the unpredictable impulses to which weak, naïve, submissive persons are prone—in short, that all these heterogeneous facts and circumstances would add up to so egregious a disaster? Disaster indeed, for on the one hand he was well aware that his sort of intriguer could prosper only at the source of power, and on the other hand, as Siri well knew, not only the prince but the maharani as well took it for granted that he would accompany the prince on this insane expedition. The weeks that followed were undoubtedly the bitterest that Siri Akbar had ever experienced.

With Prince Taor it was a very different matter.

Shaken out of his lethargy by the preparations for the
journey, he had become a new man. His familiars hardly
knew him when, with surprising competence and authority, he drew up a list of the men who were to accompany
him and an inventory of the equipment that would be
required, and personally selected the elephants that would
be taken. Yet in choosing the provisions to be stored in the
ships' holds, he showed himself to be exactly the prince
they knew. For the true character of the journey was embodied in those crates, those sacks and bales bursting with
guavas, jujubes, sesame seed, cinnamon, Golconda raisins,
orange blossoms, sorghum meal, and cloves—not to mention the indispensable sugar, vanilla, ginger, and anise seed.
A whole ship was reserved for dried or preserved fruits—
mangoes, bananas, pineapples, tangerines, coconuts, cashew
nuts, limes, figs, and pomegranates. No doubt about it, the
aims and perspectives of this expedition were of a purely
confectionary nature. The most reputed specialists were
called in. In the midst of a heady, caramellious fragrance,
Nepalese confectioners, Singhalese nougat-makers, and
Bengalese jam-makers, not to mention dairymen, who had
come down from the heights of Cashmere with goatskins
full of liquid casein, decoctions of barley, emulsified al-
monds, and balsamic resins, were hard at work.

Taor's friends thought it quite in character when in
defiance of all good sense he insisted that Yasmina should
be included among the elephants of the expedition. In
defiance of good sense, because Yasmina was a young
white elephant, blue-eyed, gentle, frail, and sensitive,
hardly equal to the fatigues of the long ocean crossing and
the ensuing marches through the desert. But Taor loved
Yasmina, and his love was reciprocated. The languid-eyed
little pachyderm had a heartwarming way of twining her

trunk around his neck when he gave her a coconut cream
puff. Taor decided she would travel in the same ship as
himself, which would also carry the entire cargo of rose
petals.

The ships were made ready in the port of Mangalore. A
heavy, gently sloping gangplank was put in place for the
elephants. But the time of departure depended on the
caprice of the winds, for the summer monsoon was long
past, and this was the period of atmospheric disturbances
that precedes the turn-about of the wind and waves. A
time of storms and torrential rains, days of gloom, when
some of the prospective voyagers wondered if the wrath
of the heavens should not be taken as an evil omen for
their journey, and some withdrew from the expedition.
But then the sky cleared, a cool dry wind blew from the
east, the winter monsoon had definitely set in. That was
the awaited signal. The elephants were embarked. This
would have been easier if it had been possible to drive
them up the gangplank all together, because then their
herd instinct would have helped. But since they were traveling on different ships this same herd instinct was a serious
hindrance, and it was necessary to employ ruse, violence,
and cajolery to get them aboard. It was Yasmina who gave
the most trouble. Seized with panic, she let out blood-
curdling roars and when the men tried to hold her, she
flung them to the ground. Taor was summoned. He spoke
to her gently and at great length; he scratched the hollow
of her forehead. Finally he tied a silk scarf over her eyes,
laid her trunk on his shoulder, and led her up the gangplank.

Each ship was given the name of the elephant it carried;
the five names were *Bohdi, Jina, Vahana, Asura,* and, of
course, *Yasmina.* One fine autumn afternoon, the five

ships, under full sail, put out of the harbor in single file. Of all those on board—men and beasts—it was Prince Taor who showed the greatest joy at embarking on this adventure and the least regret for what he was leaving. The fact is that he didn't so much as look back at the city of Mangalore as its tiers of pink brick houses on the hillside receded into the distance, as though turning away from the west-bound flotilla.

It was plain sailing. With the wind on the quarter they kept a steady starboard tack. Since they headed straight out to sea, there were neither reefs nor sand banks to be feared, and after the first few hours they were safe from pirates, who confined their attentions to coastal traffic. The expedition would doubtless have crossed the Arabian Sea without incident if the elephants had not rebelled on the very first night. The trouble was that these beasts, which had been left at liberty in one of the royal forests until they were needed, were in the habit of spending the day dozing in the shade and then at sunset of rushing to the river in a compact herd. Consequently the falling of night made them restless and, since the ships were sailing in close formation, old Bohdi's first trumpetings provoked an enormous uproar in the other ships. The noise in itself would not have mattered, but at the same time the beasts started swaying to the right and left and beating their trunks against the sides of the ships! Amidst a sound as of giant tomtoms, the ships began to roll alarmingly.

Taor and Siri, who were on board the admiral ship *Yasmina*, were able to visit the other ships with the help of a rowboat, or when the ships were close together a gangplank could be laid between them. But there was still another means of communication between ships: waving bundles of ostrich plumes in accordance with a prear-

ranged code. Taor and Siri now sent ostrich-plume mes-
sages ordering the ships to disperse, so as to stop the beasts
from stirring one another up with their noise. Only Yasmina had kept quiet, but the twitching of her ears bore
witness to the state of her emotions, and it seemed likely
that she regarded the tumult as a kind of homage addressed
to her. The following night the excitement started up
again, but was much less severe thanks to the distance between the ships.

A new trial beset the travelers on the tenth day. The direction of the wind remained unchanged, but little by little
it rose to such force that an ostrich-plume message went
out from the *Yasmina* to the other ships, ordering them to
take in sail. By nightfall the lightning-striped blackness of
the horizon made it clear that the flotilla was heading into
a storm of unusual violence. An hour later inky night descended on all five ships, cutting them off completely from
one another. Nightmarish hours followed. Just enough sail
was flown to keep the ships from taking the waves on the
beam. Gusts of wind sent them racing; for a moment they
would stop, balanced on the crest of a wave, then descend
headlong into the blue-green trough. Taor, who had been
foolhardy enough to expose himself in the bow, was half
stunned and almost drowned by an enormous wave. A
brutal baptism, in which the young man, dedicated to
sugar since infancy, encountered the saline element for the
second time. Fate decreed that his third salty trial would
be infinitely longer and more painful.

But what worried him for the present was Yasmina.
Hurled forward, backward, to the right and left at the
onset of the storm, the little albino she-elephant had roared
with fear. Now she abandoned all attempt to stand on her
feet. Her eyelids lowered over her gentle blue eyes, she lay

on her side in noisome slime, and only a faint moan issued
from her lips. Taor had been down to see her several times
but was forced to suspend his visits when a sudden lurch
of the ship sent him rolling in a pool of Yasmina's excre-
tions and she, rolling in turn, came close to crushing him
beneath her weight. But this first peril did not make him
regret his venture, for, now that he was far from Mangalore in space and time, he began to measure the meaning-
lessness of the life to which his mother had reduced him
between his jujubes and his pistachio trees. Still, he felt
remorse for the sake of Yasmina, who was clearly unequal
to the hardships of so long a journey.

Siri Akbar, on the other hand, seemed transfigured by
the tempest. Up until then he had sulked and held aloof,
but now he seemed to come back to life. He gave orders
and assigned tasks with an almost jubilant coolness. Taor
observed that his companion and number-one slave, who in
the palace ran himself ragged promoting his career with
tortuous intrigues, was magnified and one might have said
purified by the onslaught of the raw elements. For it is
true that we are always more or less the reflection of our
undertakings and frustrations. Perceiving Akbar's face in
the brief instant of a lightning flash, Taor was surprised to
discover a strange beauty, compounded of courage, lucidity, and youthful enthusiasm.

The tempest ceased as quickly as it had broken out, but
it took no less than two days of sailing around in circles to
locate three of the ships—the *Bohdi*, the *Jina*, and the
Asura. The fourth, the *Vahana*, could not be found, and
there was nothing for it but to resume the westward journey, giving up the *Vahana* for at least provisionally lost.

The voyagers must have been less than a week's sailing
from Dioscorides Island at the entrance to the Gulf of

Aden, when the *Bohdi* gave the concerted ostrich-plume
distress signal. The *Yasmina* approached and Taor and Siri
went aboard without delay. Had the old elephant been bit-
ten by insects or poisoned by spoiled food? Or was he simply unable to bear the pitching and rolling of his prison
any longer? In any case, Bohdi had gone raving, raging
mad. He charged furiously at anyone who ventured into
the hold, and when there was no one to attack, he took to
ramming the side of the hull. The situation was critical, for
what with the elephant's weight, strength, and enormous
tusks, there was reason to fear that he would sink the ship.
To bind him or kill him seemed impossible, and since he
had stopped eating there was no way of putting him to
sleep or poisoning him. True, his refusing to eat offered a
long-term hope, for he was bound to drop with exhaustion
sooner or later. But could the ship hold out until then? At
the risk that Bohdi's uproar would terrify Yasmina, it was
decided that the *Bohdi* and the admiral ship should remain
close together.

The next day, Bohdi gored himself on an iron fitting.
He bled profusely. The day after that he was dead.

"We'll have to cut up the carcass," said Siri, "and throw
the pieces overboard as quickly as possible, because we're
coming close to land and otherwise we'll be getting un-
desirable visitors."

"What visitors?" Taor asked.

Siri scanned the deep blue sky and pointed at a tiny
black cross hovering motionless in the distance.

"There they are," he said. "I'm afraid all our labors have
been for nothing."

And indeed, two hours later, a first gypaëtus alit on the
ship's topmast and looked around, turning its white, black-
bearded head in all directions. It was soon joined by a

dozen of its mates. After observing the scene, the men at work, and the gaping carcass of the elephant at some length, they descended on the hold. Terrified of the sacred birds, the sailors asked leave to take refuge on the *Yasmina*, and the *Bohdi* was abandoned to its fate. Before long its decks, masts and spars were covered with gypaëti, and the hold was awhirl with birds flying in and out.

Forty-five days after leaving Mangalore, the *Yasmina*, the *Jina*, and the *Asura* sailed into the straits of Bab-el-Mandeb—The Gate of Tears—which connects the Red Sea with the Indian Ocean. That was fair enough progress, but two ships had been lost. The voyage to Elath at the far end of the Red Sea could be expected to take thirty days. Since both men and beasts were greatly in need of rest, it was decided that the expedition should stop at Dioscorides Island, not far from the entrance to the Straits.

Never before had Taor set foot on foreign soil. He felt joyfully lightheaded as, followed by the three elephants, who frolicked happily behind him, glad of the opportunity to stretch their legs, he climbed the bare slopes of Mt. Hadjar with their meager sprinkling of thistle and gorse. Everything seemed new to the travelers—the dry, invigorating heat, the fragrant, thorny vegetation—myrtle, lentiscus, and hyssop—and even the flocks of long-haired goats, which fled in terror at the sight of the elephants. But greater still was the terror of the poor island Bedouins at the sight of these noble lords and their unheard-of monsters. Entering a village, the travelers passed tightly closed tents, in which even the dogs had taken refuge. The place seemed deserted, but the visitors were well aware that hundreds of eyes were watching them through cracks in the canvas. At the top of the mountain, which was swept by a breeze so cool that the travelers shivered despite the effort of the climb, they were stopped by a beautiful child dressed in black, who stood fearlessly in the middle of the path.

"My father, Shaykh Reza, is expecting you," he said simply.

Turning about, the boy took the lead of the column. In a rocky circus dotted with asphodel, the low tents of the nomads formed a violet, knob-studded carapace, which expanded like a lung now and then as a gust of wind lifted up the canvas.

Swathed in blue veils and wearing thonged sandals, Shaykh Reza was standing beside a fire of eucalyptus wood. After an exchange of greetings, all squatted in a circle around the fire. Taor knew he was dealing with a chief, a lord, hence his equal. But he was amazed at so much poverty. For to his mind indigence was inseparable from slavery, wealth from nobility, and it cost him a great effort to disentangle these pairs. Good manners forbade Reza to ask his guests where they came from and where they were going. The words exchanged were confined to good wishes and formulas of politeness. Taor's amazement was at its height when he saw a child bring Reza a jar of coarsely ground wheat flour, a jug of water, and a small pot of salt. With his own hands the chief mixed dough, kneaded it and, working on a flat stone, shaped it into a round, fairly thick loaf. He dug a shallow hole in the sand, shoveled coals and ashes into it, set the loaf on top of them, and covered it over with brushwood, to which he set fire. When the quick flame went out, he turned the loaf over and put on more brushwood. Then at last he took the loaf out of the hole and brushed it with a sprig of broom to remove the coating of ashes. That done, he broke it into three parts, which he divided among Taor, Siri, and him-

self. That day the prince of Mangalore, accustomed to so-
phisticated dishes prepared by an army of cooks and
cook's helpers, sat on the bare ground and feasted on gray,
scorching-hot bread that left grains of sand grinding between his teeth.

Green mint tea, saturated with sugar and poured from a
considerable height into tiny cups, brought him back to
more familiar ways. After a prolonged silence Reza began
to speak. The vague smile on his face and the simple
down-to-earth matters he spoke of at first—the journey,
food and drink—seemed to suggest that his words would be
a mere continuation of the small talk that had occupied
them until then. But Taor soon realized that this was not
the case. The shaykh proceeded to tell a story, a fable, a
parable, which Taor half understood, as though dimly perceiving in its oceanic depths a lesson applying precisely to
his case, though the narrator knew next to nothing about
him.

"Our ancestors, the first Bedouins," the shaykh began,
"were not nomads as we are today. How could they have
been? Why would they have left the sumptuous, succulent
orchard where God had put them? They had only to
stretch out their hands to gather the tastiest fruits, which
weighed down the branches with their infinite diversity.
For in that endless orchard no two trees were the same, no
two trees gave similar fruit.

"You may say that certain cities or oases still have pleasure gardens like the one I've been speaking of. Why,
rather than seize such a city or oasis and go there to live,
do we prefer to roam the desert with our flocks? Yes,
why? That's the immense question, and the answer to it
encompasses all wisdom. I will give you that answer: the
fruits of those present-day gardens are not at all like those

our ancestors fed on. Today's fruits are dark and heavy. Those of the first Bedouins were luminous and weightless. What does this mean? Fallen and degenerated as we are, it is hard for us to imagine the life of our ancestors. Just think. Nowadays there is a horrible saying that we have come to take for granted: 'A hungry stomach has no ears.' Well, at the time of which I speak, a stomach hungry for food and ears hungry for knowledge were one and the same thing, because the same fruits satisfied both hungers. Those fruits differed from ours not only in shape, color, and taste, but also in the knowledge they conferred. Some gave knowledge of plants and animals and others of mathematics; there was a geography fruit, a music fruit, there were architecture, dance, and astronomy fruits, and many more. And to those who ate of them, they imparted, along with this knowledge, the corresponding virtues: courage to sailors, gentleness to surgeon-barbers, honesty to historians, faith to theologians, devotion to physicians, patience to teachers. In those days man shared in the divine simplicity. Body and soul were molded of the same substance. The mouth was a living temple—draped in purple, with its double semicircle of enamel footstools, its fonts of saliva and its nasal chimneys, with its word that nourishes and its food that teaches, its truth that is food and drink, and its fruits that melt into ideas, precepts, and axioms. . . .

"The fall of man broke the truth into two pieces: an empty, hollow, false word without nutritive value, and a compact, heavy, opaque, and greasy food, which beclouds the spirit and is converted into paunches and double chins.

"What, then, is to be done? We nomads of the desert have chosen extreme frugality, combined with the most spiritual of physical activities: walking. We eat bread, figs, dates, certain produce of our flocks—milk, clarified butter,

cheese very rarely, meat still more rarely. And we walk.
We think with our legs. Our meditation follows the
rhythm of our steps. Our feet mime the progress of a mind
in quest of truth: a modest truth, to be sure, as frugal as
our food. We remedy the break between food and knowledge by trying to preserve them both in their extreme simplicity, convinced as we are that by elaborating them one
only exacerbates the rupture between them. Of course we
have no hope of reconciling them by our efforts alone. No.
Such a regeneration will require a power that is more than
human—I might say, divine. But we are expecting just such
a revolution, and we believe that our frugality and our
long marches through the desert are the best possible
means of preparing our minds and bodies to understand it,
assimilate it, and make it ours, whether it happens tomorrow or in twenty centuries."

Taor did not understand this whole speech—far from it.
To him it was like an accumulation of black clouds, menacing and impenetrable, but shot through with lightnings
which for a brief moment reveal tatters of landscape and
terrifying abysses. He did not understand the substance of
the speech, but he preserved the whole of it in his heart,
suspecting that it would take on prophetic meaning for
him as his journey proceeded. In any event, he could no
longer doubt that the recipe for pistachio *rahat loukoum*,
for which he had in principle left his palace at Mangalore,
was losing its reality, taking on the character of a will-o'-
the-wisp that had lured him away from his child's paradise
—or becoming a kind of symbol which remained to be
elucidated.

The ambitious Siri Akbar, on the other hand, indifferent
as he was to his master's alimentary preoccupations, retained but one lesson from his meeting with Shaykh Reza,

but that lesson shook his whole mental edifice. He had discovered the possibility of combining mobility—with the
lightness and freedom from encumbrance it requires—and a
fierce longing for power and booty. Reza, it is true, had
not said a word on this subject. But Siri had eagerly studied the ascetic severity of his face and the fierce look and
lean, hard bodies of his companions; he could guess that
they were indefatigable and inured to hardship. In the
darkness of the tents he had glimpsed the veiled silhouettes
of the women and the muffled gleam of weapons. Everything spoke of strength, speed, and a cupidity all the more
formidable because it went hand in hand with utter contempt for riches and the sweets they confer.

Both Taor and Siri were surprised, when they exchanged their reflections on board the *Yasmina*, to observe
that Dioscorides Island—where they had not left each
other for as much as an instant—had left them with totally
different thoughts and images. While seemingly sharing
the same journey, they had moved farther apart with each
passing day.

This observation was of course still truer of Yasmina,
the little blue-eyed albino elephant. Shut up for forty days
in the hold of the vessel that bore her name, she had several times thought she was dying, especially in the big
storm. Then they had slid the gangplank under her feet
and out she went. Utterly dazed, she had found herself by
the side of Jina and Asura, her lifelong companions. But
where were the two others, Bodhi and Vahana? And how
strange, dry, and sandy this country was, how steep were
its hills, how meager and thorny its vegetation! And
stranger still were those of its inhabitants she had seen, not
only for their clothing, bodies, and faces, but for the astonished, awestruck, admiring looks they cast at the ele-

phants, for such beasts had never before been seen on Dioscorides Island. In every one of the villages they had passed through the three pachyderms created a sensation. The women had fled into the houses with the small children and barricaded themselves. The men had remained impassive. But a number of young men, some with musical instruments, had chosen to escort the ponderous procession. And Yasmina, who had a head on her shoulders, had soon noticed that though she was smaller than her companions she aroused no less curiosity—in fact, she seemed to inspire a more respectful, more spiritual curiosity, awakened by her snow-white skin, softened by her azure-blue irises, and deepened by her flaming ruby-red pupils. Although lighter and less massive than the others, she drew the applause of a more select clientele with her white, blue, and red coloration. It was then that her simple heart swelled with a new and interesting pride, which was to take her far, very far, farther than reasonable.

And so the prince, the slave, and the she-elephant rode in the same ship, each inhabited by very different, but equally vague and boundless dreams.

The crossing took twenty-nine days, and no unusual event troubled the slow procession of ocher coasts, transfixed beneath a torrid sun—Arabia on the starboard, Africa on the port side—occasionally varied by volcanic mountains, deep inlets, or the mouths of dried-out watercourses.

At length they approached Elath, the Idumean port at the end of the Gulf of Akaba. Here a sensational surprise awaited them. It was the cabin boy of the *Jina,* perched on the crow's nest of the main mast, who first recognized a familiar outline among the ships at anchor in the harbor. Eager groups crowded into the bows of all three vessels.

Little by little all doubt was dispelled: it was indeed the
Vahana, which had disappeared in the big storm, and there
she was, safe and sound, waiting for her companions. How
glad they all were to see one another again! Convinced
that the other ships had gone ahead, the crew of the
Vahana had spared no effort to catch up. Actually, they
had been in the lead, and after waiting in Elath for three
days they were beginning to fear that the four other vessels had gone down in the storm.

The reunited crews might have spent the whole day
embracing one another and exchanging stories if it had not
been necessary to land the elephants and stores. Again the
strange procession attracted large crowds and again it was
Yasmina—reserved but inwardly radiant—who attracted
the choicest praises. A camp was set up not far from the
town gate, for a period of rest seemed indispensable. It was
during this short stay that a first dispute between Prince
Taor and Siri Akbar showed the prince how very much
his slave—or might it not, even now, be more fitting to say
his erstwhile slave?—had changed since their departure
from Mangalore. No doubt the dispersion of the vessels
and the emergencies inseparable from seafaring had
justified him in taking certain liberties, such as giving orders without consulting or even informing Taor. But when
it came to assembling the men and beasts on land, forming
them into a caravan, and planning their northward march
to Bethlehem, the village mentioned by the desert prophets
—the journey would evidently take some twenty days—it
seemed obvious that all authority would have to be concentrated in the hands of one man and that this one man
could only be Prince Taor. On this point all, including Siri
Akbar, were agreed. But the arrangement was not all to his
liking. After two days in camp, he came to Taor with a

suggestion that plunged the prince into an abyss of perplexity. The four ships, Siri explained, would have to wait
several weeks—if not months—for the return of the caravan. Their safety was of vital importance, for without
ships there was no way of returning to Mangalore. Therefore a small troop of men must remain on board to guard
them. So far Siri had said nothing that Taor had not
figured out for himself. But he jumped sky-high when
Siri proposed to stay behind in Elath and take command of
the guards. True, the mission was important, but it
amounted to nothing more than surveillance and required
no initiative, no special authority or intelligence, whereas
the journey northward was sure to be beset by dangers
and surprises. How could Siri, the faithful servant attached
to his prince's person, dream of not accompanying him?

Taor's surprise and dismay were so evident that Siri
could only beat a retreat. He defended himself feebly by
saying that he had merely wished to avert the dreadful situation that would arise if the prince and his companions
found no ships waiting at Elath on their return. Taor
replied that he had full confidence in the fidelity and courage of the guards he would be leaving, and that he would
never consent to part company with Siri.

As Siri came away from this interview, his face was pos-
itively disfigured with vexation.

The incident gave Taor food for thought. Since leaving
the court, he had cast off more and more of his naïveté.
Each day he practiced an operation which would never
have entered his head in Mangalore and which is indeed
most uncommon among the princes of this world. It
consisted in putting himself in the place of others and trying to figure out what they might be feeling, thinking, and
planning. Applied to Siri, this operation had revealed abys-

mal depths. He had come to the conclusion that Siri's absolute fidelity and self-abnegation were not necessarily sin-
cere—as he had thought at least implicitly up until
then—but that Siri might well be capable of calculation, of
weighing the pros and the cons, or even of treachery. By
expressing his wish to remain in Elath, Siri had dispelled
Taor's last remaining illusions. His imagination fired by
distrust, Taor wondered whether Siri might not have
wanted to be left in command of the ships so as to engage
in coastal trading on his own account—or even in piracy,
which was exceedingly profitable on the Red Sea. And
how could Taor be sure that on his return from Bethlehem
he would find his fine flotilla faithfully anchored in the
port of Elath?

At last they set out. Cradled by the gentle rhythm of his
elephant's gait, Taor continued to turn these sinister sup-
positions over in his mind. His relationship with Siri was
changed. Not so much spoiled as matured, it had become
more adult, more lucid, complicated by rancor and indulgence, endangered by its new regard for the freedom and
mystery that are in every living being; in short, it had become a true man-to-man relationship.

The first days of the travelers' slow northward progress
were marked by no noteworthy incident. They saw no
living creature or any trace of vegetation, as the elephants
trampled the reddish soil sculptured by streams that had
vanished thousands of years before. Then, little by little,
the earth became green, and more turbulent configurations
obliged the column to zigzag, to thread its way through
gorges, or follow the dry beds of wadis. Most impressive
were the monumental, evocative shapes of the cliffs, peaks,
and rocky declivities. At first the men laughed as they

pointed out to one another rearing horses, spread-winged
ostriches, crocodiles. But at nightfall they fell silent,
cowed with fear, as dragons, sphinxes, and giant sarcophagi looked down on them from the heights. The next
day they awoke in a valley of beautiful deep-green mala-
chite, which was none other than the "Valley of the
Blacksmiths" where, according to the Scriptures, twenty
thousand men had quarried stone for the temple in Jerusalem. The valley ended in a closed circus, the site of King
Solomon's famous copper mines. Now the mines were
deserted, and Taor's companions were able to explore a
labyrinth of tunnels, run up and down stairways cut out of
the rock, and climb down into bottomless wells by worm-
eaten ladders. Then at last the scattered explorers found
one another by shouting in great echoing halls, fantas-
tically illumined by their torches. Taor could not understand why this visit to an underground world, where generations of men had worked and suffered, filled his heart
with dark foreboding.

They continued their northward march. The ground
leveled off and resumed its gray color. Rocks as flat as flagstones made their appearance and soon covered the ground
uniformly. The silhouette of a tree was glimpsed on the
horizon. The closer they came to it the stranger it looked.
The heavily grooved trunk seemed enormous in relation to
the moderate height of the tree. Out of curiosity, they
measured its circumference, which came to a hundred feet.
The bark was ash color and so soft that a blade sank into it
without resistance. The short, stunted branches, bare at
that season, rose heavenward like arm-stumps raised in
supplication. The tree as a whole had something ingratiat-
ing and ugly about it—the sort of gentle, ungainly monster

that improves on closer acquaintance. As they found out later, it was a baobab, an African tree whose name signifies "a thousand years," for its longevity is proverbial.

This lone tree was the advance post of a baobab forest, through which the caravan passed in the days that followed, a sparse forest, without thickets or underbrush, presenting no other mystery than enigmatic inscriptions on some of the trunks, generally those of the most imposing size and age. These inscriptions had been cut into the soft bark. Every line was reinforced with a black, ocher, or yellow dye, and small many-colored stones encrusted in the wood formed mosaics which encircled the trunk or rose in spirals to the top. Nowhere was a face or human or animal form discernible. It was a purely abstract form of writing, so studied, so perfect that one couldn't help wondering whether it had any other meaning than its beauty.

A tree of truly imposing size obliged them by its sheer splendor to stop. Its decoration was quite fresh. Leaves, lianas, and flowers, skillfully interlaced, covered the whole trunk and rose up to the branches. The religious significance of these ornaments seemed evident, for there was something of the temple, the altar, and the catafalque in this giant tree, dressed up like an idol and raising its thousand-fingered branches heavenward like frantic arms.

"I think I understand," said Siri.

"What do you understand?" the prince asked.

"It's only a guess, but we can test it."

He called a young elephant-driver, slender and agile as a monkey. The young man nodded assent and set about climbing the trunk, finding support in the grooved bark. The others looked on in silence, and all at the same time were struck by an analogy: The driver was hoisting himself up the tree just as he hoisted himself up the side of an elephant, for, true enough, nothing was so much like an elephant as this thick-skinned gray baobab with its slender branches upraised like elephants' trunks—a vegetable elephant, just as the elephant was only an animal baobab.

The man had reached the top of the trunk, from which all the branches sprouted. He seemed to disappear into a hollow, but emerged from it at once and began to climb down, clearly in a hurry to get away from what he had discovered there. Leaping to the ground, he ran to Siri and whispered in his ear. Siri nodded approval.

"Just as I thought," he said to Taor. "The trunk is hollow like a chimney and the people here use it as a tomb. The tree is decorated this way because a body has recently been slipped into it, just as you might slip a dagger into its sheath. From the top of the trunk, one sees his face turned toward the sky. The decorated baobabs we've seen along the way are the living tombs of a tribe I heard about in Elath, the Baobali, which means 'the children, or sons, of the baobab.' They worship this tree, they regard it as their ancestor, and they expect to return into it after their death. The fact is that in its slow growth the heart of the tree absorbs the flesh and bones of the dead person, who goes on living in vegetable form."

That day they went no further, but pitched camp at the foot of the giant necrophore. All that night the strange forest of the living, upright tombs surrounded the sleepers with a black, heavy, sepulchral peace, from which they emerged in the first light of dawn haggard and trembling like men arisen from the dead. And then came a report of disaster, which plunged Taor into consternation. Yasmina had disappeared.

At first it was thought she had escaped, for at Taor's order she spent her nights free and unfettered, checked

only by her herd instinct that made her stay with the other
elephants. Besides, it was hard to imagine the young elephant letting strangers drag her away without kicking up
an uproar. Undoubtedly she had gone of her own free
will. Still, strangers must have had a hand in it, because the
two enormous coffers of rose petals, which were removed
from her back at night, had vanished with her. The only
possible conclusion was that Yasmina had been abducted,
but with her consent.

Searching parties went out. They searched in concentric
circles around the encampment, but there were no tracks
in the hard, rocky soil. As was only fitting, it was the
prince who discovered the first sign. His companions heard
him cry out and saw him running, then bend over and
pick up something between thumb and forefinger, something as light and fragile as a butterfly: a rose petal. He
held it over his head for all to see.

"Sweet Yasmina!" he said. "She has left us the finest,
most fragrant of trails to follow. Look for rose petals, my
friends! Every rose petal you find will be a message from
my little white, blue-eyed elephant. I offer a reward for
every one retrieved."

Scanning and sniffing the ground, the little band dispersed. From time to time a shout of triumph was heard.
One of the men ran to the prince with his find and received a small coin in return. But progress was slow, and
when night fell they were less than a two hours' march
from the camp, where the main body of men had remained
with the baggage and the three other elephants.

As he was bending over to pick up the second rose petal
he had found, Taor heard something whistling through the
air—an arrow; its feathers quivered as it struck a fig tree.
Taor ordered the men to stop and close ranks. A moment

later the grass and trees around them came alive and the travelers found themselves surrounded by a multitude of men whose bodies were painted green, clothed in leaves, and garlanded with fruits and flowers. "The Baobali!" exclaimed Siri. There must have been nearly five hundred of them, all aiming their bows at the intruders. Resistance was unthinkable. Taor raised his right hand in a universal code gesture meaning "peace and parley." Taking with him one of the guides recruited at Elath, Siri approached the archers, whose ranks opened before them. The emissaries vanished and did not come back until a good two hours later.

"It's amazing," Siri reported. "I saw one of their chiefs, who must be a high priest as well. Their tribe seems to be rather loosely organized. We're not too unwelcome, because our arrival has coincided providentially with the resurrection of the goddess Baobama, mother of the baobabs and grandmother of the Baobalis. Perhaps it's a coincidence. Unless the disappearance of our Yasmina has something to do with this supposed resurrection. We'll know soon enough. They're letting us pay our respects to Baobama. Her temple is two hours' march from here."

"But what about Yasmina?" asked Taor.

"Aha!" said Siri mysteriously. "I wouldn't be surprised to see her very soon."

When the little band set out, surrounded by an army of green men, who continued to threaten them with their bows, they resembled nothing so much as a company of prisoners being led away by their captors. And that is just how Taor and his companions felt.

The temple of Baobama was a large rectangular edifice with four baobabs as its corner posts and supports, richly ornamented with designs resembling those previously ob-

served on the burial trees. The thick thatch roof, the absence of windows, and the tangle of climbing plants—jas-
mine, ipomea, passion flower—all conspired to keep the
interior in a deliciously cool half-darkness. The armed men
remained at a distance, leaving the approaches to the temple occupied solely by musicians, players of reed flutes,
and drummers, who beat their calabash and antelope-hide
drums with fingers as lean and hard as drumsticks, and
human orchestras who danced furiously about with bells
on their arms and legs, copper cymbals on their heads, and
chattering castanets on their fingers. Taor and his escort
moved up to the entrance under a bamboo canopy draped
with aristolochia. Inside, they first entered a kind of vesti-
bule, which served as a treasure house and sacred wardrobe. Here the travelers saw, hanging on the walls or resting on trestles, enormous necklaces, embroidered saddle
cloths, golden bells, fringed canopies, silver headstalls, all
the gigantic and sumptuous trappings which must have
made the goddess in holiday array a living reliquary. But
for the present Baobama was stark naked, and the visitors,
who had mounted three steps to a raised platform, were
dumbfounded to discover Yasmina in person, sprawled on
a bed of roses, her eyeballs rolling heavenward in an ecstasy of delight. She seemed to have been expecting them,
for a glint of defiance and irony was discernible in her
blue eyes. In the gilded half-darkness of the temple nothing moved but two large esparto-grass sails, operated from
outside, which flapped gently to keep the air in motion.
After a long, thoughtful silence, Yasmina unrolled her
trunk, picked a date stuffed with honey out of a basket
and deposited it on her eagerly quivering tongue. Then the
prince approached, opened a silken bag and tossed a handful of the rose petals, which he and his companions had

picked up and which had guided them to that holy place, on the elephant's litter. An act of homage and submission. And that is exactly how Yasmina took it. Since Taor was within her reach, she stretched out her trunk and caressed his cheek with its tip, a gesture at once affectionate and offhand, a gesture of leavetaking and gentlest acceptance of destiny. Taor realized that his favorite elephant, deified thanks to the affinity between pachyderm and baobab, promoted to superhuman rank, worshipped by an entire people as the mother of the holy tree and the grandmother of men—he realized, in short, that Yasmina was forever lost to him and his people. The next day the travelers resumed the journey to Bethlehem with the three male elephants.

The meeting was predestined, necessary, inscribed since the beginning of time in the stars and the heart of things. It took place in Elah, a strange region, murmuring with springs, hollow with caves, bristling with ruins, a region where History had passed, upsetting everything in its path, but leaving no intelligible trace—one is reminded of those men wounded in the face and horribly disfigured, who are unable to tell their story. Yet the meeting of the three kings who were coming back from Bethlehem—on foot, on horseback, and on camelback—with the king who was on his way to the inspired village with his elephants, was bathed in a gentle but penetrating light. They met quite naturally near one of the three artificial ponds known as King Solomon's Ponds, as they were preparing, after a hot, dusty day, to go down into the water by the steps cut into the rock. And thanks to the secret affinity between the four journeys, they knew one another at once. They exchanged greetings and helped one another in their ablutions, as though conferring baptism. Then they separated

but by common accord met again that night around a fire
of acacia branches.

"Did you see him?" was Taor's first question.

"We saw him," said Gaspar, Melchior, and Balthasar in
unison.

"Is it a prince, a king, an emperor, attended by a
magnificent retinue?" Taor asked.

"It's a little child born on the straw of a stable between
an ox and an ass," the three replied.

The prince of Mangalore fell silent, struck dumb with
astonishment. There must have been some misunderstanding, he thought. For He whom Taor had come in
search of was the Divine Confectioner, the dispenser of
sweets so exquisite that they took away your taste for all
other food.

"Don't all talk at once," he said. "Or I'll never get it
straight." Thereupon he turned to the oldest and asked
him to explain.

"My story is long," said Balthasar, stroking his white
beard with a look of perplexity, "and I don't know where
to begin. I could tell you about a certain butterfly of my
childhood, which, at the other extremity of my life, I
thought I recognized in the sky. The priests destroyed it,
but I am bound to suppose that it was resurrected. And
then, too, there's Adam, two Adams if you follow me, the
white one of after the Fall, whose vacant skin resembles a
washed parchment, and the black Adam of before the Fall,
covered with signs and pictures like an illuminated manu-
script. On top of that, there's Greek art, devoted entirely
to gods, goddesses, and heroes, and the more human, more
familiar art that we are all waiting for, and of which my
young friend, Assur the Babylonian painter, will doubtless
be the precursor. . . .

"All this must seem very confused to you, who have come from so far with your elephants laden with delicacies. I shall therefore confine myself to the essentials. Enamored from childhood of drawing, painting, and sculpture, I have always come up against the uncompromising hostility of religious men, who abominate all images and portraiture. In this I am not alone. Not so long ago, we visited Herod the Great. His priests had recently fomented a rebellion over a golden eagle that he had placed over the main gate of the temple in Jerusalem. He had drowned the rebellion in blood. The eagle had perished. So had the priests. Such is the terrible logic of tyranny. I have always nourished the hope of escaping it. I have gone back to the sources of this tragedy, the one source I should say; it is to be found in the first lines of the Bible. When I read that God made man in His image and likeness, I realized that this was no futile tautology, but that those two words connoted the possibility of a dangerous, fatal break, which did indeed occur after man had sinned. Once Adam and Eve had disobeyed, their profound resemblance or likeness to God was gone, but they retained a trace of it, a face and a body which remained the indelible image of the divine reality. Ever since then a curse has weighed on that false image, which fallen man carries around with him very much as a dethroned king may continue to play with his scepter, now no better than a silly rattle. Yes, it is this image without likeness which is condemned by the Second Commandment, and which my clergy, like Herod's, persist in fustigating. But I do not believe, as Herod does, that all problems can be solved by bloodbaths. My love of the arts has not blinded me to the point of obliterating the religion in which I was born and reared. The holy texts are there, they have nourished me, and I cannot ignore them. It is true that the image can be a lie and art an imposture, and the desperate war of the priests against idolaters and iconoclasts extends to my own heart.

"When I arrived in Bethlehem, I was torn between conflict and hope."

"And what did you find in Bethlehem?"

"An infant in the straw of a stable, as my companions and I have told you, and the witnesses to that night—the longest of the year—will never cease to repeat their testimony. But that stable was also a temple; the carpenter, who was the child's father, was a patriarch, his mother was a virgin, the child himself was an incarnate God in the midst of poor mankind, and a column of light pierced the thatched roof of that wretched shelter. All that held a profound meaning for me. It was the answer to the question of my whole life, and that answer consisted in the impossible marriage of unreconcilable contraries. 'He who delves too deeply into the secrets of His divine majesty will be overwhelmed by His glory,' said the Prophet. That is why on Mt. Sinai Yahweh hid from the eyes of Moses by wrapping himself in a cloud. Well, that cloud had just dispersed and God had become visible, incarnated in a child. I had only to look at Assur to see the dawn of a new art reflected in the face of an artist. My little Babylonian painter was transfigured by the revolution that was taking place before his eyes: the simple gesture of a poor young mother, suddenly exalted to the level of a divine power. The humblest daily life—those beasts, those implements, that stable—bathed in eternity by a ray of light fallen from heaven. . . .

"You ask me what I found in Bethlehem. I found the image and the likeness reconciled, I found the image regenerated, thanks to the rebirth of an underlying likeness."

"What did you do then?"

"I knelt with all the rest, artisans, peasants, maidservants of the inn, all overjoyed. But the wonder, you see, is that each of these kneelings had a different meaning. My worship was addressed to the flesh—visible, tangible, audible, fragrant—transfigured by the spirit. For all art is of the flesh. All beauty is of the eyes, ear, or hand. And as long as the flesh was cursed, artists were cursed with it.

"Finally, I took the block of myrrh which Maalek, the sage of the thousand butterflies, had given the child that I was half a century ago, as a symbol of the accession of the flesh to eternity, and set it down at the Virgin's feet."

"And what do you intend to do now?"

"Assur and I shall return to Nippur to bring the good tidings. We shall find ways to convince not only the people, but the priests as well, and first of all that old Sheddad, encrusted as he may be in his rigid dogmas. The image is saved, the face and body of man can now be celebrated without idolatry.

"I shall rebuild the Balthasareum, but not as a repository for vestiges of the Greco-Roman past. No, we shall collect modern works, works which I, as a royal patron of the arts, shall commission my artists to create—the first masterpieces of Christian art. . . ."

"Christian art!" Prince Taor repeated pensively. "What a strange combination of words! How difficult it is to imagine this art of the future!"

"There's nothing surprising in that. Imagining is the beginning of creation. Like you, I can imagine nothing; a succession of blank centuries opens like an abyss at my feet. At the most I can conceive of the very first of these works, the first Christian painting, the one that touches and concerns us here. . . ."

"And what will this first Christian painting be?"

"The Adoration of the Magi, three kings laden with gold and purple, who have come from a fabulous Orient to bow down to a little child in a wretched stable."

During the silence that followed Gaspar and Melchior joined in Balthasar's vision. The centuries to come appeared to them as a great gallery of mirrors, in which all three were reflected, each time as interpreted by an epoch with a different genius, but always recognizable: a young man, an old man, and a black man from Africa.

Then the vision faded and Taor turned to the youngest.

"Prince Melchior," he said, "I feel you are close to me, because of our ages. And besides, your throne has been usurped by your uncle, while I, for my part, can't be sure that my mother will ever let me reign. I will therefore listen with brotherly attention to your story of the night in Bethlehem."

"Bethlehem, yes, of course," Melchior amended with the enthusiasm of his years. "But first the night in Jerusalem, because these two stages in my exile are inseparable.

"I left Palmyra with simple ideas about justice and power. To my way of thinking, there were two kinds of rulers, the good and the bad. My father, Theodenos, was the type of the good king. My uncle Atmar, who had seized the kingdom and tried to have me murdered, was the tyrant. I had no doubt about my future course. I would gather supporters, look for allies, muster an army, reconquer my father's kingdom sword in hand, and, it goes without saying, punish the usurper. A single night—the night of Herod's banquet—upset this whole beautiful program. I wish all princes who are preparing to govern could be made to read the life of Herod. What an object lesson! In his public life a just, peaceful, wise sovereign, blessed by the peasants and the artisans, by all the common people of his kingdom, a great builder, a shrewd diplomat. And behind the walls of his palace a despot and bloodthirsty madman, a murderer, torturer, infanticide. And it is no mere accident or coincidence that one and the same head, like the god Janus, shows these two faces. It was decreed by fate that every blessing conferred on the people must be paid for by an abomination perpetrated in the palace. At Herod's court I learned that violence and fear are the indispensable components of earthly power. And not only violence and fear, but a grimly contagious disease of character, compounded of baseness, duplicity, and treachery. I must tell you, Prince Taor, that after sharing a single banquet with King Herod and his court, Gaspar, Balthasar, and I were infected with that disease."

"All three of you infected with baseness, duplicity, and treachery? Speak, Prince Melchior. I want to hear that, and I hope your companions here will contradict you if you are lying."

"It's a terrible secret. All my life I will carry it bleeding and festering in my heart, for I don't see how anything can ever cure me. Very well. I'll tell you about it, and my companions can spit in my face if I am lying.

"When we told him about the star and our quest, King Herod, who had consulted his priests, informed us that Bethlehem was the goal of our journey. For the Prophet Micah had written: 'And thou Bethlehem in the land of Juda, thou art not the least among the princes of Juda, for out of thee shall come a Governor that shall rule my people.'⁹ To the three questions we had brought with us he added one of his own that has been tormenting him on the threshold of death, the question of his succession. To that

question as well as ours, he said, Bethlehem must supply
the answer. And he charged us as his plenipotentiaries to
identify this heir, to honor him, and then to bring him
word in Jerusalem. We intended to do his bidding in all
loyalty; we didn't want it said that this tyrant, who had
been flouted and deceived throughout his reign, every one
of whose crimes can be explained if not justified by an act
of treachery, had on his deathbed been betrayed once
again by foreign kings whom he had entertained
magnificently. But then the Angel Gabriel, who had
played the majordomo of the stable, begged us to go
straight home without passing through Jerusalem, because,
so he said, Herod was nourishing dark designs with regard
to the Child. I talked it over with the other princes: What
were we to do? I thought we should keep our promise.
Not only as a matter of honor, but because we knew what
lengths the King of the Jews could go to when he thought
himself betrayed. By reporting to him in Jerusalem, I
argued, we could allay his suspicion and forestall great
misfortunes. But Gaspar and Balthasar insisted on doing
Gabriel's bidding. For once an archangel tells us what to
do! they cried out. They were two against one, and I was
the youngest and poorest, so in the end I gave in. But I
regret it, and I think I shall never forgive myself. And
now, Prince Taor, I've told you how, having approached
the powerful, I feel soiled for all time."

"But then you went to Bethlehem. What did Bethlehem
teach you about power?"

"By the example of the Crib the Archangel Gabriel,
who was watching over the Child, taught me the strength
of weakness, the irresistible gentleness of the nonviolent,
the law of forgiveness, which does not abolish the law of
talion, but infinitely transcends it. For talion prescribes

that the vengeance must not exceed the offense. It is a way station between natural anger and perfect concord. The kingdom of God will never be established once and for all. The key to it must be forged slowly, and we ourselves are that key. In view of all this, I laid the gold coin struck with the effigy of my father King Theodenos at the Child's feet. It was my only treasure, my only proof that I was the legal heir to the throne of Palmyra. In relinquishing it, I renounced the kingdom to search for that other kingdom promised me by the Savior. I shall withdraw into the desert with my faithful Baktiar. We shall found a community with all those who wish to join us. It will be the first city of God. There we shall meditate in the expectation of His coming. A community of free men with no other law than the law of love. . . ."

He turned to Gaspar, who was on his left.

"I have just uttered the word 'love.' But how can I fail to recognize that my African brother has a far better, purer and more compelling right than I to speak of that great, mysterious emotion? For wasn't it for love, King Gaspar, that you left your capital city and traveled so far northward?"

"Yes," said Gaspar, king of Meroë, "it was for love, because of love, impelled by love's heartache, that I crossed deserts. But you mustn't suppose that I ran away from a woman who didn't love me, or that I was trying to forget an unhappy love. If I had thought that, Bethlehem would have taught me otherwise. To make it clear, I shall have to take you back . . . back to the incense, to the use I made of incense one night when we—the woman I loved, her lover, and I—were clowning to amuse ourselves. We had painted our faces grotesquely, and smoke rising from censers enveloped us in fragrance. I have no doubt that the

combination of sacred smoke with that degrading scene
contributed to opening my eyes. I realized. . . . What did
I realize? That I should have to go away, I'm sure of that.
But the deeper meaning of my journey dawned on me
only when I saw the Child. For in my heart there was indeed a great love, a love compatible with incense, because
it aspired to flower in worship. As long as I was unable to
worship, I suffered. The sage with the lily had said to me:
'It is Satan weeping over the beauty of the world.' In reality, I myself was weeping over an unappeased love. With
each passing day I found Biltine weaker, lazier, stupider,
more deceitful and frivolous. To cleanse her of all this
wretched humanity I'd have needed an immense, inex-
haustibly generous heart. At least I never held it up to her.
I knew that I myself, that my own soul-lessness was to
blame for the poverty of our adventure. I didn't have
enough love for both of us, that's all! I ought to have irrigated her cold, dry, calculating heart with luminous tenderness, and I couldn't. What the Child taught me—but I
had guessed as much, my heart had an intimation of the lesson—was that a love that is worship is *always* shared, because its radiance makes it irresistibly communicative.
When I approached the Crib I laid the coffer of incense at
the Child's feet, for he is the only being on earth deserving
of that sacred homage. I knelt down. I touched my fingers
to my lips and threw the Child a kiss. He smiled. He held
out his arms to me. Then I knew the perfect encounter between the lover and the beloved for what it was: this
tremulous veneration, this jubilant hymn, this marveling
fascination.

   "And there was something more, which for me, Gaspar
of Meroë, surpassed all the rest in beauty—a miraculous

surprise which the Holy Family had obviously prepared in the expectation of my coming."

"What was that surprise, King Gaspar? I am consumed with perplexity and impatience."

"Very well, I shall tell you. Balthasar told you just now that he believed in the existence of a black Adam, the Adam of before the Fall, and that only the other Adam, the Adam of sin, was white."

"I have indeed heard a passing allusion to the black Adam from his lips."

"At first I thought Balthasar had said that to give me pleasure. He is so kind! But in bending over the Crib to adore the Child, what do I see? A black baby with kinky hair, with a sweet little flat nose, in short, a baby just like the African babies of my country."

"First a black Adam, then a black Jesus!"

"Isn't it logical? If Adam didn't turn white until after he had sinned, mustn't Jesus in his original state be black like our ancestor?"

"But what about his parents? Mary and Joseph?"

"White, I assure you! As white as Melchior and Balthasar!"

"And what did the other people say when they saw this miracle, a black Child born of white parents?"

"Well, you see, they said nothing, and as I didn't want to humiliate them, I made no reference to the black Child I had seen in the Crib. To tell the truth, they may not have looked very closely. It was rather dark in that stable. Maybe I was the only one who noticed that Jesus was a black. . . ."

He fell silent, moved by his retrospective vision.

"What do you mean to do now?" asked Taor.

"I shall share Bethlehem's marvelous lesson of love with all who are willing to listen to me."

"Good. Begin with Prince Taor. Give me my first lesson in Christian love."

"The Child in the Crib, who became black, the better to welcome Gaspar, the African king. There's more in that than in all the love stories I know. That beautiful image teaches us to become like those we love, to see with their eyes, to speak their mother tongue, to *respect* them, a word which originally meant *to look at twice*. Thus exalted, pleasure, joy, and happiness fuse into love.

"If you expect another to give you pleasure or joy, does it mean that you love him? No. You love only yourself. You want him to serve your self-love. True love is the pleasure we get from another's pleasure, the joy that springs up in us at the sight of his joy, the happiness it gives me to know that he is happy. Pleasure from pleasure, joy from joy, happiness from happiness—that is love, nothing more."

"But what about Biltine?"

"I have already sent a courier to Meroë with the order to set my two Phoenician slaves free at once. Let them do as they please. I for my part will be more than satisfied with the happiness I shall have given Biltine."

"Lord Gaspar, I hope you won't take offense, but it seems to me that you have lost much of your attachment to that woman since your visit to Bethlehem. . . ."

"I love her no less, but with a different kind of love. This new love may suffuse us both with happiness, but it is powerless to degrade either of us—Biltine, for example, by curtailing her freedom, or me by making me consume myself with jealousy. Perhaps Biltine will prefer Galeka to me. Then she will leave me, but only after giving me the happiness of her happiness. I shall feel no bitterness, because I shall have lost all desire to reduce her to the state of an object by exerting my right of ownership over her."

"Friends Balthasar, Melchior, and Gaspar," said Taor, "I must humbly own that I grasped very little of what you have said. Art, politics, and love, as you are planning to practice them from now on, strike me as keys without locks and locks without keys. To tell you the truth, I find within me no very keen interest in these things. Each of us has his own preoccupations, and the Child, with an amazingly accurate divination of our nature and character, knows how to respond to them all. Consequently, what he says to one in the secrecy of his heart is unintelligible to the others. As for me, I can't wait to hear how he will speak to me. For you see, it was neither a museum, nor a usurper, nor a woman that sent me on my way, it was. . . . No, I won't try to explain, you'd think I was making fun of you and you'd laugh at me or get angry. You alone perhaps, King Balthasar, are indulgent and open-minded enough to understand me and acknowledge the possibility of destiny disguising itself as a trifling tidbit. The Child, I am sure, is waiting for me, with His answer all ready for the Prince of Sweets, come to Him from the Malabar Coast."

"Prince Taor," said Balthasar, "I am touched by your confidence. I admire your naïveté, but it frightens me. When you say 'the Child is waiting for me,' I take it to mean above all that you are the waiting child. As for the other Child, the one in the Crib, I must warn you that he won't wait for you much longer. Bethlehem is a mere crossroads, a place of comings and goings. You are the last

to arrive, because you've come further than the others. I
wish I could be sure of your not arriving too late."

These wise words spoken by the wisest of the kings were
salutary for Taor. The very next day his caravan started
out for Bethlehem in the first light of dawn and would no
doubt have arrived there by nightfall if it had not been
delayed by a serious incident.

First a storm beat down on the mountains of Judea,
transforming parched wadis and rocky gorges into raging
torrents. Men and elephants might have welcomed a
refreshing shower if the resulting quagmire had not im-
peded their progress. Then suddenly the sun reappeared
and a dense mist rose from the water-logged soil. The travelers were shaking themselves in the noonday sun when a
desperate trumpeting froze their blood. For they knew
what every sort of elephant's trumpeting meant, and they
knew beyond any possible doubt that the sound they had
just heard meant terror and death. A moment later the elephant Jina, who was bringing up the rear, rushed forward
at a gallop, trunk in the air and ears spread fanwise,
crushing everything in his path. Several men were killed,
others wounded, and the elephant Asura was toppled over
with his load. Considerable time and effort were needed to
put order into the chaos that followed. Then a column
started out in poor Jina's tracks, which were not hard
to follow in that sandy soil interspersed with thornbushes.
Suddenly gone mad, he had galloped a long way, and night
was falling when the men finally caught up with him. First
they heard a loud buzzing sound and traced it to a ravine a
hundred cubits deep; it was as though a hundred beehives
had been hidden there. The party went closer. The insects
were not bees but wasps, and the only hive in sight was

poor Jina's body, clothed in a thick layer of wasps—a black-and-gold caparison, that sizzled like boiling oil. It was easy to figure out what had happened. The load of sugar Jina was carrying had melted in the rain, covering his hide with thick syrup. The proximity of a colony of wasps had done the rest. Of course, their stings couldn't penetrate the elephant's hide, but there were the eyes, the mouth, the ears, and the tip of the trunk, not to mention the tender, sensitive organs under the tail. The men were afraid to go near the unfortunate animal. The most they could do was to make sure he was dead and that his cargo of sugar was beyond saving. The next day, Taor, his retinue, and the two remaining elephants made their entry into Bethlehem.

The great stir provoked by the official census, which had obliged whole families to register in their place of origin, had lasted only a few days. After a period of general confusion the itinerant population had gone home. The people of Bethlehem fell back into their old habits, but the streets and squares were still littered with the vestiges of carnivals and fairs—straw, animal droppings, smashed crates, rotten fruit, disabled carts, sick animals. Taor's elephants and retinue aroused little interest among the tired and jaded adults, but there as everywhere a crowd of ragged children formed around them, begging and marveling all in one. The innkeeper the three kings had told him about informed Taor that the man and woman had taken the Child and gone their way after fulfilling their legal obligations. In what direction? He didn't know. Northward, no doubt, to Nazareth, that was where they had come from.

Taor took counsel with Siri. Siri wanted just one thing, to hurry back to Elath where the ships were moored, and

quietly wait for the monsoon wind that would take them
back to Mangalore. He argued the sorry state of the caravan, three elephants lost out of five, some men killed,
others sick or vanished—possibly kidnapped, possibly run
away—their funds and provisions pitifully depleted, as
Draoma the treasurer could bear witness. Taor listened
with amazement. This was the language of common sense;
he recognized it, having spoken it himself not so long ago.
But a great change had taken place in him. Exactly when?
He couldn't say—and Siri's argument sounded to him like
some childish, old-fashioned fairy tale, without the
slightest bearing on the present situation and its urgent requirements. What requirements? To find the Child and
open his heart to Him. Taor could no longer help seeing
that the preposterous original aim of his expedition—to find
the recipe for pistachio *rahat loukoum*—concealed a profound, mysterious design, which was indeed in some way
related to it, but infinitely transcended it, just as the
spreading mustard tree,[10] which comforts the weary with
its shade, transcends the tiny seed from which it grows.

Accordingly, Taor was preparing, regardless of anything Siri could say, to head for Nazareth in the north,
when the serving maid of the inn told them something that
put him and Siri in agreement for the time being. It was
she who had cared for the young mother and bathed and
swaddled the newborn babe. Now she told the travelers
how she had heard the man and woman talking over their
plans. It seemed they were heading southward in the direction of Egypt, to escape a great danger they had been
warned of. What danger could threaten an obscure carpenter without power or money, traveling with his wife
and baby? Taor remembered Herod. Siri, for his part, felt
that this journey, begun as a pleasure trip, was becoming

steadily more sinister, and saw black clouds gathering over it.

"Master," he entreated, "let us go south without delay. That is the direction both of Elath and of the Holy Family's flight." Taor acquiesced, but said they would not set out until the following day, for he had thought of something merry and good to do in Bethlehem.

"Siri," he said. "Among all the things I have learned since leaving my palace, there is one that I was far from even suspecting and that afflicts me particularly now: many children are going hungry. In every town and village we pass through, our elephants attract crowds of children. I look at them and see how thin, frail, and emaciated they are. Some carry bellies as swollen as wineskins on legs as thin as drumsticks, and I know this is just one more symptom of starvation, perhaps the gravest. So here's what I've decided. We overloaded our elephants with delicacies intended as an offering to the Divine Confectioner of our imagination. Now I know we were mistaken. The Savior is not as we expected. Besides, I see our provisions dwindling from day to day, and with them the troop of pastry cooks and confectioners in charge of them. We shall arrange for a great night feast in the cedar wood overlooking the city and invite the children of Bethlehem."

The joyful ardor with which Prince Taor assigned duties to his followers put the finishing touches to Siri's consternation, for it convinced him that his master was raving mad. The pastry cooks made fires and set to work. Beginning early next day, the smell of cake and caramel invaded the streets of Bethlehem. Because of this, Taor's men, who went from house to house inviting the children to the feast, were well received. Actually, all the children were not invited. The prince had talked the matter over

with his advisers. Parents were not wanted, and that elimi-
nated children too small to leave home or eat by themselves. But the prince was determined to go down as far as
possible on the age scale, and the limit was finally set at
two years. The older children would help the youngest.
No sooner had the sun sunk below the horizon than the
first groups appeared in the cedar wood. Taor was moved
to see that these simple folk had done their utmost to
honor their benefactor. The children were washed,
combed, and dressed in white robes, and some were
crowned with wreaths of roses or laurel. Taor had often
heard groups of little rascals screaming and yelling as they
chased one another up and down the alleys and stairways
of these villages, and he expected his feast to be a noisy, tu-
multuous affair. Wasn't his purpose in inviting these poor
children to give them pleasure? But they were visibly
overawed by the cedar wood, the torches, and the great
table with its precious plate. Hand in hand, they approached with quiet dignity and took the places assigned
to them. They sat up straight on the benches and rested
their little closed hands, but not their elbows—they had
strict orders about that—on the edge of the table.

They were not left waiting long. Soon they were served
fresh milk flavored with honey, because, as everyone
knows, children are always thirsty. But drinking arouses
the appetite, and, as they looked on wide-eyed, heaps of
delicacies appeared: jujube jelly, ramekins of rich cream
cheese, pineapple fritters, dates stuffed with walnut meats,
litchi-nut soufflés, mango tarts, medlar paste, Dionysian cus-
tards flavored with wine of Lydda, succulent frangipane
cakes, and a hundred other marvels, combining the Indian
tradition with recipes picked up in Idumea and Palestine.

Filled with wonder, Taor looked on from a distance.

Night had fallen. Resinous torches scattered here and there bathed the scene in a soft, golden light. Amid the blackness of the cedars with their massive trunks and enormous branches, the large, festively laid table and the children in their linen robes were an island of impalpable, unreal brightness. An onlooker might have wondered whether this was a band of pleasure-loving children indulging themselves or a flight of innocent, disembodied souls hovering like a fragile constellation in the night sky. And as though this feast of the chosen must inevitably be accompanied by the torment of the excluded, a great cry of pain was heard rising from the unseen village.

The rich assortment of delicacies on the table were only a prelude. They were soon forgotten when four men arrived with a gigantic edifice, a masterpiece of confectionary architecture, resting on a wooden platform. Built of nougat, marzipan, caramel, and candied fruit, it was a faithful replica of the Mangalore palace, with ponds of syrup, statues of quince paste, and trees of angelica. Nor had the original five elephants been forgotten; there they were, molded of almond paste and fitted with tusks of rock candy.

Greeted with an ecstatic murmur, this apparition only added to the solemnity of the feast. And to Taor it seemed so charged with meaning that he couldn't resist the temptation to make a short speech.

"Children," he began. "You see this palace, these gardens, these elephants. That is my country, which I left to come here to you. And it's no accident if all this is reproduced here in sugar. Because my palace was a lovely place, where everything conspired to produce enchantment and delectation. But why, you may wonder, did I say *was* rather than *is*—so betraying a presentiment, not

that the palace and its gardens are no longer there, but that
I shall never see them again. My departure, incidentally,
was also connected with sugar. I set out to conquer the
recipe for pistachio *rahat loukoum*. But more and more
clearly I glimpsed something great and mysterious at the
bottom of this childish pretext. Since leaving the Malabar
Coast—where a cat is a cat and two and two is four—I seem
to have ventured into a garden of onions, for here every
thing, every animal, every person has an apparent meaning, which conceals a second sense which, when deci-
phered, points the way to a third, and so forth and so on.
And something very similar seems to have happened to me,
for I have the impression that in a few weeks the simple,
foolish youth who said goodbye to Maharani Taor Mamore, has become an old man, full of memories and
precepts. And I don't believe I have come to the end of
my metamorphoses.

"There, this palace of sugar . . ."

He broke off and took hold of a golden shovel shaped
like a yataghan, which a servant held out to him.

". . . must be eaten, in other words, destroyed . . ."

Again he broke off, for from the unseen village a thousand piercing cries could be heard as though an army of
chicks were having their throats cut.

". . . destroyed, and I think one of you should strike
the first blow. You, for instance . . ."

He handed the shovel to the child nearest him, a little
shepherd boy with black curls that encased his head like a
helmet. The child looked up at him, but didn't budge. At
this a countryman went up to Taor and said: "My lord,
you have been speaking Hindi, and these children understand only Aramaic." Whereupon the countryman said a
few words in Aramaic. The child took the golden shovel

and without a moment's hesitation brought it down on the nougat dome of the palace, which collapsed into the inner courtyard.

It was then that Siri appeared, unrecognizable, in tatters, covered with ashes and blood. He ran to the prince and drew him away from the table.

"Prince Taor," he gasped. "This country is cursed. I've always said so! An hour ago Herod's soldiers occupied the village, and they've been killing, killing, killing, without mercy!"

"Killing? Who? Everybody?"

"No, but maybe that would be better. They seem to have orders to do away with all male children under the age of two."

"Under two? The babies, the ones we didn't invite?"

"That's right. They cut their throats, even in their mothers' arms."

Taor hung his head with grief. Of all the tribulations he had suffered, this was the worst. But why had such a thing happened? Herod's orders—that was the story. He remembered Prince Melchior, who had wanted the Kings to keep their promise and report the outcome of their mission to Herod in Jerusalem. That promise had been broken. Herod's trust had been betrayed. And it was well known that the tyrant could go to any lengths when he thought himself flouted. All the male children under two. What would that add up to in this small but prolific population? The child Jesus, now on his way to Egypt, had escaped the massacre. The old despot's blow had missed its aim. But his innocent victims would be innumerable!

Absorbed in laying the sugar palace to waste, the children took no notice of Siri. At last they had come to life; they were talking and laughing with their mouths full and quarreling over choice morsels. Withdrawing into the shadows, Taor and Siri watched them.

"Let them enjoy themselves while their little brothers are dying," said Taor. "They will learn the horrible truth soon enough. As for me, I don't know what the future will bring, but I have no doubt that this night of transfiguration and massacre marks the end of an age in my life, the age of sugar."

The Salt Hell

When the travelers passed through the village in the livid dawn, it was enveloped in silence interspersed with rare sobs. The massacre, it was rumored, had been the work of Herod's Cimmerian legion, a body of red-faced mercenaries from a land of mist and snow, who among themselves spoke an impenetrable language. It was to them that Herod entrusted his most gruesome missions. They had vanished as suddenly as they had come.

Taor averted his eyes to keep from seeing some half-starved dogs lapping up a puddle of blood on the threshold of one of the huts. Siri insisted on a southeasterly course, preferring the Judean desert and the Dead Sea steppes to the military garrisons of Hebron and Beersheba, through which the direct route would have taken them. They went steadily downhill, at times so steeply that the elephants' feet dislodged great masses of gray earth. By the end of the day, white, granular boulders made their appearance. The travelers examined them. They proved to be blocks of salt. Then came a forest thinly settled with white, leafless bushes that seemed covered with frost. The branches were as brittle as porcelain. They too were salt. Finally the sun sank behind the travelers, and in a gap between two mountains they saw a distant patch of metallic blue: the Dead Sea. They were setting up their camp for the night when a

sudden gust of wind—such as often occurs at dusk—
brought them a strong smell of sulfur and naphtha.

"In Bethlehem," said Siri gloomily, "we passed through
the gate of hell. We have been going deeper into Satan's
Empire ever since."[11]

Taor was neither surprised nor alarmed. Or if he was,
his curiosity outweighed his fear. Since leaving Bethlehem,
he had been busy comparing two radically opposed images, which had appeared to him at the same time: the
massacre of the little children and the feast in the cedar
wood. He was convinced that the two scenes were united
by a secret affinity, that despite the contrast between them
they were in some way complementary, and that if he
could manage to superimpose one on the other a great light
would be shed on his own life and perhaps on the destiny
of the world. Children had been massacred while other
children, sitting around a table, were partaking of succulent fare. In this Taor saw an intolerable paradox, but also
a key full of promise. He felt certain that his experience
that night in Bethlehem was a preparation for something
else, a clumsy, somehow abortive rehearsal of another
scene in which two extremes—feast of love and bloody
immolation—would merge. But he barely glimpsed the
truth through a dense cloud which his meditation was
powerless to dispel. Just one word floated to the surface of
his mind, a mysterious word which he had recently heard
for the first time, but in which there was more equivocal
shadow than limpid teaching, namely, the word "sacrifice."

The next day the travelers resumed their downward
journey, and the further down they went, through ravines
and over rocky slopes, the more the stagnant air became
charged with alkaline fumes. At length the Dead Sea

spread out at their feet, the mouth of the Jordan to the north, and straight ahead, towering over the eastern shore, the rugged slopes of Mount Nebo. The travelers were struck by a strange phenomenon: the blue surface of the water was sprinkled with white dots, as though a strong wind were churning up the waves. And yet the leaden air was quite still.

Though their planned itinerary would have taken them some distance from the Dead Sea, they couldn't resist the attraction that any body of water—pond, lake, or ocean—has for people who have been traveling through the desert. They therefore decided to proceed eastward to the Sea and follow the coast southward. When they came within an arrow's flight of the beach, the water called them with its purity and oily calm. Men and beasts made a rush for it. The swiftest of the men plunged at the same time as the elephants. A moment later the men came out again, rubbing their eyes and spitting with disgust. For that lovely translucent, though hardly transparent water, that chemical-blue water traversed by syrupy ribbons, is saturated not only with salt, so much so that salt substitutes for sand on the beach and bottom, but also with bromine, magnesia, and naphtha—a witches' brew that glues the mouth, burns the eyes, opens freshly healed wounds, and covers the body with a viscous coating that becomes a carapace of crystals when it dries in the sun. Taor, who was one of the last to reach the water, wanted to try it. Cautiously he sat down in the warm liquid—and floated, as though held in place by an invisible armchair. More like a boat than a swimmer, he paddled about with his hands. When he came out, he was horrified to find those hands bathed in blood. Siri explained: "You must have some old cuts and bruises that haven't fully healed. This water seems to be uncom-

monly hungry for blood. When it sniffs out a patch of
delicate thin skin, it breaks through and helps itself." Taor
had realized that in no time. The trouble was that he had
no recollection of any scar on his hands—whatever Siri
might say, he felt sure that his palms had started bleeding
of their own accord, or in response to some mysterious
command.

He had no difficulty, on the other hand, in clearing up
the mystery of the white caps on the surface of that water,
which was much too sluggish to churn up foam. In reality
they were great mushrooms of white salt, rooted in the
bottom and emerging at the top like reefs. Every new
wave that passed over them added a fresh layer of salt.

The shore where the travelers pitched their camp was
strewn with whitened tree trunks that suggested the skeletons of prehistoric animals. Only the elephants seemed to
have adapted themselves to the oddities of this Sea, which
the prophet had called "the great lake of God's wrath."
Immersed to their ears in the corrosive brew, they showered one another with their trunks. Night was falling
when the travelers witnessed a little tragedy, which made a
deep impression on them. The surface of the water had
turned leaden in the dusk. A great black bird came flying
over from the opposite shore. It was a rail, a migrant
denizen of marshy country. Outlined against the phospho-
rescent sky as though drawn with India ink, it seemed to
have more and more difficulty in flying and to be rapidly
losing height. It had no great distance left to cover, but the
noxious fumes from the water were inimical to all life.
Suddenly, in a last access of frenzy, the wing beats grew
faster, but the bird hovered motionless in midair. Then it
plummeted as though struck by an unseen arrow, and the
waters closed over it without a sound, without a splash.

"Cursed, cursed, cursed!" cried Siri, shutting himself up in his tent. "Accursed country! Here we are more than eight hundred cubits below sea level. Everything in this place conspires to remind us that this is the kingdom of the demons. I wonder if we shall ever get out of it alive."

The disaster that struck the next morning seemed to confirm his dark forebodings. First it was discovered that the last two elephants had disappeared. But the search was soon broken off, for beyond the shadow of a doubt there they were in plain sight: two enormous mushrooms of salt shaped like elephants had swollen the ranks of the saline concretions that had formed in the shallow water. By showering each other with their trunks, they had encrusted each other with thicker and thicker layers of salt, and after pursuing their ablutions well into the night they had grown too heavy to move. There unquestionably they were, paralyzed, asphyxiated, crushed under their burden of salt, but safe from the ravages of time for several centuries, several millennia.

The disaster was irremediable, absolute, for these were the expedition's two last elephants. Thus far the survivors had been able to take over the greater part of the lost elephants' cargo. That was no longer possible. Enormous quantities of provisions, arms, and goodies were abandoned for want of carriers. But graver still, the men whose whole function and purpose in life had been the care of these beasts no longer felt attached to the expedition, and the rest, all the rest, suddenly realized that the pachyderms were far more than beasts of burden, namely, the symbol of their native land, the incarnation of their courage and loyalty to the prince. The day before, the men who had pitched their tents on the shores of the Dead Sea could still be described as the caravan of Prince Taor of Mangalore.

That morning it was a mere handful of derelicts, hoping
against hope to save themselves, that started southward.

It took them almost three days to reach the southern
end of the Dead Sea. They passed gigantic cliffs pierced
with caves, many of which must at some time have been
inhabited, for access to them was provided by paths that
were obviously the work of man, stairways dug in the
hardened soil and crude ladders or gangplanks made of
rough-hewn tree trunks. But since in the absence of rain
and vegetation these installations would have endured for
centuries, there was no way of knowing whether they had
been abandoned and if so for how long.

As the travelers proceeded, they noted that the shores of
the great lake were gradually converging and foresaw that
they would soon come together. At this point they were
stopped by a scene of eerie, grandiose sadness. The place
was undoubtedly a once magnificent city, but it would
have been an understatement to call what was left of it a
ruin. The word ruin suggests the slow, gentle action of
time and the elements, the eroding rain, the parching sun,
the roots that split and lichens that devour stones. This was
very different. Clearly this city had been blasted in a single
instant, blasted in the radiance of its prime. Palaces, terraces, porticoes, theaters, covered markets, arcades, an
enormous square centering on an artificial pond ringed
with statues—the fire of God had melted them all like wax.
The stone had the black sheen of anthracite, its surfaces
seemed vitrified, its angles planed, its edges rounded as by
the heat of a thousand suns. Not a movement, not a sound .
disturbed the sleep of this great necropolis; one would
have thought it uninhabited if not for a population in its
image: the silhouettes of men, women, children, and even

of dogs and asses, which the apocalyptic blast had projected and imprinted upon the walls and streets.

"Not another hour, not another minute in this place!"
sighed Siri. "Taor, my prince, my master, my friend—this
is the last circle of hell. But are we dead and damned? No,
we're alive and innocent! There's no reason for us to stop
here! Our ships are waiting at Elath."

Taor paid no heed to Siri's supplications, for his attention was held by other indistinct but imperious voices that
had been buzzing in his ears since leaving Bethlehem. More
and more clearly he saw his life arranging itself in stages or
levels, each showing an evident affinity with those preceding it, but also a surprising originality, at once forbidding
and sublime. And in each of these levels he was bound to
recognize himself. Fascinated, he saw his life metamor-
phosed into a destiny. For now he was in hell, but hadn't
the whole story begun with pistachio nuts? Where was he
going? How would it all end?

They had come to a temple. Nothing remained of it but
steps, truncated columns, and further on a great stone
cube, which must have been the altar. Taor mounted the
steps of the parvis—as worn as if armies of angels or demons had trodden them—and turned to his followers. He
felt only tenderness and gratitude for these compatriots,
who had followed him faithfully into an adventure of
which they understood nothing. But now it was time for
them to understand, to stop being irresponsible children,
and make up their minds for themselves.

"You are free," he said. "I, Taor, prince of Mangalore,
release you from all allegiance to my person. The slaves
among you are free. Those of you who are bound by
word or contract, I discharge you from all obligations.

Faithful friends, if no imperious conviction impels you to follow me, I adjure you to sacrifice yourselves no longer. We embarked on a journey that promised, precisely because of its frivolous purpose, to be pleasant and of limited duration. Did that journey ever begin? Sometimes I doubt it. In any event, it ended on a certain night in Bethlehem, while some children were feasting and their brothers dying. Since then, another journey, my personal journey, has begun. I don't know where it will lead, nor whether I shall journey alone or with a companion. It's up to you to decide. I'm not sending you away, and I'm not holding you. You are free."

Without another word he stepped back into their ranks. For a long while they made their way through narrow, winding streets, past tumbledown hovels. Finally, as night was falling, they crowded into what must have been the inner garden of a villa, but was more like a dungeon than anything else. Swift scurrying sounds told them they must have disturbed a family of rats or a nest of snakes.

From the events that followed Taor concluded that he had slept for several hours. He was awakened by loud steps punctuated by the sounds of a staff tapping on paving stones. Lights and shadows danced on the wall, apparently cast by a swinging lantern. The sounds died down, the lights faded. But he couldn't get back to sleep. A little later the sounds and lights were repeated, as though a watchman were making regular rounds. This time the man came into the garden and dazzled Taor with his raised lantern. He was not alone; another figure stood behind him. The man with the lantern took a few steps and bent over Taor. He was tall, clad in a black robe that contrasted sharply with the pallor of his face. Behind him his companion waited, holding a heavy staff. The other

straightened up, stepped back and inspected the ruined
garden. Then his face lit up and he burst into a loud laugh.

"Noble strangers!" he said. "Welcome to Sodom!"

And he laughed again, louder than before. Finally he
turned about and went as he had come. But Taor, who had
had a good look at the other figure in the dancing light of
the lantern, was filled with consternation. Naked, he
thought, but he was far from the truth. The man was red,
blood-red; muscles, sinews, and throbbing blood vessels
stood out all over his body. No, the man was more than
naked, he was flayed, a living but skinless man with a staff,
walking about in Sodom by night.

Taor passed the next hours in a twilight state, compounded of sleep, lucidity, and intermittent hallucinations.
But the sounds coming from the city—the rumbling of
wagons, the footfalls of beasts on paving stones, cries,
oaths, the muffled roar of crowds and traffic—were quite
real and proved that Sodom was still inhabited, teeming
with a secret nocturnal life. As the day dawned, the life
died away. Looking around him in the light, Taor saw he
had but one companion by his side. Siri no doubt? He
couldn't be sure, for whoever it was was sleeping, wrapped
in a blanket up to his hair. Taor touched his shoulder, then
shook him and called him by name. A rumpled head
emerged from the blanket. It wasn't Siri, it was Draoma, a
colorless nobody, to whom Taor had never paid any attention, who lived in Siri's shadow, scrupulously performing
the delicate and essential functions of bookkeeper and treasurer to the expedition.

"What are you doing here? Where are the others?" the
prince asked him eagerly.

"You gave us our freedom," said Draoma. "They've
gone. Most of them to Elath with Siri."

"Did Siri say why he was leaving?"

"He said this place was cursed, but that you had to stay for some inexplicable reason."

"He said that?" cried Taor with surprise. "It's true that I can't make up my mind to leave this place until I've found what—without knowing it—I came here to look for. But why didn't Siri speak to me before leaving me?"

"He said it was too hard. He said your little speech confronted us with a diabolical choice: leave like thieves or stay."

"So he left like a thief. I forgive him. But why have you stayed? Have you alone remained faithful to your prince?"

"No, my Lord, no," Draoma admitted frankly. "I'd gladly have gone too. But I'm responsible for the treasury, and you must approve my accounts. I can't go back to Mangalore without your seal. Especially in view of our expenses, which have been considerable."

"And as soon as I've set my seal to your accounts, you too will run away?"

"Yes, my Lord," said Draoma, unabashed. "I'm only a poor bookkeeper. My wife and children . . ."

"Never mind that," Taor broke in. "You shall have my seal. But let's get out of this hole."

In the raging light of the rising sun, the city revealed forms that had not been seen since its destruction, but unreal, spectral, ghostlike—not towers, columns, or roofs, but enormous black shadows projected on flagstones flushed with the sunrise. As he trod the shadows, Taor was lifted by a feeling of happiness that he made no attempt to explain to himself. He had lost everything: his sweets, his elephants, his companions; he had no idea where he was

going, but his destitution and availability for whatever
might come his way made him drunk with joy.

An indistinct clamor—the grumbling and grunting of
camels, muffled blows, oaths, groans, drew him to the
south of the city. Prince and bookkeeper came to a large
open field, where a caravan was about to set out. The draft
camels, crude ropes tied around their lower jaws, looked
about them with haughty melancholy. With their hobbled
forelegs, they could only take short, hurried steps. The
hobbles were removed, but that was to load them. Bending
first their forelegs, then their hind legs, they sat down,
grunting with exasperation. The cargo—consisting exclusively of salt—was lashed into place. The salt was transported in translucent rectangular slabs, four to a camel, or
else in molded cones, packed in palm-leaf matting. The
loading area opened directly onto the desert, and in spite
of himself Taor was reminded of a seaport—Elath or
Mangalore—where a fleet was making feverish preparations
for a long voyage. For nothing so much resembles a monotonous voyage on a calm sea as does the passage of a caravan over yellow dunes stretching to the horizon.

Taor watched a caravaner who was skillfully twining
and knotting ropes to secure a camel's load. Suddenly half
a dozen soldiers hailed the man and surrounded him. Taor
failed to understand the argument that followed. The soldiers dragged the caravaner away. A fat man, with a merchant's counting beads twined around his neck, followed
the scene. He seemed to be looking for a witness to share
his righteous indignation. Catching sight of Taor, he cried
out, "The scoundrel owes me money. He was getting
ready to leave with the caravan. They stopped him just in
time."

"Where are they taking him?" Taor asked.

"To the judge, of course."

"And then what?"

"Then what?" said the merchant impatiently. "The judge will order him to pay me what he owes; but he can't, so it's the salt mines for him."

And shrugging his shoulders at so much ignorance, he ran after the soldiers.

Salt, salt, nothing but salt. Since Bethlehem, Taor had heard nothing but that word, an obsessive word of one syllable like wheat, rice, tea—basic foodstuffs, charged with symbolic value and defining as many different civilizations. But though there are wheat, rice, and tea civilizations, is a salt civilization imaginable? Isn't this crystalline substance cursed with a caustic bitterness that makes it impossible for anything good or living to come of it? While following in the wake of the soldiers and their prisoner, Taor questioned Draoma.

"Tell me, Draoma, what in your opinion does salt stand for?"

"Salt, my Lord, is a commodity of the utmost value. Just as there are precious stones and precious metals, salt is a precious crystal. In many regions it serves as a medium of exchange, a coinage without an effigy and therefore impervious to the power and fraudulent manipulations of princes. Hence an incorruptible coinage, but one that can only be used in absolutely dry climates, for it has the disadvantage of melting away at the first rain."

"Incorruptible by man, but at the mercy of the first rain shower!"

Taor admired the genius of this crystal, which not only had any number of contradictory attributes, but could even loose the tongue of a simpleminded bookkeeper and give him wit.

Still followed by the fat merchant, the soldiers and their prisoner had vanished behind a jutting wall. Taor and his companion discovered a narrow stairway which they too descended. At the bottom, a sloping corridor led to a spacious cellar which, to judge by its buttressed walls and vaulted ceiling, must have belonged to an imposing building. A silent crowd came and went, taking no heed—except by their silence—of the tribunal which was in session in a semicircular recess. With passionate interest, Taor observed the men, women, and children about him—all Sodomites, secret inhabitants—unless their neighbors merely disregarded them by virtue of a tacit agreement—of the accursed city, survivors of a population which the fire of heaven had exterminated a thousand years before. "This race," he thought, "must be indestructible, if God Himself was unable to destroy them." He searched their faces and forms for the distinguishing marks of the Sodomite race. Their leanness and air of strength made them seem tall, though they were hardly above middle height. Even in the women and children neither bloom nor tenderness was discernible; their bodies seemed hard and weightless, and their facial expression, suggesting instant readiness to utter sarcasms, had a certain charm but also inspired fear. "The Devil's beauty," Taor thought, for he did not forget that this was a minority, condemned and hated for their customs. But their whole mien and bearing made it clear that they were resolutely committed to their way of life. Their attitude was free from provocation, but not without pride.

Taor and Draoma approached the tribunal, which was to judge the caravaner. A small groups of idlers formed around the soldiers and the complainant. Then Taor no-

ticed a woman whose face was ravaged by grief; four small
children were clinging to her. And to one side he saw
three figures dressed in red leather and brandishing alarming utensils, whose amiable smiles were belied by the ob-
viousness of their function.

The trial went off quickly, for the judge and his asses-
sors hardly listened to the defendant's answers and arguments. "If you put me in prison, I won't be able to work at
my trade," he said. "And if I don't work, how can I pay
my debts?"

The complainant replied with a sneer, "We'll provide
you with a different kind of work."

The verdict was no longer in doubt. The debtor's wife
screamed and his children wailed. At that point Taor
stepped forward and asked leave to speak.

"This man," he said, "has a wife and four small children, who will be punished severely and most unjustly if
he is condemned. Would the judges and the complainant
permit a wealthy traveler, temporarily in Sodom, to pay
the sum owed by the defendant?"

Taor's offer created a sensation. A crowd quickly gathered around the tribunal. The presiding judge motioned
the merchant to approach. They talked briefly in an un-
dertone. Then the judge struck his desk with the flat of his
hand and demanded silence. The stranger's offer, he announced, was accepted on condition that the sum be paid
at once and in unimpeachable currency.

"What is the sum?" Taor asked.

A murmur of astonished admiration passed through the
crowd. This generous stranger didn't even know what he
was letting himself in for.

The merchant took it on himself to reply.

"I am willing to waive the interest accruing from the

delay and the legal expenses I have had to incur. I will also rectify downward to the nearest round number. In short, I shall be satisfied with thirty-three talents."

Thirty-three talents? Taor had no idea of the value of a talent, or of any other currency, but the figure thirty-three struck him as moderate and reassuring. Thus it was with perfect equanimity that he turned to Draoma and ordered him, "Pay!" The crowd's curiosity was now concentrated on the bookkeeper. Would he really do the magnificent deed that would liberate the insolvent debtor? The purse that he drew from under his cloak seemed absurdly small, but not nearly as disappointing as the words he uttered.

"Prince Taor," he said, "you didn't give me time to account for our expenses and losses. Since our departure from Mangalore they have been enormous. For instance, when Bohdi was abandoned to the gypaëti . . ."

"Spare me the details of our journey," Taor interrupted. "Don't beat about the bush, just tell me how much you have left."

"Two talents, twenty minas, seven drachmas, five silver shekels, and four obols," said the bookkeeper in one breath.

Laughter went up from the crowd. So this high-and-mighty foreigner was a mere imposter. Taor went red with rage, but he was much angrier at himself then at the laughing audience. Good God! Less than an hour ago he had been relishing his destitution as a new and unhoped-for youth, a gift of destiny; his poverty and freedom were as heady as a new wine he was tasting for the first time. And faced with a challenge—this man ruined by debt, this woman with four children to care for—he had conducted himself like a prince rolling in wealth, who sweeps away all obstacles with a mere sign to his treasurer. He raised his hand and asked leave to speak again.

"Lord Judges," he said, "I owe you an apology, first of all for not having introduced myself. I am Taor Malek, prince of Mangalore, son of Maharaja Taor Malar and Maharani Taor Mamore. This accounts for the ridiculous—I admit it—scene you have just witnessed: In all my life I have never touched or even seen a coin. Talent, mina, drachma, shekel, obol—are so many words of a language I neither speak nor understand. Thirty-three talents—is that the sum needed to save this man? It never entered my head that I could be short of money. I haven't got it? Never mind. I have something else to offer you. I'm young, my health is good. Too good perhaps, to judge by my paunch. Most important, I have neither wife nor child. I solemnly ask you, Lord Judges, and you, the complainant merchant, to let me take the prisoner's place in your prisons. I shall work until I have earned enough to repay this debt of thirty-three talents."

The crowd had stopped laughing. The enormity of Taor's sacrifice imposed silence and respect.

"Prince Taor," said the judge, "you were unaware just now of the magnitude of the sum needed to redeem the debtor. The proposition you are making now is infinitely graver, for you are offering to pay with your body and your life. Have you thought it over? Mightn't you be acting out of spite because the people laughed at you just now?"

"Lord Judge, the heart of man is opaque and mysterious, and I cannot swear to what lies hidden even in my own. As to the motives for my action, I shall have plenty of time to ponder them during my captivity. I can assure you, however, that they are lucid, firm, and irrevocable.

Once again I offer to serve, in this man's stead, the time needed for the payment of his debt."

"So be it," said the judge. "Your will be done. Affix the irons."

The executioners knelt at Taor's feet with their tools. Draoma, who was still holding the purse, cast terrified looks in all directions.

"My friend," Taor said to him, "keep this money. It will come in handy on your trip! Go. Return to Mangalore, where your family is waiting for you. I ask only two things of you: First, don't say one word in Mangalore about what you have seen here, or about the fate reserved for me."

"Yes, Prince Taor. I shall keep silent. And what is your other request?"

"Come and embrace me, for I don't know when I shall see anyone from my country again."

They embraced. Then, trying in vain to conceal his haste, the bookkeeper vanished into the crowd. The executioners completed their work at Taor's feet, and the freed prisoner abandoned himself to the effusions of his family. As Taor was being dragged away, he turned once again to the judge.

"I know," he said, "that I must work for the sum of thirty-three talents. But how much time does one of your prisoners need to earn that sum?"

The judge was already immersed in the next case. The question seemed to startle him.

"How much time a prisoner in the salt mines needs to earn thirty-three talents? Why, everybody knows that: thirty-three years, of course!" He shrugged his shoulders and turned away.

Thirty-three years. An eternity! The prospect made

Taor's head swim. He reeled and fell in a faint. He was
still unconscious as they carried him to the salt caverns.

All new prisoners in the salt mines were subjected to the
same regime. Even the most rugged among them found the
new life and surroundings so hard to bear that drastic mea-
sures were needed to prevent suicide. The shackled newcomer was lodged in an individual cell and force-fed
through a tube when necessary. Long experience had
shown that the harshest methods of acclimitization tended
to be the most successful. The initial crisis of despair could
last from six days to six months, but even after it was surmounted the prisoner was not permitted to see the light of
day for another five years. During that time he came into
contact with no one but other salt miners, subjected to the
same conditions as himself, and his diet of dried fish and
brackish water remained unvaried. Clearly, it was in this
connection that Taor—the Prince of Sweets—underwent
the most painful reform of his tastes and habits. From the
very first day his gullet was scorched with thirst, but this
was a mere thirst of the throat, localized and superficial.
Little by little, it vanished, but only to give way to a
different thirst, less mordant perhaps, but more profound,
more fundamental. It was no longer his mouth and throat
that cried out for fresh water, but his entire organism;
every one of its cells suffered from radical dehydration
and joined in a silent chorus of protest. As he listened to
the inner clamor of his thirst, he knew that if he lived to
be set free it would take all the rest of his life to quench it.

The salt mines consisted of a vast network of tunnels,
vaults, and quarries carved out of rock salt, a buried city—
doubly buried because directly over it was the likewise
buried city of Sodom. The work force was divided among

three departments. There were diggers, carriers, and finishers. The carriers brought great blocks from the bottom, and the finishers cut them into whitish slabs. The diggers excavated and explored—a process that had been going on for centuries and showed no sign of ever ending. The rock salt was so hard that no props were needed, but there were still surprises and dangers to be feared. From time to time, dark, weird shapes would appear on a wall or ceiling, a giant cuttlefish, a sick horse with swollen limbs, a nightmare bird, known to the miners as "ghosts." They were pockets of clay, caught in the salt as air bubbles may be caught in crystals. When a "ghost" appeared in the course of excavation, the diggers, who had no way of gauging its size, were obliged to circle around it. And sometimes one of these monsters, lurking motionless in the bowels of the mountain, would lose patience with the bustlings and pinpricks of the human ants and explode in a peal of thunder, drowning a whole mine in tons of liquid clay.

There were ninety-seven mines in all. The salt works provided the cargo of two caravans that left Sodom each week. In addition to the slabs from the mine, there were also cones, molded in wooden forms from sea salt collected from sun-dried ponds. Because the work in the salt marshes was done in the open air, the miners coveted it as an approximation to normal life. By dint of toadying, an underground worker sometimes got himself transferred to the marshes. But the mine didn't release its slaves so easily. The miners had lived too long in darkness. The glaring sunlight burned their skin and eyes, and suffering from skin lesions and incurable ophthalmia, they were forced to return underground. The worst injury is to become so adapted to injury that no cure is possible. Corroded by the permanent action of the salty dampness, the skin of some miners became so thin so diaphanous—comparable to the membrane that covers a wound before it has fully healed— that they looked as if they had been flayed. They were known as red men, and it was one of these that Taor had seen on the night of his arrival in Sodom. As a rule, they went naked—for they could bear no clothing, least of all the corrosive salt-soaked clothing of the miners—and they so dreaded the sun that they ventured out only at night. Thanks perhaps to his Indian origin, Taor did not suffer this general excoriation, but his lips became like parchment, his mouth dried out, and his eyes filled with sores that oozed down over his cheeks. At the same time, his paunch melted away and his body became that of a bent and shriveled old man.

For a long time he knew only the immense cave, as large as the interior of a temple, where he cut and scraped the slabs of salt, the damp tunnels that led from one part of the mine to another, and most of all the strange, white-walled chamber where he ate and slept with some fifty others and where prisoners spent their leisure hours carving tables, chairs, cupboards, and kennels out of rock salt—and even, by way of ornament, statues and chandeliers.

After a period of total confinement, the duration of which he could not judge, he was allowed out into the daylight. At first it was to participate in fishing expeditions, for fish was the prisoners' only food. A strange sort of fishing, to be sure, since those waters suffered no animal or vegetable life. It was done at the northern end of the Dead Sea, close to the mouth of the Jordan. It took three days to get there and four to carry the baskets of fish back.

Taor was deeply impressed by the way the Jordan

flowed into the Dead Sea and vanished, absorbed by its
heavy waters, for in this he saw the image of a death
agony. The river comes along singing merrily, laden with
fish, shaded by balsams and tamarisks alive with birds.
With the impetuosity of youth it hurls its murmuring
waters into the future, and the future that awaits it is grim.
First the river tumbles into a gorge of yellow earth which
pollutes it and breaks its flow. From then on it is no better
than a greasy, opaque sludge, rolling slowly to its death.
The branches of the bushes that persist in lining its banks
are stunted and already caked with sand and salt. In the
end the Dead Sea swallows up a sick river and digests it
entirely, letting nothing escape, for the Dead Sea has no
outlet. Further on, the powerful, circling flight of fishing
eagles betokens still another tragedy. Asphyxiated by the
salt water, the river fish—for the most part bream, barbels,
and sheatfish—rise to the surface by the thousands and lie
there belly up, though not for long; saturated with salt,
they soon sink like stones. It is these dead, petrified fish
that the prisoners tried to gather with nets, often strug-
gling to fight off the eagles, infuriated by the intrusion. A
strange sort of fishing indeed, macabre and unreal, quite in
keeping with the accursed scene.

But stranger still was the harpoon hunt, unique of its
kind, in which Taor also took part. Slowly the boat was
rowed to the middle of the Sea—to one of the spots where
it was known to attain its greatest depth. An experienced
man stood in the prow, leaning forward and looking into
the syrupy water. A harpoon attached to a rope lay within
reach. What was he looking for? A furious black monster
that inhabits no other waters, the acephalotaurus, or head-
less bull. Suddenly, in the thick of the metallic liquid, its
revolving shadow was sighted. Growing rapidly larger, it

rushed at the boat. The men overpowered it and hoisted it on board. In reality, the beast was a great lump of asphalt. Spewed out by the bottom and driven upward by the density of the water, it rose swiftly to the surface. These asphalt monsters had an infuriating way of attaching themselves to boats and clinging by a thousand elastic threads. To remove them the Sodomites used a repellent mixture of male urine and menstrual blood. This asphalt was precious, not only for caulking ships, but also for its medicinal properties, and a good price could be had for it.[12]

An occupation that seemed quite useless and gratuitous, however, was the gathering of the apples of Sodom, which grew on the layers of saliferous gypsum and marl deposited by the overflowing of the asphalt lake. These poisoned fields are the home of a thorny bush with frail, pointed leaves, that yields a fruit similar to the wild lemon. It looks inviting, but its appearance is a cruel trap, for when ripe it is swollen with a corrosive juice that takes the skin off your mouth and when dried it crumbles into a gray powder that looks like ashes and irritates the eyes and nose. Taor never found out why he was made to gather this strange fruit.

In the course of these expeditions, he looked for the beach where he had spent the night with his men on the way down from Bethlehem. All the landmarks he remembered seemed to have been effaced. He couldn't even find the two salt elephants—which would have been hard to miss. He felt as though his entire past had been destroyed. And yet for a last time it rose up before him, in the most unexpected and absurd form imaginable.

One day a portly man, puffed up with self-importance, turned up in the sixth mine, which was Taor's. His name was Cleophantes, and he hailed from Pisidian Antioch in

Asia Minor, which, as he never tired of pointing out, must
not be confused with the Syrian Antioch on the Orontes.
Distinctions of this sort gave you the man in a nutshell:
raising his forefinger like a schoolmaster, he inflicted them
on anyone who would listen. He enjoyed special privi-
leges, because, or so he claimed, he had been brought to his
present pass by a series of misunderstandings that would
soon be cleared up. And the fact is that he was never
shackled or shut up in a cell by himself and that he disappeared at the end of the week. What attracted Taor's attention was that this Cleophantes described himself as a
confectioner by trade, specializing in Levantine sweets.
One night when they were lying side by side, Taor
couldn't resist the temptation to ask him:

"Tell me, Cleophantes. Do you know what *rahat loukoum* is?"

The confectioner of Antioch gave a start and looked at
Taor as though seeing him for the first time. What could
this human derelict have in common with *rahat loukoum?*

"Why," he asked, "are you interested in *rahat loukoum?*"

"It's a long story."

"*Rahat loukoum,* I must tell you, is a noble, exquisite,
and subtle delicacy, which would be out of place in the
mouth of a human wreck like you."

"I haven't always been a human wreck, and you probably won't believe me when I tell you that I once ate a
piece of *rahat loukoum,* of pistachio *rahat loukoum,* to tell
you the whole truth. I can also tell you that I left home resolved to learn the recipe, and paid dearly for my determi-
nation. But, as true as you see me here before you, the recipe is still unknown to me. . . ."

At last, among this human flotsam, Cleophantes had

found an interlocutor worthy of his culinary learning. He
swelled up with pride.

"Have you ever heard of gum tragacanth?" he asked.

"Gum tragacanth? No, I can't say I have," Taor admitted humbly.

"It is the sap of a shrub of the genus *astragalus*, found in
Asia Minor. When steeped in cold water, it swells and
takes on the aspect of a thick white mucilage. This gum
tragacanth serves important purposes in the higher spheres
of society. Apothecaries use it in cough lozenges, barbers
in hair oil, and laundresses as a stiffener. Confectioners
make it into a jelly. But it finds its apotheosis in *rahat
loukoum*.

"Rinse the gum in cold water. When the gum is dis-
solved, place it in a jar for ten hours. Next, heat some
water in a large receptacle that will serve as a steamer.
Pour the contents of the jar into a pot and place the pot in
the steamer. Stir the gum constantly with a wooden spoon,
skimming from time to time, until it is thick and creamy.
Strain it through a fine sieve and let it stand for another
ten hours. Then heat it again in the bain-marie and add
sugar, rose water, and orange-flower water. Keep stirring
the mixture until it forms a ribbon when you let it slide off
the spoon. Remove from the fire and allow to stand for
one minute. Pour the paste onto a marble slab, cut it into
squares, and insert a nut kernel in each square. Keep in a
cool place until the squares harden."

"Yes, but what about the pistachio?"

"What pistachio?"

"It was pistachio *rahat loukoum* I had in mind."

"Nothing simpler. Pound your pistachio nuts as fine as
possible in a mortar. Mix them into the paste instead of the

rose water and orange-flower water. Does that satisfy you?"

"Yes. Yes indeed," Taor murmured dreamily.

For fear of offending his companion, he didn't tell him how remote *rahat loukoum* seemed to him now: the husk of an infinitesimal seed that had overturned his life, transpiercing it with fearsome roots, whose flowering promised to fill the heavens.

The high society of Sodom had no scruples about applying to the mine administration for prisoners to perform demeaning tasks or provide temporary help in exceptional circumstances. The administration frowned on such practices—which demoralized the prisoners, they thought—but could not refuse the requests of prominent persons. So it was that Taor, clad in the livery of a waiter or a cupbearer, became acquainted with the masters of Sodom in the course of long dinner parties to which they invited one another. These functions—which appealed to his alimentary bias—offered him an incomparable observation post. Ignored by hosts and guests alike, he saw, heard, and took note of everything. If the personnel managers feared that these hours spent in an atmosphere of effete luxury would undermine the physical and moral stamina of the salt miners, they were mistaken, at least where Taor was concerned. Indeed, the former Prince of Sweets found nothing more invigorating than the spectacle of these men and women, who were not the salt of the earth because, as they themselves said, there was no earth in Sodom, but the salt of the salt. Not that he felt unreserved sympathy for these damned souls with their abrasive spirit of negation and derision, their inveterate skepticism and deliberate arro-

gance. They were too patently prisoners of their age-old
attitude of disparagement and denigration, which they re-
spected scrupulously as their only tribal law.

For a time Taor was attached to the service of a couple
who lived on a grand scale and whose dinners were attended by the most brilliant and caustic personalities of
Sodom. Their names were Semazar and Amraphelle.
Though husband and wife, they looked as much alike as
brother and sister, with their lashless eyes and unblinking
lids, their insolent upturned noses, thin, sinuous, sneering
lips, and the two bitter wrinkles that scarred their cheeks.
Faces, aspark with intelligence, which always smiled and
did not know how to laugh. A harmonious couple, no
doubt, but after the manner of Sodom, and an uninformed
observer would have been surprised at the atmosphere of
vigilant malice they maintained between them. With the instinct of an unerring marksman each was constantly on the
lookout for the other's weak spot, which once detected became the target for a cloud of poisoned darts. Relations
among Sodomites were governed by the unwritten law
that the greater their love the more cruelly they tormented
one another. Indulgence meant indifference, benevolence
contempt.

Taor moved like a shadow through these enormous, hermetically sealed rooms, where the Sodomites banqueted all
night. Toxic-colored liquors distilled in the Asphalt Lake
laboratories fired imaginations, swelled voices, encouraged
cynical gestures. Abominable things were said and done;
Taor couldn't help witnessing them, but he did not take
part. He understood that Sodomite civilization was rooted
in three closely related factors: salt, the telluric depression,
and a certain erotic practice. As for the salt mines and
their bassitude, Taor had experienced them in his body and

soul for so many years that the day would soon be at hand —if it were not already—when he would have lived longer in this hell than anywhere else. That sufficed no doubt to give him a certain abstract, intellectual understanding of the Sodomite spirit. He remembered how, when taking his first steps in the blasted city, he had observed that the usual relief, the elevations usually seen in a city, were replaced by projected shadows. Thrown into the subterranean life of this city, he had later come to realize that the elevations profiled by these shadows had not only been flattened beneath Yahweh's foot, but had also been turned about, converted into negative values. Thus every elevation was inverted into a similar but diametrically opposite depression. And this inversion had its equivalent in the Sodomitic spirit, which saw all things as black, angular, trenchant shadows, plunging to vertiginous depths. In the Sodomitic view all elevated vision was converted into fundamental analysis, all ascendance into penetration, all theology into ontology, and the joy of acceding to the light of intelligence was frozen by the angst of the nocturnal researcher, who excavates the foundations of being.

But Taor's understanding went no further, and he was well aware that the two elements of Sodomitic civilization known to him—salt and telluric depression—would have been no more than unrelated accidents, had Eros not enveloped them in its carnal warmth and density. There could be no doubt that, for want of being born in Sodom and of Sodomite parents, that sort of love would always inspire him with instinctive horror, and that the admiration he could not deny these people would always be mingled with pity and revulsion.

And so he listened attentively as they glorified their loves, but he lacked the sympathy without which such things cannot be fully understood. They rejoiced at having escaped the horrible mutilation of the eyes, sex, and heart—symbolized by circumcision—which the law of Yahweh inflicts on his people to make them unfit for all sexual activity apart from procreation. They had nothing but irony for the fanatical procreationism of other Jews, which leads inevitably to all manner of crime, ranging from abortion to the abandonment of children. They recalled the infamy of Lot, the Sodomite who had repudiated his native place and opted for Yahweh, only to be made drunk and raped by his own daughters later on. They rejoiced in the sterile desert where they lived, in its crystalline substance with its geometrical forms, and in the pure, fully assimilated food they ate, thanks to which their intestines, instead of functioning like sewers clogged with filth, were hollow columns, the props and centers of their bodies. According to them, the two *o*'s of Sodom, like those of Gomorrah, but in a different sense, signified the two opposing sphincters—oral and anal—of the human body, the alpha and omega of life, which communicate with each other, echo and call out to each other from end to end of man, and the sexual act of the Sodomites is the only fit response to this great and somber tropism. They also said that in sodomy the sexual act, instead of being confined to a cul-de-sac, is hooked up to the intestinal labyrinth, irrigates every gland, stimulates every nerve, stirs every entrail, and finally discharges full in the face, so transforming the whole body into an organic trumpet, a visceral tuba, a mucous ophicleide, with infinitely ramified coils and volutes. All this was not quite clear to Taor, but he understood the Sodomites better when he heard them say that sodomy, instead of subordinating sex to the propagation of the species, exalts it by directing it into the royal road of the digestive system.

Because sodomy respects the virginity of young girls and does not threaten wives with the dangers of childbearing, it enjoyed special favor with the women and formed the basis of a veritable matriarchy. Indeed, the entire population worshipped a woman—Lot's wife—as their tutelary deity.

Tipped off by two angels that the fire of heaven was about to descend on the city, Lot betrayed his fellow citizens and fled in time with his wife and two daughters. They were forbidden to look behind them. Lot and his daughters obeyed. But his wife could not restrain herself from looking back to bid a last good-bye to her beloved city, which was perishing in the flames. Her tender gesture was not forgiven—Yahweh turned the poor woman into a pillar of salt.[18]

On their national holiday, the Sodomites celebrated her martyrdom by gathering around the statue, which for the last thousand years had been fleeing from Sodom, but so reluctantly that a torsion of her whole body made her face the city—a magnificent symbol of courage and fidelity. The people sang hymns, danced, copulated "in the good old-fashioned way" around the Salt Mother, as she was affectionately termed—and covered this impetuous yet motionless woman, enveloped in the hard spiral of her petrified veils, with all the flowers the country had to offer: desert roses, fossil anemones, quartz violets, and sprays of gypsum.

Some time later a new prisoner was brought to the sixth salt mine. His florid complexion, comfortable girth, and most of all the look of horror with which he viewed this underground realm—all showed that he had just been wrenched away from the green earth and the smiling sun. He still had about him the good smell of life on the surface. The red men surrounded him, felt his skin and questioned him. His name was Demas and he came from a village near the Waters of Merom, a small lake through which the Jordan flows. Since the region is marshy and rich in fish and aquatic birds, he lived by hunting and fishing. If only he had stuck to his home country! But driven by the hope of larger catches, he had gone down the Jordan, first as far as the Lake of Gennesaret, where he had stayed a long time, and then continued southward through Samaria. After stopping in Bethany, he had finally followed the river to its mouth, where it loses itself in the Dead Sea. "Cursed country! Disgusting animals!" he moaned; and what abominable people he had met. Why hadn't he turned back? Why hadn't he returned to the green, smiling north? Instead, he had quarreled with a Sodomite and split his skull with an ax. The dead man's companions had seized him and dragged him to Sodom.

Convinced that they had got as much as they could out of the foreign prisoner, the red men soon abandoned him to the despair and prostration that newcomers always went through before resigning themselves to their gruesome fate. Taor took him under his protection, cajoled him into taking a little food, and made room for him in his salt cubbyhole. Lying side by side in the mauve night of the salt mines, racked with fatigue but unable to sleep, they would talk for hours.

That was how Demas happened to mention a preacher he had heard on the shore of the Lake of Gennesaret and in the country around the town of Capernaum, and whom

the people most often referred to as the Nazarene. At first
Taor pretended to ignore this talk of the preacher, but a
warm, bright flame was kindled in his heart, for he knew
that this was the Child he had missed in Bethlehem and for
whose sake he had refused to leave the country with his
companions. He pretended to ignore the preacher, as a
fisherman pretends to ignore a magnificent fish that he has
been pursuing for years but is afraid of frightening, now
that he has finally caught up with it, for he knows he will
need the greatest gentleness to coax it into his net. With
unlimited time ahead of him, Taor let Demas's memory
distill, drop by drop, everything he knew about the Nazarene, either from hearsay or from seeing it with his own
eyes. Demas told him about Cana where Jesus had turned
water into wine for the wedding guests and how in the desert He had appeased the hunger of a great multitude with
five loaves and two fishes. Demas had not personally
witnessed these miracles. But he had been present on the
lake shore when Jesus bade a fisherman row him out into
the middle and cast his net. The fisherman had complied
reluctantly, for he had fished in vain all night, but this time
so many fish were caught in his net that he thought it
would break. Demas had seen that with his own eyes and
bore witness.

"It looks to me," said Taor, "that the Nazarene's main
interest is in feeding His followers."

"Maybe so," said Demas, "but you mustn't think that
the men and women around Him are always glad to accept
His invitations. In fact, I once heard Him tell a rather bitter
parable, possibly inspired by the coldness and indifference
of people He wanted to shower with gifts. A generous rich
man went to great expense to prepare a succulent dinner
for his friends and relatives. When everything was ready

but no one came, he sent a servant to remind the guests of
his invitation. Each one had a different pretext for declin-
ing. One had to inspect a field he had just bought, another
had to try out five new teams of oxen, still another was off
on his honeymoon. The generous rich man then sent his
servants out into the streets and squares to invite all the
beggars and cripples, the halt and the blind they met,
"Lest," he said, "the succulent dishes I have prepared go to
waste."

On hearing that, Taor remembered the words he himself had spoken after listening to the stories of Balthasar,
Melchior, and Gaspar, and to be sure, he must have been
divinely inspired, for after confessing that he felt terribly
remote from the artistic, political, and amorous preoccupations of the three kings, he had expressed the hope that
to him, too, the Savior would speak a language consonant
with his innermost being. And now, by the mouth of poor
Demas, Jesus was telling him—whose whole life, even his
great journey to the Occident, had hinged on alimentary
preoccupations—stories of a marriage feast, of multiplied
loaves, of miraculous fishing, of banquets given to the
poor.

"And that's not all," Demas went on. "Let me tell you
about a sermon He delivered at the synagogue in Capernaum. It's so amazing that I still find it impossible to believe, though my witness can be trusted to the hilt."

"What is He supposed to have said?"

"He is supposed to have said literally: 'I am the living
bread which came down from heaven. Except you eat the
flesh of the Son of man, and drink His blood, ye have no
life in you. Whoso eateth my flesh and drinketh my blood
dwelleth in me and I in him.' Those words provoked a

scandal and most of those who had been following Him dispersed."

Taor was silent, dazzled by the terrible clarity of those sacred words. Groping in a light too glaring for his spirit, he saw the events of his past life take on a new relief and coherence, though he was far from understanding everything. All at once the feast he had given the children in Bethlehem and the massacre of the infants seemed related and seemed to throw light on each other. Not content with feeding people, Jesus had sacrificed His own self and fed them His own flesh and blood. It was no accident that the feast and the human sacrifice in Bethlehem had taken place simultaneously: these were two aspects of one and the same sacrament. And suddenly he found justification even for his own presence in the salt mines. For to the poor children in Bethlehem he had given only delicacies transported by his elephants, but to the children of the poor insolvent caravaner he had made a gift of his flesh and his life.

But never did the words of the Nazarene as reported by Demas touch Taor more deeply than when they referred to fresh water and gushing springs, for every cell in his body had been crying out with thirst as long as he could remember, and all that time he had had nothing to drink but brackish water. What then was the emotion of this man tortured by the salt hell when he heard these words: "Whosoever drinketh of this water shall thirst again, but whosoever drinketh of the water that I shall give him shall never thirst; but the water that I shall give him shall be in him a well of water springing up into everlasting life." No one knew better than Taor that this was no metaphor. He knew that the water which stills the thirst of the flesh and

the water which flows from the spirit are not different by
nature, unless one is torn asunder by sin. And he remembered how Shaykh Reza on Dioscorides Island had spoken
of food and drink capable of satisfying body and soul at
the same time. Indeed, everything Demas said fitted in so
well with Taor's thinking, responded so well to the questions he had always asked himself, that he felt sure it was
Jesus Himself who was speaking to him through the mouth
of this fisherman from the Waters of Merom.

And then one night Demas told him how Jesus, on returning from Tyre and Sidon, had climbed the mountain
known as the Horns of Hatim because it is situated near
the village of Hatim and is shaped like a saddle, concave in
the middle and raised at the ends. And there Jesus taught
the multitudes and said: "Blessed are the poor in spirit, for
theirs is the kingdom of heaven. Blessed are the meek, for
they shall inherit the earth."

"What more does He say?" Taor asked in a soft voice.

"He says: 'Blessed are those which do hunger and thirst
for justice, for they shall be filled.'"

No words could have been addressed more personally to
Taor, the man who had suffered thirst for so long in the
name of justice. He begged Demas to repeat and to repeat
again those few words that summed up his whole life. He
let his head fall back on the smooth mauve wall of his al-
cove, and then a miracle occurred. Oh, a modest, unassum-
ing miracle, which could have no other witness than Taor:
out of his corroded eyes, from under his festering eyelids,
a tear rolled down over his cheeks. It fell on his lips, and
he tasted it. That tear was fresh water, the first drop of salt-
less water he had tasted in more than thirty years.

"What else did He say?" he insisted in an ecstasy of
eagerness.

"He said: 'Blessed are they that mourn, for they shall be comforted.'"

Life in the salt mines was more than Demas could bear, and he died soon afterward. His body joined many others in the great mortuary salting vat, where salt crystals, perpetually at work, dried out the flesh, killed all germs of putrefaction, and transformed dead bodies, first into stiff parchment dolls, then into statues of brittle, translucent glass.

And the succession of nightless days resumed, each so identical with the last that the same day seemed to begin over and over again without hope of an end or conclusion. And yet one morning Taor found himself alone at the north gate of the city. His sole viaticum consisted of a linen shirt, a bag of figs, and a handful of obols. Had the thirty-three years of his debt elapsed? Perhaps. Taor, who had never been able to reckon, left the matter to his jailers. Even his feeling for the passage of time had become so blunted that all happenings since his arrival in Sodom seemed synchronous.

Where was he to go? The question had already found its answer in Demas's stories. First get out of the Sodom depression, climb up to the normal level of human life. Then make his way westward to Jerusalem, where he seemed most likely to find the trace of Jesus.

His extreme weakness was compensated in part by his light weight. A puppet of skin and sinew, a walking skeleton, he floated over the ground as though supported by angels to the right and left of him. What gave him the greatest difficulty was the state of his eyes. A waxy pus oozed from his bleeding lids and formed thin, hard scales as it dried. Unable to face the daylight, he tore off a piece

of his robe and tied it around his forehead, leaving only a
narrow rent through which he could dimly see his path.

Although the Dead Sea was well known to him, it took
him seven days to reach the mouth of the Jordan. There
he turned westward. On the twelfth day, he came to
Bethany, the first village he had seen since his liberation.
After living for thirty-three years among the Sodomites
and their prisoners, he delighted in watching men, women,
and children who seemed human and moved naturally in a
landscape of verdure and flowers. Indeed, the sight was so
refreshing that he was able to take off his blindfold. He
asked one passerby and then another if he knew a prophet
by the name of Jesus. The fifth person he questioned sent
him to a man who was said to be a friend of Jesus. His
name was Lazarus, and he lived with his sisters Martha and
Mary Magdalene. Taor went to the house of this Lazarus.
It was closed. A neighbor told him that this was the four-
teenth day of Nisan and that many pious Jews had gone to
Jerusalem to feast the Passover. Jerusalem, said the man,
was less than an hour distant, and though it was already late
there was a good chance of finding Jesus and his friends at
the house of a certain Joseph of Arimathea.

Taor started out. At the end of the village he was over-
come by weakness, for he had not eaten that day. A short
while later, however, he started off again, sustained by a
mysterious power.

An hour, the man had said. It took him three, and it was
dark night when he entered Jerusalem. He spent quite a
while looking for Joseph's house, which Lazarus' neighbor
had described rather vaguely. Would he arrive too late as
he had in Bethlehem, in a past which had receded to the
ends of his memory? He knocked at several doors. Because
it was the Feast of the Passover, the people answered

gently in spite of the late hour. At last a woman opened and said yes, this was the house of Joseph of Arimathea. Yes, Jesus and his friends had met in a room on the upper story to feast the Passover. No, she was not sure if they were still there. He could go up and see for himself.

Once again he had to climb. He had been climbing since he left the salt mine, but his legs no longer carried him. Nevertheless, he climbed and opened a door.

The room was empty. Once again he had come too late. People had eaten at this table. There were still thirteen wide, shallow goblets, each with a squat foot and two handles. In some of the goblets there were still a few drops of red wine. And on the table there were still a few pieces of the unleavened bread which the Jews eat at Passover time in memory of their fathers' flight from Egypt.

Taor's head reeled. Bread and wine! He reached for a goblet and raised it to his lips. He picked up a piece of unleavened bread and ate it. Then he toppled forward, but he did not fall. The two angels, who had been watching over him since he left the salt mines, gathered him into their great wings. The night sky opened, revealing a sea of light, and into it they bore the man who, after having been last, the eternal latecomer, had just been the first to receive the Eucharist.

POSTSCRIPT

1. Now when Jesus was born in Bethlehem of Judaea in the days of Herod the king, behold, there came some wise men from the east to Jerusalem,

2. Saying, Where is he that is born King of the Jews? For we have seen his star in the east and have come to worship him.

3. When Herod the king had heard these things, he was troubled, and all Jerusalem with him.

4. And when he had gathered all the chief priests and scribes of the people together, he demanded of them where Christ should be born.

5. And they said unto him, in Bethlehem of Judaea, for thus it was written by the prophet:

6. And thou Bethlehem, in the land of Juda, art not the least among the princes of Juda; for out of thee shall come a Governor, that shall rule my people Israel.

7. Then Herod, when he had privily called the wise men, inquired of them diligently what time the star appeared.

8. And he sent them to Bethlehem, and said, Go and search diligently for the young child; and when ye have found him, bring me word again, that I may come and worship him also.

9. When they had heard the king, they departed; and lo, the star which they saw in the east went before them, till it came and stood over where the child was.

10. When they saw the star, they rejoiced with exceeding great joy.

11. And when they were come into the house, they saw the young child with Mary his mother, and fell down, and worshipped him; and when they had opened their treasures, they presented unto him gifts: gold and frankincense and myrrh.

12. And being warned of God in a dream that they should not return to Herod, they departed into their own country another way.

13. And when they were departed, behold, the angel of the Lord appeared to Joseph in a dream, saying, Arise, and take the young child and his mother, and flee into Egypt, and be thou there until I bring thee word; for Herod will seek the young child to destroy him.

14. When he arose, he took the young child and his mother by night and departed into Egypt,

15. And was there until the death of Herod, that it might be fulfilled which was spoken of the Lord by the prophet, saying: Out of Egypt have I called my son.

16. Then Herod, when he saw that he was mocked of the wise men, was exceeding wroth, and sent forth and slew all the children that were in Bethlehem, and in all the coasts thereof, from two years old and under, according to the time which he had diligently acquired of the wise men.

Matthew, 2:1–16.

These lines from the Gospel according to St. Matthew are the only mention of the three kings in the Holy Scriptures. They do not figure in the Gospels of St. Mark, St. Luke, or St. John. The number three has generally been inferred from the three presents mentioned: gold, frankincense, and myrrh. All the rest, including the names Gaspar, Melchior, and Balthasar, derive from legends and apocryphal writings. Thus the author has felt free to invent the lives and characters of his heroes on the basis of his Christian education and the rich iconography inspired by the Adoration of the Magi.

Concerning King Herod the Great, on the other hand, we

are amply informed, chiefly by the Jewish historian Flavius Josephus (A.D. 37–100). The chapter on Herod in the present book was inspired largely by Josephus's *The Jewish War*, but I have also drawn on other sources, in particular the studies of Jacob S. Minkin and Gerhard Prause.

The legend of a fourth king, who started from farther away than the others, missed the event in Bethlehem, and wandered until Good Friday, has been told several times, in particular by the American pastor Henry L. Van Dyke (1852–1933) and the German Eduard Schaper (born in 1908), who was inspired by a Russian Orthodox legend.

Notes

1. Paul Nizan.
2. Muhammad Asad.
3. The balsamodendron myrrha.
4. Today the Caspian Sea.
5. "And they built a place of exercise in Jerusalem, according to the laws of the nations, and they made themselves prepuces and departed from the holy covenant and joined themselves to the heathens and were sold to do evil."

(I Maccabees, I, 15–16)

6. 1,000 feet.
7. In 31 B.C.
8. Deuteronomy 12:10.
9. Matthew 2:6.
10. For the mustard tree, see Matthew 13:31–32.
11. The surface of the Dead Sea is 400 meters below that of the Mediterranean and 800 meters below Jerusalem.
12. Flavius Josephus, *The Jewish War*, IV, 8, 4.
13. Genesis, Chapter 19.